THE ACTOR

Harrison

ERIKA VANZIN

Want to get more FREE from Erika?

Sign up for the author's New Releases mailing list and get "Backstage" for free! You will periodically receive news and offers.

Follow this link to get started:
https://hello.erikavanzin.com/welcome/

To my readers.
You are the reason
my dreams found their wings
and soared to reality.

CHAPTER 1

Harrison

I drive my Ferrari up to Stone Canyon Road in Bel Air. The night is a bit chilly, considering it's not even mid-January, but the heated seats feature is a perk I wanted in my car even if I do live in Los Angeles.

The estate I'm driving to is nestled between the trees dotting this neighborhood. Kevin Peterson, the producer hosting this party, couldn't wait to show off this new mansion he purchased a few months ago, after his divorce from his ex-wife became final. When a Hollywood producer personally invites you to a party at his house, you can't say no.

For an actor like me, networking is vital to continuing to work in this industry, so even though it's Wednesday and tomorrow morning I have an appointment with my agent, here I am, wearing my best shirt and trousers, driving my luxurious car in Los Angeles traffic, hoping they have valet parking because it's a pain in the ass finding a spot up in these hills. I don't think Kevin kept his guest list limited to a few close friends.

When I reach the gates, I'm immediately surrounded by paparazzi taking pictures of the guests arriving at the party. Flashes almost blind me and I'm glad I'm driving slowly, trying to figure out where to park, because they're so close I could probably run over someone.

The gates are open and a couple of security guys in black suits are keeping the unwanted photographers at bay. Or at least they pretend not to want them here, the truth is everyone here benefits from their job. If you aren't worthy of the gossip magazines, your career is probably free-falling into the pit of anonymity, and climbing back out of that pit is painfully difficult.

"Harrison!" I hear them calling me, and I school my face into a bored expression. Photographers are vital for every Hollywood actor, but the trick is to pretend they're bothering you.

I spot the guy in a black suit who, when he first sees me, turns pale, then smiles and waves at me. I stop my car in front of him, turn off the engine, step out and give him the keys. He gives me a keyring with the number twenty-five carved on it.

"Thank you." I smile while he walks around my car and sits behind the wheel.

I have no idea how that poor guy will find a spot to park my car, but when he turns it on, he lightens up. I don't know how many chances he has to drive a Ferrari, but considering he works at these parties, I think he more than enjoys a ride in a luxury car.

I walk up the marble steps of the mansion toward its ten-foot, iron and glass front door and the two marble columns on either side of the massive two story. If he wanted something to show off his status as a rich dude in Hollywood—he nailed it.

I give my name to the security guy at the door who checks his list then motions to the mansion behind the door. "Enjoy the party, sir."

"Thank you." I smile.

The music is blasting from the living room, visible through the foyer with its double marble staircase leading upstairs, while a massive seven-foot statue of Aphrodite greets me in the middle of the marble floor. A sparkling gargantuan chandelier attached to an iron and glass dome in the ceiling looms over the statue, dwarfing it.

"Jesus Christ," I murmur walking into the house and keeping out of reach of the fixture.

"Are you wondering if it will come crashing down by the end of the night too?" Aaron's voice makes me turn around.

I smile at my friend and stroll toward him. "It's, how can I say, unique."

He chuckles and I follow him into the heart of the party. I watch him elegantly making his way to the bar and I can't help but notice the difference between him and the host of this party. They're both famous producers in Hollywood, but while Aaron is classy and doesn't show off his money, the other is obnoxious and tacky. They couldn't be more different.

"Have you been here long?" I shout over the loud music.

He shakes his head. "Just long enough to take in the crowd."

I glimpse around at the people he's referring to, taking a good look at the crowded space. There are a lot of people I know, from A-list actors and actresses to a bunch of producers, directors, and insiders. There are also a lot I don't know, some looking like this is not their first gig, others gawking at every famous person in the room.

"Did anyone stay home tonight?" I grin and Aaron laughs.

"When you have a new toy to show off, you want to reach out a bit farther than your neighbors. At the end of the day, everyone in this industry has a house like this. You have to call the new faces in town if you want to impress someone." He sips the glass of wine he grabs off the tray of the waiter in a black suit and white shirt.

I nod, knowing exactly what he means. After years in this industry, you see so many outrageous and crazy things nothing fazes you anymore.

"Are you here for networking or just for pleasure?" Aaron asks.

I shrug. "I'm in between jobs, so I thought it would be helpful to pop in here for a bit. I saw a couple of directors I want to chat with. You? Are you working tonight?"

"Dakota's here because she's auditioning for a role in a movie coming up this summer, so she's sweet-talking the director and producer. I thought it could be a productive night for me too. You know, there are a couple of projects I'm interested in and the people involved are here too." He doesn't sound convincing.

"You're keeping an eye on her, aren't you?" I chuckle.

He rubs a hand over his face and nods. "God, yes. There are so many assholes in this room that I want to be here in case she needs me."

I bark out a laugh. I understand his jealousy, not because I have doubts about Dakota, but because there are a lot of perverts in this industry. He's one of the few producers with a moral compass who doesn't require an actress to suck his dick to get a part.

A flock of five girls wearing their best party dresses approaches us with dreamy gazes and coy smiles. The blond one puts a hand on my arm and leans in.

"We *love* your movies! We're *huge* fans." She puts a smug smile on her face.

"Really? Which one's your favorite?" I ask, knowing they don't really watch my movies. They probably saw the massive, action-packed franchise, but nothing else I did, not even the one that won me the Oscar. But it's fine. It's part of the game. They profess their love for me, take pictures, put them on social media, and my name gets out there. No different from the paparazzi, they're just better dressed.

"*All* of them! We can't choose just one, that's not fair." She puts a hand over her chest and pretends to be shocked while her friends nod.

I chuckle, playing their game. They have no idea how many times I've heard this excuse. If you really like someone's work and you want to have a conversation with them, you can at least do your homework. Watch just one of my movies, then you can talk about it. I'm not here to give them a pop quiz about all of my roles.

"I'm glad you love them. Thank you, I really appreciate your support," I say sincerely.

They may not be interested in me as an actor and only in me as a status symbol, but I really do appreciate their support. It's people like them that keep my name out there and allow me to keep working in this industry. It's depressing, sure, but it's the least I can do to keep doing the work I love.

"Do you mind if we take a picture together?" she asks and I smile.

It took them less than two minutes to get to what they really wanted. "Sure, I saw a photo booth over there we can use." I point to the corner of the room where a small crowd is waiting to use the spot with the perfect setting for an Instagram picture.

I turn toward Aaron, who is hiding a smug smile behind his champagne glass. I give him a don't-even-try-to-comment look and he innocently shakes his head.

"I'm going to take a picture with these lovely ladies," I announce, eliciting some giggling from the girls.

"Don't let me take you away from your groupies." He winks at me and I scowl at him.

"See you in a few minutes."

"Are you sure about that? They look like they want a bit more than a picture," he teases.

I turn toward the expectant girls and take in their ages. They're young, way too young for me. They're probably legal, but with all the makeup, dresses, and high heels they probably look older than they are. I don't know if they're even twenty-one. I sure as hell wouldn't give them something to drink.

"More than sure. Jail is not my favorite vacation spot." I raise my eyebrow.

"Yes, you should probably keep your hands to yourself," he agrees.

We make our way to the other side of the massive living room, walking around waiters with champagne and dodging tipsy dancers. We don't say a lot while we wait our turn for the photo booth. The girls mostly whisper into each other's ears and giggle, casting furtive glances in my direction. I smile, make some small talk, but the time is dragging out so long until it's almost awkward standing here without saying a word. If I needed confirmation that they're young, really young, this is it. A more experienced woman would have probably already dragged me somewhere more private to have a quickie.

"This is us!" I say with too much enthusiasm when the last couple comes out of the booth.

We enter the space and I'm horrified to find a love seat to put my ass on. No way I can fit with all five girls on there.

"Ladies, sit, please!" I bow to let them walk in.

"You can sit with us!" the blond chatty one suggests.

"I would never let a girl stand while I sit. My mom raised a gentleman." I don't give in to the suggestion.

They giggle and reluctantly sit down, but at least they don't make a fuss. The camera in front of us is automatically triggered when you press a button, so when they push it and strike a pose, I stand behind them raising my hands so everyone can see I'm not groping teenagers and then smile at the camera.

It takes thirty seconds for the set of photos and then they decide to get a digital copy on their phones. I take the opportunity while they're focused on their mobiles to say goodbye and bolt out of the booth.

It's easy to disappear into the crowd that seems even larger than when I arrived. I spot a familiar figure on the dance floor and I reach her, putting my hands on her hips and grinding her ass to the beat of the music.

"Hey, beautiful." I kiss her cheek.

She turns her head and smiles. "Hey, handsome!" She kisses me back.

I filmed a couple of projects with Samantha. We had fun working together and also hooking up from time to time.

"I saw you with Kevin's teenage daughter. She's young, like really young!" she teases me.

"I swear, I kept my hands high and visible in the picture." I keep dancing with her while she turns around and laces her hands around my neck.

She is gorgeous in this silver sequined dress. If I play my cards right, I won't be alone tonight.

"Good, because they are barely legal." She winks at me while she keeps grinding to the music.

My hands travel to her lower back, skimming over the naked skin. "Are you here with someone?" I lower myself to talk into her ear, feeling my erection growing in my pants.

"Yes, with my husband," she answers back against my ear.

I freeze. "Your what?"

"My husband, he's over there." She points to a bunch of producers chatting between each other.

"Since when do you have a husband?" I ask in disbelief, completely stiff in the middle of the dance floor. The other people surrounding us are too engrossed in the music to pay attention to us.

"A couple of weeks." She frowns. "I thought you knew."

"Well, obviously not. Why are you grinding against my boner if you're married?" I ask in disbelief.

"Because you're hot? A lot of times I get off watching your shirtless compilation on YouTube," she admits like it's the most normal thing in the world and my heart sinks into my stomach.

This is my life. Approached by fans way too young to have a conversation or married women who use fan videos of me shirtless to pleasure themselves. While sometimes this is flattering because, no matter what, some confessions boost a man's ego, on the other hand, nobody takes me seriously.

I'm the good-looking actor that takes his shirt off in the first fifteen minutes of the movie and stays like that for the other ninety. Nobody remembers that when I won an Oscar, I spent the entire movie stuffed into a black coat, the only skin showing was my face and hands. People seem to have forgotten I can actually act.

Don't get me wrong, I like fame and the movies I star in, but sometimes I'd like something that showcases my skills more than my abs.

A middle-aged man with a beer belly hidden under his jacket approaches us, and I realize I'm still hugging Samantha way to close for a married woman.

"Can I dance with my wife?" he asks, smiling sweetly at her.

"Sure," I blurt out jumping back way too fast to be smooth and waving at the couple that doesn't even pay attention to me.

I march to the bar where I left Aaron and find him chuckling. He probably saw everything that happened on the dance floor.

"Fuck my life," I mumble, waving down the bartender to order something stronger than champagne.

"Not your best night, I guess," he jokes.

"Shut up, please."

This night perfectly summarizes my last few years. I have a life most people envy. I'm rich, famous, and I don't have any problems meeting women. The thing is, nobody takes me seriously. I'm a stereotype, a cliché: the shallow Hollywood star, good for fucking and taking off my shirt on screen but nobody stays around long enough to dig under the surface.

Fuck. My. Life.

CHAPTER 2

Sienna

"Are you kidding me?" I stare horrified at the crowd in front of me.

Dozens of people dancing to loud music in the middle of the tackiest house I've ever seen. The taxi dropped Harper and me in front of the mansion's gates where hordes of paparazzi wait for the last celebrities to show up. They paid little attention to us, taking some picture but not flooding us with flashes when we walked through the gate.

Harper and I are not rich and famous. She's a waitress at one of the many clubs in the city, while she auditions for roles waiting for her breakthrough role, and I am the penniless indie director struggling to pay the rent. This is why we've been roommates since I arrived here ten years ago, barely eighteen, with a dream to become the most famous director in the world.

The 'becoming a director' part has worked out these last ten years; I'm still working on the 'most famous' part. Which is why I'm in the middle of the most hideous party Hollywood could spawn. I landed a contract with the producer who's hosting this nightmare for a movie I want to direct. Hence, I'm here squeezed into a cheap dress, trying to impress the Hollywood bigwig. A recipe for disaster.

"Is that a pole dancer?" Harper asks pointing to a corner of the room where a half-naked woman is sensually dancing around a pole. She is the most gorgeous creature I've ever seen, but she seems utterly out of place here with these famous pigs ogling her while a bunch of actresses try to catch their attention.

"It appears so," I sigh, and she casts a glance at me and smiles.

"Don't even think about it. You at least need to show your face to Kevin. He invited you here, you go over there and smile at him."

"I don't know what you're talking about." I'm sure she can read my desire to disappear from this place as soon as possible.

One thing I've never liked about this industry is that you have to attend parties like these. They're so fake and you have to kiss asses to get what you want. If you're a woman, you have to suck at least a couple of dicks if you want to be taken seriously.

This is why I never made a big splash in Hollywood. I'm not willing to compromise and I have to fight like hell just to land an indie movie with a low budget and a lot of extra work. But I'm happy with that. I don't want to mix my art with mediocre blockbusters that just fatten the pockets of big production companies.

"You look like you want to bolt any second now. Don't do it. You fought tooth and nail for this project. By some miracle you got the attention of one of the biggest producers in Hollywood; don't waste this chance because you're allergic to this industry," she says with a serious expression.

She's right. I played my cards right. I used all the connections I had to gather a bigger budget for this movie and I'm willing to do anything to bring it to the screen. Well, almost anything. I'm not going to have sex with anyone for it.

"Let's find Kevin and see what we can work on," I suggest, reaching out my hand and inviting her to lead the way.

We make our way to the middle of the dance floor, dodging people grinding against each other. I swear to God I saw Harrison Bates putting his hands on Samantha Wild. Doesn't he know she's married? The truth is, he probably doesn't even care. He's the golden boy of Hollywood, with his perfect blond hair and striking blue eyes. He represents all the reasons why I don't like this industry when it comes to big names.

"Here you are!" Kevin's booming voice diverts my attention from pretty boy.

"I promised you I'd come, and here we are!" I shout over the loud music.

He laughs at my response and I can see Harper next to me chuckling. Am I so predictable that everyone thought I wouldn't come?

"I was sure you'd stay away from this place," he remarks.

"If you want, I can walk out and you'd never know I was here," I suggest, more as a hope that he agrees than an actual joke.

He laughs. I don't.

"No. Walk around, mingle with people. We need more money for your movie. Shake your pretty ass in front of some rich producer and open his wallet," he suggests and I feel my skin crawl.

Kevin is one of those who wouldn't say no to an offer for a blowjob in exchange for some favors. He wouldn't push it on you, but if you offer, he'll gladly oblige. This is why he's celebrating his divorce. He's also someone with an exceptional nose for good movies. If he smells something worth his money, he puts in every effort for it to succeed. That's why I put up with him—his misogynist remarks, his fake tan, and that hair that's way too dyed for his age.

"I'm not kneeling in front of your friends," I point out and he rolls his eyes.

"I know you don't do those things, but it never hurts to be nice."

"I'm always nice!"

"No, you're not," both Kevin and Harper say in unison.

I look at my friend in disbelief.

"Don't pretend you don't know what I'm talking about. I've seen grown men walking away crying after talking to you," she remarks and Kevin laughs.

"It's not my fault they're so insecure they can't take having their flaws pointed out," I scoff and they both roll their eyes this time.

"Just be nice and bring home some money. We need it," Kevin says before turning around and walking away.

The truth is I don't know what to do. I'm awkward in these situations and when I'm nervous I tend to blurt out everything that's on my mind. It's not like I try to offend people on purpose, but I tend to say what I think and sometimes those things aren't nice.

"I saw a director I want to talk to. See you in a bit?" Harper asks.

"Wait! You can't leave me alone!" I plead.

She raises a scolding eyebrow.

"Okay," I concede. It's not like I'm a toddler who has to be supervised all the time, but I feel more confident when I have her around.

She disappears between famous Hollywood actors and waiters serving champagne. I make a turn and scan the crowd, looking for a group of people big enough they won't notice if I slip into the conversation. I spot some not too far from me—a couple of well-known actresses, three producers with their wives, an award-winning director, and two other men I don't know. I approach the circle as they're talking about something I don't get so I just listen to the conversation.

A couple glances at me, but the cheap dress I bought two years ago at the mall and the unfamiliar face don't grab their attention, and they just keep talking about their weekend at Saint Barts. Another couple just got home after a three-week retreat in Aspen. I can't even think about not working for three weeks straight. If that happened, it would mean one of my projects flopped and I'd be desperately looking for something else to take its place.

I listen to their problems about yachts being too big to fit into some ports, pet therapists that can't understand why their dog keep stealing food from their plates, or the embarrassment of their credit card being declined while they were buying art in Dubai.

Their problems are so far from mine that I could be an alien from another planet. The most challenging experience I had this week was finding five hundred dollars to pay the plumber for a problem with my kitchen sink our landlord refused to fix.

"What did you do this weekend?" one of the wives asks me, her fake cleavage pushed high by the corset of her thousand-dollar dress distracting me from looking her in the eyes.

"I went to a friend's opening exhibit at an art gallery. She's a painter," I blurt out.

She lightens up. "That's lovely! Where is it? Maybe I can pass by and take a look. I'm in desperate need to replace some art pieces in our house." She seems genuinely interested.

"The Spirit Gallery in Burbank," I answer and the conversation around me dies down.

Every eye is focused on us and I can see more than a few looks of pity aimed at me. The woman who asked the question seems a bit surprised but she recovers like a champ.

"There are art galleries in Burbank? I didn't know that. It's not on my usual route to the yoga studio." She smiles sweetly to try, maybe, to make me feel less uncomfortable. She is not succeeding. I feel like every eye is on me, scrutinizing my fifty-dollar dress and the hair Harper tried to fix up a bit before we came here.

"Quite a few, actually," I answer.

"Lovely," she says, and the conversation dies down in an embarrassing silence.

"Sorry, I have to go…over there," I blurt out when I can't take it anymore. I walk away as fast as I can without looking like a maniac or tripping in these heels. I walk to a corner next to a photo booth and try to regain my composure.

How can Kevin think I can ask these people for money when I have nothing in common with them? They have a lifestyle so far from the reality I'm used to, I can't even strike up a conversation with them, let alone find a way to ask them for money.

I take a deep breath and try to regroup. I need that movie, I believe in this project, and I know it can be a massive success. I can overcome my insecurities for a couple of hours, just enough time to get some support from these rich people.

I look around to find another group of people, maybe smaller this time, less intimidating. I swipe my gaze over the familiar faces and my eyes land on the only one I'm not interested in tonight: Harrison Bates.

He's at the bar talking to Aaron Steel, smiling and having a blast. He's comfortable at this party, because these are *his* people, not mine. He's so full of himself he struts around like he owns the place. I hate him. Or rather, I hate what he represents in Hollywood.

He comes from a rich family, private schools, best college in the country. He could have done anything, but he stomped his feet like a kid when his dad told him being an actor wasn't a real job and did it out of spite.

"If you keep looking at him like that, he'll catch on fire." Harper's amused voice makes me turn toward her just in time to see the smirk on her face.

"I hate him."

"You don't even know him."

I stare at his perfect body wrapped in an electric blue shirt that makes the color of his eyes pop even more. Not that I can see them from this far away, but I've looked at them so many times driving around Los Angeles when his movies come out, plastered all over the huge billboards, that I'm positive he chose that color to appear even more attractive.

"He is a daddy's-boy who got this far because of his father's connections."

"I would call him daddy." She giggles and I throw her the stink eye. "Oh, come on. Don't tell me you don't find him attractive. He's like a Greek god walking on earth!"

He is. He is a wet dream for every woman in this room, but that doesn't mean I want to fuck him.

"So what? He's evil incarnate. He keeps using his body, taking off his shirt to make money. He's the reason why there aren't many good movies around. He makes more money being naked than acting."

"Wow. That was harsh." I turn toward her and she's frowning at me.

I sigh. "Maybe it's harsh but it's the truth. Production companies don't pick up worthy scripts anymore, because they make more money if they put some naked dude on screen that has millions of followers on social media. Harrison got where he is because he's got rabid fans drooling over him as soon as he shows his face anywhere. Any kind of merchandise they put out with his face on it gets sold out in minutes. Minutes."

She crosses her arms over her chest and raises her perfectly plucked blond eyebrow. "Are you jealous of him, Sienna?"

I scoff. "No, I'm not jealous. I'm pissed because I'm here begging people to give me money for a really good movie and he got money thrown at him because he smiles and winks in front of the camera. It's not fair. I don't want to be like him, I just want to have the same fighting fair chance at success."

"Well, he was unbelievably good in the movie that won him the Oscar," she points out.

"He was lucky."

"Okay, now you're just bitter. It wasn't luck, he *is* talented."

"He was lucky to have a damn good script, with a damn good director that pushed him to do more," I snap, my blood boiling under my skin.

"Now you're the one being unfair. He won the Oscar as best actor, but the movie didn't win. That means something."

I don't answer because I think the movie was great, but the one that won was objectively better. It was a tight competition that year.

"So, tell me why he didn't win any other Oscar. Tell me why, if he is so good, does he only do movies that are barely mediocre. Action-packed franchises that leave nothing to the future generations. Maybe because he was lucky that one time and then he couldn't nail any other audition where some skill was required? But he's here in his Ferrari, and all he has to do is snap his fingers to get the money he needs."

She says nothing after my outburst, but she's not looking at me. When I turn around and follow her gaze, my eyes meet Harrison's. He is staring at me like he's looking into my soul.

A heat rises from my chest and hits my cheeks. My breath catches in my throat and I almost stop breathing. My heart starts hammering in my chest and I'm almost sure he can read my mind and pick up all the hateful thoughts I just poured out against him.

He frowns like he can't figure out why I hate him so much and I feel a bit guilty because, at the end of the day, I'm someone who wants to play fair and it's not fair how I treated him tonight, even if he didn't hear me.

I turn toward Harper, to see if she's noticed him staring at me, and I find her smiling.

Fuck. My. Life.

CHAPTER 3

Harrison

"Who the hell is that?" I stare at the gorgeous woman on the other side of the room trying to kill me with her gaze.

Damn, I've never seen someone look at me like I just shit on their plate. She's throwing daggers at me while she chats with the blond next to her. Her raven black hair falls down in waves behind her shoulders and the tight red dress hugs her curves like it's painted on her gorgeous luscious body. She's one of the most beautiful women I've ever seen in my entire life, and I swear to God, I've had the chance to see a lot of them.

"Who?" Aaron asks, scanning the crowd.

"The goddess with black hair and a killer body in a red dress next to the photo booth."

He follows my gaze and smirks. "That, my dear, is Sienna Mackey, an indie director who's got her hands on one of the hottest projects around right now."

I turn my attention back to my friend. "Really?"

He chuckles. "Don't be so surprised, she is really good at her job."

"I'm not surprised at that, but at the fact that there's still a hot movie to film out there," I point out.

Aaron studies me for a long moment. "You should really change managers."

"Tell me about it," I mumble. "How do you know about this project?" I ask louder.

He sips the whiskey he just got from the bartender and frowns. "I tried to get my hands on it, to produce it and distribute the movie through the streaming platform, but she didn't even want to hear about it. She wants to send it to festivals and try that route."

Very few people turn down an Aaron Steel proposal. He is big in this industry, and has the power to make or break a career. He is also a good guy, so it's not like he stabs you in the back if he doesn't get what he wants, but still, there are few people that pass up a chance to work with him. The line of people at his studios, waiting to work with him, is so long that if he asks you about your project, you drop everything and come crawling with a smile.

"It's gnawing at you, isn't it?" I bump my shoulder with his, grinning.

"You can say that. It's a very good movie, but Kevin got there first and he's not giving it up." He chuckles.

"Kevin as in, this Kevin?" I point at the ugly house where the party is hosted.

He nods. "She's probably here because they need a bit more money to start the project."

This gets my full attention. Indie movies are famous for their low budgets and lack of adequate funds. The fact that one of the most influential producers in this industry is putting out his cash to make it happen and looking for someone else to chip in means this thing could be huge.

"You're sure it's a very, very good project?"

He gives me a curious look. "Absolutely. Oscar-worthy good."

The excitement bubbling in my chest almost makes me smile. I glance back at the goddess again and I can't snuff the hope blooming inside me. Oscar-worthy is the only thing I can think about. I need this. I need a project that can make me feel useful.

"Is there a male role?" I ask my friend.

He nods. "Are you interested?"

I shrug and grin at him, then push away from the bar counter I'm leaning on.

"Where are you going?" He frowns at me.

"To give my agent a reason to be pissed off with me."

"Isn't that the norm?" He laughs and I wink at him while I make my way to Sienna.

I walk across the room without moving my eyes from hers. I pay no attention to people who try to stop me to chat or whatever they want. She's my only target and her eyes are growing wider and wider as I get closer to her. When I'm at arm's reach, she takes a step back as her friend giggles. I wink at the blond and then turn my full attention to Sienna who studies me with a mixture of suspicion and annoyance.

"Hello, there," I purr with my signature charming smile spreading across my lips.

I know, I'm playing dirty, but I want to know this woman and the movie she's working on. I don't leave anything to chance. I'm not here to play fair, I'm here to show the world what I can do, and she's my chance.

"What do you want?" she asks harshly and I'm a bit taken aback. My smile wavers a bit, but I force it back in place.

Her friend is full on giggling by now, trying—and failing—to hide it behind her hand. Sienna glares at her too. I'm almost glad I'm not the only one on the receiving end of her fury.

"Just trying to be friendly." I keep my pleasant tone, but my nervousness is gripping my stomach. I'm worried it will show, sooner or later.

"I don't have time for small talk with Hollywood sellouts like you," she blurts out and her friend gasps in response.

"Sienna!" she scolds.

The blow is so low it takes me a few moments to process what she said and answer her hostile insult. "Wow. You don't even know me." I drop my sweet tone and charming smile.

"Isn't it true that you get paid millions to take off your shirt and star in movies?" she asks with venom in her tone.

The punch to the gut takes my breath away. I know what they think about me in the industry, but nobody has ever been so blatantly honest and brutal in saying it to my face.

"I won a fucking Oscar for best actor." I can't hide the disbelief and rising temper in my voice.

We've never spoken before this moment and I don't know what her problem is, but I don't deserve this treatment. Maybe she's pissed off because this is a shitty day for her, but I don't care.

"A long time ago. Why haven't you won anything else since?" She raises her eyebrow as her friend blurts out a "*Jesus Christ*" under her breath.

"Why? Have you won anything with your work?" I spit back. I'm done getting insulted by someone I don't even know.

"Plenty of awards," she scoffs.

"And yet here you are, begging for money because you can't pull off your next movie. Isn't it ironic that you're begging from the Hollywood elite, where you clearly don't fit in?" I fight back with maybe more harshness than necessary, but I'm done with her.

The fury on her face is so strong I'm almost sure she's going to punch me in the face, but I don't give her a chance to reply. I turn around and march back to Aaron who's looking at me with confusion. When I reach him, I'm fuming.

"Well, that was fast!" He studies me.

"That was an unbelievably long time in her presence, if you ask me," I spit angrily and regret it as soon as his eyebrows shoot up in surprise.

"What did she say to piss you off?"

I summarize our conversation and the more I repeat it, the angrier I get and the more surprised Aaron is.

"Wow, that was quite a ride." He glances over at her, frowning.

"Tell me about it. Sadly, it's no different from what people say about me behind my back in this industry, but she was spitting it in my face like she wanted to hurt me. I don't even know her!"

"Not everyone in this industry thinks that about you. A lot of people appreciate your talent. The weird thing is she wasn't so rude when I met her. She blurts out a lot of stuff when she gets nervous, I got that too, but she was never that harsh. Distrustful of this industry, sure, but never mean or rude." He seems to study her from afar to figure out what happened.

Tonight was a big no since the start, but I couldn't imagine I could stoop so low. "It doesn't seem *she* has a high opinion of me."

He shakes his head. "I'm not to trying to defend her or anything, but I think she's just fed up with this industry and you're exactly what this industry represents. A white rich man with everyone bowing at his feet. You don't have a problem with finding the next job. You receive hundreds of proposals. On the other hand, she's an attractive woman trying to be taken seriously by a bunch of assholes trying to stick their cock into her instead of recognizing her value." He's not completely wrong.

"Okay, but I'm not one of those assholes. She judged me before even speaking to me. It's not fair."

"It's also not fair that she has to struggle to make a name for herself in Hollywood when she's way more talented than a lot of men thriving in this industry." He raises an eyebrow.

He's right, but it doesn't mean it hurts any less. What she said hit way too close to home.

"Do you know where Kevin is?" I ask Aaron when a very bad idea forms in my head.

"Over there, why?" He points toward a group of people gathered by the pool.

I say nothing, but start walking toward the back door, Aaron hot on my heels.

"You're not doing something stupid like getting her fired, are you?" he asks worriedly.

"No! God, she bruised my ego, but I'm not that much of an asshole. Jesus Christ, you really think I would do something like that?"

"Just asking. You're marching furiously toward her only producer, you never know."

I realize I must look like an angry rhino charging the crowd. I slow down and pull myself together before putting a smile on my face and approaching Kevin.

"Here you are, I was looking for you!" I grin at his surprised smile.

"I thought I saw you around here. I'm glad you came." He turns around, leaving the conversation with a director and a couple of other producers and giving me his full attention.

"I love this party and your house is amazing!" I put maybe a bit too much enthusiasm in my words but he doesn't seem to notice.

His smile broadens. "This will be my bachelor retreat. I can finally party as much as I want without my wife complaining about the women coming and going."

His wife was probably complaining about the ones who were coming and going in his bed, but I don't point it out.

"I'm sure you'll enjoy your new freedom." I wink and he laughs.

"I'll make sure you'll be on the guest list."

"I can't wait!" I really don't want to be here, but I can't say it out loud.

He glances behind my back and notices Aaron a ways behind me, talking with one of the actors enjoying the party. He's not looking at us, but I know he's assessing the situation. I saw him a bit worried about my mission and I can't blame him. I'm not here to talk about the party.

"Are you here to steal my project?" He motions toward my friend with a smirk.

"I'm here with a proposal," I say with a smug smile plastered on my face.

He turns toward me with a mixture of boredom and curiosity that perfectly fits his character. He can't show how interested he is or he'll give me an advantage in this conversation. Something like that would never happen in Hollywood, especially around big sharks like him.

"I had the chance to talk with Sienna about her new project." I kick myself when I realize I should have asked Aaron more about it. I was so focused on getting back at her I didn't think that far ahead. I didn't think at all.

"Really? She's very proud of it." He smirks, not saying anything else, waiting for me to reveal my cards.

"I know! She wouldn't stop talking about it. She blurted out so much the only thing that came to mind was, *I need to know more*!" I pull off my best performance of a person enthusiastic about a new idea he's just heard about.

Kevin seems genuinely surprised. Maybe because he didn't expect her to push this with me. I have no idea if he knows that she hates my guts. It's difficult to gauge what his position is in this project, besides putting up the money. For all I know they could be lovers who share a hatred for me.

When the thought crosses my mind, my stomach squeezes uncomfortably. I never considered this could be the case. I probably look like a fool. She strikes me as someone with way too strong an opinion to appeal to someone like Kevin, who likes them docile and submissive, but you never know.

"Really?" He raises a pleased eyebrow.

Not helping, Kevin. You are not useful with your cryptic responses.

"She's a firecracker, isn't she?" I can play this game too, asshole. I can talk for hours about nothing until you drop dead, knowing shit about me.

"She is!" He smiles broadly.

I nod expectantly and he finally gives in.

"She's so invested in this movie she would be crushed if it didn't get made," he admits.

Here we go. Talk about money, Kevin. I know this is your favorite language.

"Is there any chance it will fall through?" I pretend to be surprised. Aaron told me they need more money. This is why she is here.

"Can I tell you something in confidence?" He makes a big deal of glancing at Aaron and then at me, like he's putting a lot of faith in me not telling anyone about it. "The funds are not enough for this movie. It's a big project and we spent a lot to acquire the rights for the script. Now we're tight for the production costs, let alone the promotion," he almost whispers conspiratorially.

He is good. He is really good. He doesn't go straight to the point in asking for cash. He makes you feel like you're helping a poor director achieve their dream. What he doesn't know is that I came here precisely to play this game. I already know I want to put money in it. I just need to know how.

"Are you serious? Is it *that* good?"

He nods once, then sips his champagne for a more dramatic effect. "That good."

"Listen. I could look into it. I know a company trying to branch out with their investments. I can try to talk to them, if you want. Maybe they have some marketing budget to relocate. They did some other indie movie, but nothing this big." I try to sound uncertain.

"It's worth a try. They're not some controversial company that would cause a backlash, are they?" He pretends to be worried. The truth is that even a scandal is free publicity in this industry.

"No, please, don't even think something like that. They deal in premium healthy dog food."

He chuckles. "A business that will skyrocket in the future."

Tell me about it. I know very well where that company will go.

"You can say that. Listen, give me a couple of days to look into it and if they're interested, I'll have them call you. I can give them your phone number, right?" I lay down my trap.

"Give them my personal one, I will take care of it."

And here we go. I have him exactly where I want him—bent over a pile of money.

"Sure. Not a problem at all."

When I walk into the house and find Aaron at the bar counter, he looks at me like I just murdered someone. He studies my appearance as though trying to spot blood on my hands.

"Do I want to know?" he finally asks.

"Healthy Dog LLC is going to make a movie!" I clap my hands smiling.

"Isn't that the company where you're a silent investor?"

I gasp. "I didn't think about that! What a coincidence."

He frowns. "Do they know about that?"

"Why should they know about it? I found an investor for their movie. Does it matter where the money comes from? As long as everything is legal, money is money."

He shakes his head, disapproving. "It will backfire, you know that, right?"

"Probably, but I'll think about that when it happens."

I hope it won't hurt too much.

CHAPTER 4
Sienna

I refresh the festival's website page for the millionth time. It's not there. My short movie and my name are not in the list of the ten finalists that will be shown at the festival in front of avid fans of indie movies and some Hollywood bigshots.

I'm not discouraged because I think my work isn't good enough for the festival. I know it is, but the competition is fierce this year. I know every single person on this list and they are all great directors, even the less famous ones. There were more than four thousand entries. I'm not in the top ten, but maybe I'm eleventh or twelfth.

The problem is the twenty-thousand-dollar prize and the sponsorship for the next movie. I need that money, because I'm running out of savings to pay for this apartment and I will soon be in serious trouble.

And *that* sponsorship. I'm not sure how much it covers, but a bit of money on the new movie wouldn't be bad.

"Are you still staring at that page?" Harper's incredulous voice comes from the front door.

I was so focused on whining at my defeat I didn't even realize she came home. She is staring at me wide eyed.

"Maybe," I mumble guiltily.

"I went out three hours ago!" she points out.

"I lost track of time." I make an excuse but the truth is that since the party at Kevin's house seven days ago, I crawl from my bed to the couch without finding the courage to call him. Staring at this page is another way to avoid my fate.

"Listen, you fucked up. Royally. Get over it. You can't go back to that party and find someone to give you money for the movie. Find another way," she says, sitting down on the coffee table in front of me.

She's right, I know it, and I usually don't sit around beating myself up for what went wrong. I wake up the next day and fight like hell until I find some way to get my movie done. But this time I feel overwhelmed. It's the biggest project I've got myself into and the pressure is high. *Welcome to Hollywood!*

"I know, it's just that I'm not cut out to be the charming goddess who charms people into doing what she wants. Give me a movie to film, I know exactly what to do and I thrive doing it. Ask me to smile and charm my way into someone's wallet, I'm not even sure where to start."

"Oh, I have no doubt about that," she scoffs.

I feel a pang of guilt inside my chest. That was the worst screw-up that night. I may not like Harrison Bates but I have no excuse for how I treated him.

"I know I was rude," I mumble.

"Rude?" She raises an eyebrow, scolding me.

"Okay. I was savage. I know I made a mistake." I finally concede.

But she's not finished. "You destroyed that poor guy. He looked like you kicked him in the balls and then spit on him lying there on the ground."

I know. I've never treated someone like that but I was panicking and I blurted out all the thoughts I have about him, getting even more riled up when he defended himself.

"You should apologize to him." It's not the first time she suggests that but I die of shame every time I think about doing something like that. He probably wouldn't accept my apology and kick me to the curb instead.

"Do I look like someone that has celebrities on speed dial?"

She rolls her eyes and stands up. "You work in Hollywood, how hard is it?"

"I work in the *suburbs* of Hollywood!" I shout while she strolls to her room, chuckling.

As if my week wasn't already bad enough, someone decides that screwing with me would be fun and my phone lights up with Kevin's name, throwing daggers at me.

"You have got to be kidding me," I breath out, grabbing my phone, unsure if I should answer or let it go to voicemail. "Screw it!" I say before pressing the green button.

"Hi, Kevin," I chirp more confident than I feel.

"Come to my place, we need to talk," he says curtly before hanging up.

When a man tells you *We need to talk* it's bad news. But when the man who holds your entire career in his hands tells you that, it's pack-your-bag-and-leave-the-country kind of news.

"What happened?" Harper's frowning face peeks around the door jamb.

"Kevin called. He wants to meet me at his place," I explain.

"So what?"

"I don't know, maybe he wants to kick my ass for how I acted at his party?"

"Possible. But it could also be good news," she offers.

Sometimes I don't know how she can keep up this positivity. I prepare myself for the worst-case scenario every time someone calls me. I want her optimism sometimes, but then I remember I don't handle receiving bad news very well.

"I wish." I stand up from the couch I crawled onto hours ago.

"Take a shower, you stink." She winks at me before going back into her room.

I smell the hoodie I've worn since I don't know when. "Jesus Christ." I wrinkle my nose at the pungent scent.

An hour and a half later I hop out of my beat-up Civic and walk to the front door. My car stands out like a sore thumb in this place even though the house looks even more hideous than the night of the party.

I walk to the front door and ring the bell. After what seems like hours, Kevin comes to open the door. He beckons me into his home and closes the door behind me without removing the phone from his ear. He doesn't speak but he is frowning at something someone is telling him on the other end of the line.

I follow him through the spacious living room, even more massive now that there aren't dozens of people dancing in it, and walk through the patio door to the table by the swimming pool.

He moves a chair for me to sit and then walks away from my prying ears to the other side of the garden to bark orders at the phone.

If this is the mood of this conversation, it's better I stand up and leave before I end up dead and buried under the palm tree. As if he senses I'm about to bolt, Kevin turns around and waves at me, and then at the table. I don't know if he's having a stroke or telling me to eat something from the banquet displayed in front of me.

Not sure what to do, I skip the sandwiches and cakes, and go for a safer plate of grapes and strawberries. It's barely the end of

January, but the sun is warm today and it's nice to sit here and enjoy this weather.

I put some fruit on a plate and try to eat something, but I'm so nervous I almost choke on the first grape.

When he finally ends the conversation and walks to the table, he throws his phone on the marble surface and sits down at the head of the table.

"Piece of shit," he grits out and I don't know what to say.

I'm scared if I ask what's going on he'll bark at me and make the situation worse, but I'm also worried that if I say nothing he'll take my silence as apathy and that's worse.

I go for, "They usually are," agreeing with something I have no idea about, but not taking a clear position with an opinion that requires knowledge of the situation.

Kevin takes this as an invitation to vent his frustration. "Can you believe they pulled out from the agreement after they signed a contract? I will sue their asses. I will milk every penny from them and they will have to wipe their asses with their bare hands because I'll leave them with nothing," he barks.

It's a disgusting image to have at a dining table full of delicious food, but I don't complain out aloud.

"That's awful!" The comment can apply to a lot of things. The deal that went to ashes, the suing part, and also the ass wiping bit.

"I know! Now I have to find someone who can step in one week before the first day of filming. One fucking week. Can you believe that?"

I shake my head in disbelief. How can I tell him that I fucked up at his party and I don't even have anyone signing on for our project? Let alone dropping it. This is the end of my career.

He then asks like he just realized he's a bad host, "Have you eaten something? The new housekeeper overdid it when I told her you were coming."

He wouldn't feed me if he wanted to kill me, right? "I just got some fruit."

"Good." He starts to fill his plate with sandwiches and cakes, adding nothing more.

"Kevin, is there a reason you wanted me here?" I ask, a bit puzzled and a bit eager to have this done. He wants to end my career in Hollywood? Okay, but just do it, not torture me with this nonsense.

He frowns at me like he doesn't remember why he called me here and then he says, "We're making the movie, didn't I tell you on the phone?"

My heart starts to race in my chest. "How? When? No, you didn't say anything, you just called me here and ended the conversation. What the hell happened?"

I'm so confused I don't even know if I'm happy, scared or just freaking out. I thought the party was a waste of time. Well, on my part it was, but Kevin clearly worked his magic. When the realization hits, I'm glad I'm seated because I would have ended up sprawled on the floor.

"A company that has nothing to do with this industry wants to branch out with their investments and bring a new brand awareness to their products so they decided to give the movie industry a chance," he explains.

"I don't understand. Do we have to show their products in the movie? Or do they want something else?" I'm a bit confused.

"They want a percentage of the gross income, and they are okay with the *sponsored by* clause when we promote the movie. No product placement in the movie."

"Okay. I can deal with that."

"Good, because they dropped the entire sum that we need. Well, a bit more because I pushed a bit higher, but they didn't complain, so I'm good with that." He chews at a piece of sandwich and then he points to my plate. "Aren't you eating?"

I shake my head. "I'm too nervous to eat. I can't believe we found someone!" I hope he doesn't get offended at the *we* part of the sentence.

If it was up to me everything would have ended up in flames.

"Well, not we. *You* found someone." He keeps chewing the sandwich without paying much attention to my puzzled face.

"What do you mean? I didn't find the company."

He waves his hand, dismissing my concern, and bites another piece of that damn sandwich. Isn't he even a bit focused on this conversation?

"Harrison Bates was enthusiastic about what you told him about the movie and found this company that was investing in movies," he explains like it's the most normal thing in the world while I choke on air.

"He what?" I manage to spit out while coughing.

Kevin waves, grabbing the attention of one of his staff inside, and asks for a bottle of wine, not paying attention to me almost dying at his table. I have no idea what Harrison has in mind, but I'm pretty sure nothing good will come of this conversation. I humiliated Harrison Bates seven days ago. I bruised his ego and busted his balls. It's impossible he found something positive about that conversation. We didn't even talk about the movie. But I talked with Aaron about it. He was the one spilling the beans with his friend. God, I hate Hollywood.

"He was so excited he ran to me to find out more."

"I bet he did," I murmur under my breath. "What's the catch? What did he want?"

"We didn't sign with him, we signed with the company. They put up the money," he says.

"Really?"

"I signed a couple of hours ago, so yes. I'm pretty sure it was the company name on the contract, not his."

A mixture of excitement and doubt is running through my veins. The thrill I got at the news is becoming suspicion at a very fast pace. We fought, we were at each other's throats, and now he is gifting me this movie? Like hell is he doing something out the goodness of his heart.

"So, what's the deal with him?"

"He's going to star in the movie. He will be the main character." He drops the bomb chewing on a piece of cake.

"Like hell he is!" I blurt out.

"Yes. It's in the contract. They give us the money, he'll be the lead," he continues with an angelic calm while I'm about to explode.

"We already have a lead!" I raise my voice.

"I beg your pardon?" He turns slowly and gives me his full attention.

I shrink in my chair. "Sorry, I didn't mean to disrespect you, but we have the perfect actor for that part. How can we put *Pretty Boy* in something so dramatic? We can't take off his shirt!" I ask calmly, the opposite of how I feel inside where I'm smoldering with anger.

He chuckles and smirks. "Maybe it was a very bad fuck for you, but he enjoyed it and he gave us the money. So, suck it up and enjoy the ride."

"I didn't fuck him! And no, I don't enjoy the ride. I'm the director and I have a say in the casting choices. I don't want him in my movie." I stand my ground.

I didn't make it ten years in this industry by accepting everything they impose on me.

"Well, sweetheart, his role is included in the contract. No Harrison Bates, no money. No money, no movie."

"I'll find other investors." I'm scraping the bottom here. There is no chance I can find someone for that sum.

"Listen. I don't care if you have a problem with him or not. He's here to stay. You, on the other hand, are not irreplaceable. He is Hollywood royalty. He has fans that will do anything to watch this movie. He's the one pushing it high, not you. You're good, but I can find a million good directors out there willing to work with me and Harrison Bates. You want to do this movie? Good. I'll put you at the wheel. You want to complain? Feel free to find another job." He never raises his voice, never lose his composure during his speech, but the message is no less clear.

If he has to decide between Harrison Bates and me, I'm easily replaceable. I'm the one with no power to negotiate this project. I have to consider myself lucky that Harrison Bates wants to work with me or I will be out of a job.

I don't know what his agenda is, if he wants to sink this movie with a mediocre performance out of spite because I humiliated him, but I won't make his life easy. If he thinks he can do whatever he wants because he's Hollywood's golden boy and everyone will bend to his whims, he'll regret every single decision he's ever made.

I fought tooth and nail to climb this fucking mountain. I'm almost there, and I won't let an arrogant asshole ruin everything I worked for these last ten years.

"Fine. I will work with *Pretty Boy.*"

CHAPTER 5

Harrison

I sit alone on one of the chairs set up for the table read. It's been a month since the company I partially own signed the contract to give money to make this movie but I'm still nervous. I asked them to keep my involvement with them quiet, but I expect every day to get a call from Sienna telling me I'm an asshole.

Aaron would say that this is my conscience screaming at me to come clean, but I'm not famous for following other people's advice. I was so angry that night I thought *Fuck it! I don't care*. But the more time that goes by, the more I feel a bit guilty about it. There should be another guy waiting in this chair to start filming this movie. Someone less famous than me that needs this job a lot more. It's the only thing I feel guilty for. Not the fact that I forced my way into this movie.

I need this movie more than anyone else. Not for money, but for the script. As soon as I got it in my hands, I knew it was going to be the greatest challenge I've ever faced but also the greatest reward. My agent was mad because I signed on for something I won't be paid much for. To be honest, considering the money I put into this project, unless it becomes the greatest movie in history, I'll probably lose money on it.

What my agent doesn't understand is that I don't care about money. I need something to drag me out of the pit I have fallen into and that *he* makes me dig deeper and deeper with every blockbuster movie he makes me do. I can't take it anymore. I'm tired of being the joke of Hollywood Hills. And this is my chance.

I studied the script, I learned my part, I made notes where we can make it better. It's a great movie, but it can be better. I *want* it to be better.

The door opens and Viola, the actress who will star opposite me in this movie scans the empty long rectangular table surrounded by two rows of chairs. She lights up in a smile when her eyes land on me.

"Hello! Nice to meet you," she says, walking around the table and extending a hand when she reaches me. I stand up, smile, and greet her.

"Nice to meet you too. It's a pleasure to work with you."

"Oh, shut up. You're the star here. I barely pulled off a couple of good movies and a lot of commercials." She playfully swats my shoulder and sits down next to me.

"Well, they were good movies."

She snaps her head toward me, wide-eyed. "You watched them?"

"Of course, I did! Not having the chance to audition together or test the waters about your style, I went through them at least a couple of times." She seems surprised that I took the time to watch them.

This is something I see a lot. Nobody expects me to come prepared on set and they all look surprised when I actually know what I'm doing. It's frustrating. In the beginning I felt humiliated, but I've learned to let it go and not let it affect me.

The door swings open again and this time half dozen people come in chatting—two other actors we will work with and others I don't know. They all wave and greet us with big smiles and the tension I was harboring inside slips away.

I love the table reading because this is the most intimate part of making a movie. We're all here, seated around the table, reading the script, taking notes, changing things and getting to know one other. But the best part is we all share the same excitement of starting something new, something amazing, almost magical.

There is a buzz of energy in this moment that's irreplaceable. The wrap at the end of the movie is great because you celebrate the end of months of hard work and long hours, but the expectation at the beginning of a project is even better.

Fifteen minutes later, everyone has arrived, including Sienna, who since she stepped foot inside this room has not acknowledged my presence.

"Thank you everyone for being here today," she starts with a warm firm voice and a smile. "This movie will be big. This movie will be great. And you know why? Because we hand-picked every single one of you because you are the best. We spent days going through names, casting for the actors, and in the end, we chose the best. That's why this movie will be great. Because *you* are the best!" She concludes and the small crowd cheers and whistles.

I don't miss the backhanded insult that comes with this pep talk. I wasn't chosen—hand-picked as she put it—I was signed into this movie by a contract she couldn't turn down. I deserve it, but that doesn't mean it hurts any less.

Like every other time life slams its fist in my gut, I put a smile on my face and clear my throat. "Well, we have the best director, so I think that's another reason we'll be great."

She turns to me as the others clap. It's the first time she's looked me in the eyes and, while she is smiling, her dark, almost black eyes turn ice cold. She looks spectacular in those tight jeans and fitted button-down red shirt, even better than the night of the party, but her coldness is something that leaves a mark on my skin.

She says nothing, just nods and goes back to what we were doing. I swallow my pride and take a deep breath before digging out my script and the notes that come with it.

The reading is a blood bath. At least for me. We are two hours into it and Sienna has shot down every single suggestion I've made. The only time she accepts a proposal I make is when the writer says that it's actually a good idea and reasons with Sienna until she changes her mind.

It's a continuous push and pull between us that became uncomfortable for everyone one hour ago. I'm sure half the people in here think if this is the tone we've set for the movie, working with us on set will be a nightmare. And I don't blame them. I would think it too.

"Why is she so angry with you? Did you piss in her coffee?" Viola next to me whispers while Sienna and Pam, the writer, discuss a change in the script.

I can't hide a half laugh that comes out halfway between a grunt and a scoff. "I don't know. Ask her," I mumble under my breath.

"For what it's worth, I think that they're great suggestions."

I feel my chest expand with pride. I'm glad at least she understands I put a lot of effort in. I hope the others in the room understand it too.

"Thank you. I studied this script carefully and I think it's great." I smile and wink at her.

"Excuse me, Harrison." Sienna's voice feels like a bucket of icy water dumbed over my head.

I turn toward her with a smile, even if I'm boiling inside. I want to stand up and walk out of this room, but that would be a bit too much of a diva attitude I can't afford right now.

"If you want to be somewhere else, instead of here reading this project, you can go. I'm sure I can find someone to read your part and finish it," she says coldly.

A few people shift uncomfortably in their chairs. The tension between us is palpable and everyone senses there's a beef between the two of us. You'd have to be blind and deaf not to notice it.

"Oh, no. Don't worry. I'm *exactly* where I want to be," I say with a sweet fake smile.

Sienna's jaw twitches when she clenches her teeth. She's so angry with me I almost feel the waves of fury hitting my chest. I can see Viola next to me trying to hide her smile behind the printed pages of script. Some gazes dart back and forth between us, trying to see if we're going to openly fight or just keep this passive-aggressive vibe going all day. At this point, I want to fight and shout in each other's faces, but I won't be the one starting it.

"Please, stay focused on your part and don't distract the other people doing their job." She scolds me like a fourteen-year-old caught glimpsing at his phone in class.

"I was just telling Viola how amazing it will be to work with you over the next months," I spit out with a smile.

Viola loses her shit this time and grunts, trying not to laugh. I know my remark is childish, but she had two options: suck it up and work peacefully with me or go to war and make it awkward and difficult for everyone. She chose the latter and I'm not taking her shit without fighting back.

I was the one insulted that night, but I'm here, doing my job like the professional I am.

By the end of the table read we are all tired and ready to wrap this day. Regardless of what's happened between me and Sienna, the mood is still one of excitement for this movie.

While we read our parts aloud and go through the different proposals and suggestions, we can feel the scenes coming together in a visual way. We visualize every aspect of the script and make the best of this time around this table.

I have ten full pages of notes written in my notepad and when we come to the next scene, I'm already prepared for battle.

I raise my hand and I can feel everyone holding their breath.

"Do you have a suggestion, Harrison?" Sienna asks with an exasperated tone.

If she hadn't fought every single one of my ideas, she probably would have the energy to listen to me.

"Yes, I do." My voice is laced with fake sweetness.

"Go ahead," she mutters.

She will never refuse to listen to a proposal. It's not who she is. She gives everyone the chance to voice their opinion because she really cares about what people have to say. She's not one of those high-and-mighty directors who thinks they know it all and everyone else is a mere pawn for their success. She believes in cooperating to make things better. I saw it in this meeting. I saw how she frowns in concentration while she tries to come up with a solution accommodates other people's suggestions, smiling proudly when it works.

She loves this job. I'm the problem.

"We have to rewrite this scene."

"Why on earth do we have to do that?" she asks, baffled.

"You can't make the sex scene fade to black. It's a cathartic moment and you are cockblocking it. No pun intended," I say and someone chuckles.

She seems to count to ten to avoid exploding in my face.

"I'm not transforming this movie in a cheap romcom. There is no romance in this movie, love can't become the focus at the end of it," she hisses.

"I wasn't talking about love. I'm talking about sex," I point out. "This movie is about a single father who loses his only daughter in a car accident. When he sues the company that made the child's car seat they flip the table, accusing him of negligence and manslaughter for the death of his own daughter. He spends the entire movie trying to prove his innocence while grieving the death of his only child. A person who watches this movie goes through raw, painful, grief, anger and despair. You can't fade to black on the only moment he finally fucks a bit of his pain out of his system. Quite literally in this case." I can see a lot of people nodding in approval at my proposal but Sienna doesn't budge.

I can see it in her expression that she won't take my suggestion and I'm almost ready to play the *I will cut your funding* card until she speaks.

"Do you feel the need to be naked in every movie? Seriously, what's wrong with you? If your main purpose in life is to show off your body, I suggest you find another kind of movie where you can play naked."

The blow hits me square in the gut. Nobody is breathing for a long moment, and I'm not either. No matter how hard I try to crawl out of this pit, there is someone ready to shove me down again. I lower my gaze and try to focus to find the words for a reply, but nothing comes.

"Actually, I think this is a good idea," Viola intervenes. "I have the same note on my script because I was surprised that after everything he went through, he doesn't get the break he clearly deserves. I vote for the full sex scene."

I feel her leg press against mine under the table and I smile, hoping she understands how grateful I am.

"You'll be mostly naked in that scene, are you comfortable with that?" Sienna asks Viola, still not conceding an inch.

Viola scoffs. "In my movie debut, I had a two-minute scene with a full-frontal nude shot where you clearly see my vagina for thirty-eight seconds. I think I'm past being shy in front of the camera." Someone barks out a laugh. "If the scene isn't just meaningless sex, I think it adds to the narrative, not cheapen it."

I stay silent as I observe Sienna take in a deep breath and think about it.

"Actually, I already rewrote the scene because I thought it was missing something, and I removed the fade to black. He's right. The protagonist needs a bit of a break and the audience needs to see it too."

Sienna thinks a bit more and finally agrees. "Fine. But nothing vulgar."

Everyone lets out a sigh of relief.

The rest of the reading goes on quite smoothly. We're all tired and wanting to wrap it up and go home. When Sienna finally lets us out, someone bolts out of the room like a college kid ready for spring break.

Sienna's eyes land on mine and she pins me with a stern look. "A word," she says when people start to leave the room.

Viola gives me a little sympathetic nudge and then waves at me before walking out.

When we're alone, Sienna lets the mask drop and shows all her loathing toward me. "I don't know how you convinced them to put you on the contract, but if you think you're going to sink this movie by undermining my authority or playing a mediocre part, you are very mistaken."

I shake my head and smile sadly. She really hates my guts and I don't even know why. Just for being *me*? I'm the Hollywood golden boy and she is struggling. I get that. But I'm not doing it on purpose.

"You can sleep easy tonight. I'm here to show you and all those people who think I'm a failure, that I'm actually a damn good actor," I hiss in her face before walking out of the room and slamming the door behind me.

This will be the hardest movie I have ever filmed and I'm not sure I can endure it.

CHAPTER 6

Sienna

"Cut!" Ellen, the assistant director, shouts for what seems like the millionth time today. I look at her next to me and see the pained expression on her face.

This isn't working. This scene is the last in a long list that isn't working. We are ten days into filming and twenty-five since my brutal fight with Harrison at the table read and nothing changed. We keep fighting and shooting the scenes over and over. We are already late in the schedule and we're barely at the beginning. Kevin has already called me twice to yell at me about costs sky-rocketing and less budget for promotion.

I don't even have to say anything to Ellen and she yells "Re-set!" to do it all over again. People start bustling around the set to put everything as it was in the beginning of the scene, ready to film it for the eighteenth time today. I can see on everyone's faces here they're not happy about how this shooting is going and I feel the anger growing in my belly.

As a director, it is my job to direct the scene exactly how I want it, but to do so, I have to communicate with the actors about what I want, and Harrison and I are clearly not communicating.

I'm losing control and credibility on my own set.

I stand up and approach Harrison, who is looking at my scowl. I take a deep breath trying to dampen my fury before reaching him and making things worse.

"Okay. There is clearly something not working in this scene," I say in a low voice, to avoid everyone witnessing our confrontation. It's already bad enough that I can't make him do what I want.

"Oh, you think so?" He raises a challenging eyebrow.

"Why can't you get angry? I mean, you're furious with me, can't you put a some of that into what you're doing?" I raise my voice a little more than before. If he thinks he can mock me, he will learn soon enough how mistaken he is.

He scoffs, making my nervousness expand in my stomach.

"Because I shouldn't get angry in this scene, can't you see it?" He explains it like I'm five years old.

"They just told him he has to show up to defend himself on trial, how can't he be angry?" I start to lose my calm and it shows in my rising voice.

"Exactly! The scene should be soft. He is defeated, desperate, hopeless. He shouldn't be angry, he should want to kill himself!" he shouts and I lose my shit.

"Really? We all agree that your character should be angry, but you stubbornly keep doing this halfway whining thing that sounds like a kid throwing a tantrum. Get your shit together and get fucking angry!" I shout back.

"Everyone? Everyone thinks I should be angry or *you* think? Because it's clear as day, after seventeen takes, that *everyone* is fucking wrong!"

I turn around and march away. That's it. I can't stand him accusing me of being wrong in front of everyone.

"Where are you going?"

"To cool off a few minutes before I rip your head off with my bare hands!" I shout back without turning around.

I walk off the set and go straight into my trailer. The place is crammed with papers that the production requires and I have to move around a few folders stuffed to the brim to find a small spot on the green couch to sit down. I plop on the soft cushion and rub the heel of my hands over my eyes before slipping my fingers into my hair and tightening them into a fist. I will end up bald by the end of this movie if Harrison keeps challenging me like this all the time.

A soft knock and the sound of the door opening draws my attention. Ellen's black curly hair pops up from behind the mini fridge next to the entrance.

"Are you okay?" she asks stepping in and closing the door behind her.

"By the end of this filming one of us will end up murdered and the other in jail," I say, defeated.

She smiles, softening those big dark brown eyes that make her look even sweeter than before.

"He's famous for voicing his concerns on set and pushing to change things to the way he wants them," she states.

I never paid attention to those rumors because they tend to be spun from only one side of the story, without painting the reason for the other side. But this is way too close to what I'm experiencing with him to ignore them completely.

"And what do the other directors do?"

She shrugs. "They usually give him a lot of freedom to do whatever he wants."

I scoff. "Of course, they do."

She smiles again and leans against the counter in front of me.

"What do they say about him, besides his artistic stances?"

At this point, it's better to be prepared, knowing all of the gossip surrounding him, considering we have to live on set for the next few months.

"That he's picky and makes unreasonable requests like a vegan menu, but then he eats chicken. Something fancy that costs quite a bit more, but that it's irrelevant on the big scale of those projects. When you have a multi-million budget, you don't worry about a few hundred thousand dollars on top of the catering."

"Are the chickens on his shit list too? Or maybe he just thinks they're vegetables," I joke, but it doesn't feel funny. His diva attitude pisses me off.

She laughs and shakes her head. "I don't know, but I know that he eats a lot of salads when on set."

"He's probably on a diet to keep his perfect body free of fat." Like he needs to be fit to film this movie.

"I don't know what is it, but you need to find a way to work with him if you don't want to end up even more behind on the schedule," she points out.

I rub a hand over my face and sigh. "Is it crazy that I want to recast the role? I'm tempted to call Kevin and say we tried but we couldn't work it out."

She thinks about it for a long moment. "It's the beginning. It's easier to do it now than wait longer and have to reshoot more scenes, but you have to talk to Kevin about it. He's the one with a handle on the budget."

I nod and think about it. "I'll come back as soon as I hear from Kevin," I tell her and wait for her to leave before grabbing my phone and calling the number that's flashed way too many times on my screen these last ten days.

"What?" he answers abruptly on the third ring.

I don't beat around the bush, it's useless with him. "What happens if I recast Harrison right now?" I sound way more confident than I feel. Years in this industry have taught me to never look weak.

There is a moment of silence on the other end and I almost think he hung up. I have to look at the screen to see that he's still there. Not a good sign for me. When he pauses like this it means two things: he didn't hear me or he's preparing to shout at me. No in-between. In either case, it's bad for me because I don't know if I'm brave enough to repeat my request without stumbling on my words, or if I have the strength today to deal with his fury.

"Oh, it's a very easy answer to your question: you will lose the money from the contract and have to pay the penalty for breaching it. Do you fucking have the money to pay them back? Do you? Because I sure as fuck don't!" he barks out without leaving me time to react. "I don't give a shit about what you have to do. Suck his dick, fuck him, do whatever you want but make it happen. Film this fucking movie and don't complain. You are the fucking director, the movie is yours, get your shit together and work with him!"

Well, that went more or less as expected. Even the cursing was tame compared to some of his outbursts. The truth is, he's right. Instead of thinking about recasting I should take my set back and kick Harrison's ass for not doing what I tell him.

But today I'm too tired to even think of fighting with him. Again. So I just walk out of the trailer and face him.

"Do the scene however you want. Do it more softly or upside down. I don't care. It's late, we have to shoot it again tomorrow anyway, so just do it and come back tomorrow with a different attitude because I'm fucking tired of your tirades," I say as soon as I find him seated alone.

He studies me like he wants to say something but then thinks twice about it. Maybe it's because he sees my tired face or those of his colleagues on this set. He understands he can't push again and again because we are all tired already and we have a long way ahead of us. I don't wait for him to say anything, but turn around and walk back to my chair next to Ellen.

I follow Harrison with my gaze when he goes back to the set. "Ready to shoot one last time for today!" I shout and everyone scurries into their positions.

"Rolling!" Ellen shouts to let the camera operators know we're ready to shoot. The set is dead quiet.

"Action!" I yell and the scene unfolds in front of us and the cameras.

Harrison is facing Viola and this time his posture is less tense, like he is defeated, something I can relate to right now. His voice is soft, incredulous, almost like the fight has left him at the umpteenth obstacle life threw at him.

I glimpse at Ellen and she is staring enraptured at Harrison's close-up on the monitor. I don't know if it's because he's one of the handsomest men I have ever encountered, or if it's because he is giving us the rawest performance of his life.

He is so deep into his character that I can't see where Harrison ends and his character begins. It's like he is feeling every single emotion in his chest and pouring it out on screen. I haven't seen him like this since we started filming, this magic that lives inside him and makes him shine throughout the scene. I have to admit, this is very good acting he is gifting us.

When the scene rolls to an end I call "Cut!" and everyone holds their breath. I can feel it deep in my bones that all eyes are on me. I turn toward Ellen and she's smiling. She saw it too. She saw that this one was a very good take.

"What do you think? Am I the only one who think we can call it a day?" I whisper to her and she shakes her head.

"That was a freaking good shot!" she confirms and I smile back at her.

A bit of tension leaves and the grip of my stomach relaxes slightly.

"That was good. We move on tomorrow with the next scene," I say out loud and everyone seems to let out a collective sigh of relief. Even Harrison's shoulders slump and he smiles a bit while Viola squeezes his arm before leaving the set.

He seems to stay a bit longer, maybe to enjoy the feeling of this moment, almost incredulous that it worked. Then he walks out, looking down without making eye contact with anyone. I wonder why, considering he just proved he was right. He should be boasting about it with everyone, but instead he seems almost ashamed.

"That was a great performance," Ellen says to me as she packs her things and gets ready to go home.

"It was," I agree.

"You should tell him that," she suggests and I know she's trying to smooth things between us.

This is the first time I've worked with her, but I'm starting to appreciate her mission to make things easier for me. Maybe because she is a woman in this industry and she knows how challenging is to be here, and some help is always appreciated.

"I will." And it's not a lie. I'm someone who gives credit for a job well done.

I walk out with her and reach my trailer as she goes to talk to the production assistant. When I slump onto the couch, I'm so tired I almost call it a night and go home. But when I take a look at tomorrow's schedule I stand up, grab the cold brew stored into my fridge, pour it into a cup and let the caffeine do its magic while I prepare for tomorrow.

It's way past midnight when a knock at the door startles me. "Who is it?" I ask a bit worried. Not that I'm concerned about someone attacking me in my trailer, especially after knocking, but still, I feel the tension gripping my stomach.

"It's Harrison, can I come in?"

"Yes, sure," I answer, puzzled. I didn't expect him at all.

He steps in and I can see his red eyes and tired face. He removed his makeup, but he's every bit as handsome as when he's made up for the scene. I guess good genes help a lot in this industry.

"What are you doing still here? It's late and you have an early shoot tomorrow," I say as he leans against the counter in front of me.

He's so tall the trailer appears almost suffocatingly small with him in it.

He shrugs. "I lost track of time."

He's evasive, but I decide not to push for more.

"You should go home and rest. Tomorrow will be another long day," I say a bit too harshly than intended.

He flinches a bit at my tone and I feel a pang of guilt in my chest. I should try to smooth things over, not be the bitch who makes a reputation for herself on set.

"I saw the lights on and I thought to step by to thank you for letting me do the scene like I wanted to today," he replies softly.

I'm surprised by his words. He could have said, "I told you so," but instead he chose a peaceful approach.

I nod. "It was a great performance. You were right. You did good."

He smiles and his eyes soften a bit. Two small dimples appear on his cheeks, giving him an almost boyish look. I wonder how deep they go when he pulls off a full grin.

"So you admit I was right" He's not mocking me, just stating the truth.

"I don't have a problem admitting I was wrong. I'm not a cold bitch." I want to add *like you think I am*, but I refrain from fueling further discussion.

"If you had let me when I asked you in the beginning, we would have finished a lot sooner." He bites out the remark and I feel the anger rise in my stomach.

Before I say anything I'll regret tomorrow morning, I point at the door. "Goodnight, Harrison."

He studies me for a long moment then smiles, shakes his head, and walks out the door waving goodnight without looking at me.

I stare at the door for way too long, trying to figure out the meaning of our conversation. Fighting with Harrison is something I can handle. Shouting and being at each other's throats feels familiar. This conversation we just had? It's more unsettling than anything else and I don't even know if it was good or bad.

CHAPTER 7
Harrison

The morning was a nightmare, like every morning since I started filming this damn movie. The only thing that gives me the strength to come here day after day is knowing this is a really great script. I may not agree with Sienna most of the time, but I really enjoy playing this part. I can show off all my skills, play a fully developed person in all his raw emotion and shine in it.

Sienna has relented a bit on telling me how to play my part. Since the discussion we had a week ago, where I proved that my vision of the character was better than hers, she's given me more freedom in doing what I believe is better for the movie. Not that I don't have to fight for it every single time, but at least now she lets me try. Sometimes I'm right and sometimes she is.

The thing is, other than our disagreements, she's a good director and we work well on her set. Everyone is happy and they got over our continuous bickering. The only one exhausted by the whole situation is me. And her, I suppose. I don't think I'm the only one suffering the blow of our dislike for each other.

"Is that Alfredo sauce on the chicken?" I ask the girl behind the counter at the catering trailer.

She smiles at me and nods vigorously. "Yes! It's homemade."

I shake my head and I see the disappointment on her face. I know this is their specialty for today, but the sauce is a big no for me.

"Is this pasta vegan?" I ask pointing at the second inviting bowl next to the chicken.

I'm starving. I ate this morning at home before coming to the set, but I had to be here at four to get ready for an early shooting at five. It's past noon now, and I'm running on fumes.

"Think so..." she says, uncertain, her small shoulders slumping in defeat.

"You think or you're sure?" There's a harshness in my voice I'm not able to hide. I'm tired, and starving. I can't help it and I feel a pang of guilt when she blushes a bit.

I know what she's thinking. I'm a spoiled movie star throwing a tantrum. I get that a lot when it comes to eating on set.

"I have to ask my boss," she almost whispers, intimidated.

"You know what? Just give me a salad. No dressing or anything." I try to smile at her and not make her feel guilty, but I'm sick and tired of eating just a salad on set because there isn't a vegan alternative.

"Just a salad? If you want, I have a fabulous Caprese back there. Just fresh tomatoes and mozzarella with a bit of olive oil and basil. It doesn't have many calories, I promise." She seems reinvigorated by her new idea.

I shake my head. "Just the salad, please." I say without a smile this time. I want to explain it's not a matter of calories, but the person I assume is her boss appears behind the counter.

"Is there a problem here?" he asks, carefully watching the exchange between me and the girl who is now blushing and lowering her gaze.

"No problem. I was just wondering if you can add a vegan alternative to the menu. Just one dish, nothing fancy," I add when

I see him frowning.

"The salad is vegan," he says and I can't tell if he's serious or mocking me.

"I know. Besides the salad, I mean," I say through my teeth.

"I have to speak with the production. I'll let you know." He dismisses me and turns around to go back to his business.

This is the first time in my life that I got *I-will-let-you-know*ed by someone over salad and a freaking meal.

I grab my plate and turn around, not bothering to say bye to the girl behind the counter, and avoid the table where some of my colleagues are eating. When I reach my trailer, I slam the door shut behind me and open one of the cabinets where I keep my snacks. I find the last packet of rice cakes. I sigh and sit down to my sad portrait of a lunch.

"Mr. Bland, I introduce you to Miss Bland," I murmur opening the package and using the crunchy rice to help me scoop up a bite of the greenery.

I'm halfway through my second bite when the door of my trailer flies open and a very angry Sienna stomps in. I can't deal with her right now, not when I'm already eating a fucking salad for lunch.

"Can I have a bit of privacy?" I ask, annoyed. She can't barge in without knocking, I'm not her freaking kid.

"I want an actor that doesn't act like a diva, but I guess we don't always get what we want, do we?" she retorts, crossing her arms over her chest. She looks like the goody-two-shoes scolding the rebel in her group. Cute, if she wasn't my own personal nightmare at the moment.

"What the hell is your problem?" I bark. Being already nervous doesn't help to keep my temper at bay. I have limits too and she is pushing all my buttons.

"My problem?" she scoffs.

"Yes, your problem," I hiss angrily.

"My problem is that I'm already on a tight budget and I have to work with a diva that wants to eat vegan."

I feel the anger rising in my chest. "Unfuckingbelievable!" I shout, unable to keep my voice low. "It's my third day of eating a freaking salad and I barely make it through the afternoon because I'm hungry, but it's my fault? I asked for a meal, not a banquet laid out in front of me. One. Fucking. Meal!"

"Congratulations! The salad is vegan!" she shouts back. "Do you know how much it costs to add a vegan menu at the catering company? Do you have any idea or are so used to gigantic productions that you completely forget how is to work in smaller projects? I have news for you, sweetheart. Here, everyone does their part. If I give you a vegan menu, I have to fire someone to cut costs." She is so angry her face is tomato red and the blood vessels bulge on her neck.

Accusing me of not caring about the people I work with, demanding special treatment, is a low blow. It hits me in the gut and it hurts.

"You know what? The problem is, you're an inexperienced director playing with a bigger production. You don't know how to deal with me or any of the people working here. I bet when the guy told you that adding a vegan menu meant revising the contract to cover the extra cost, you shit your pants. But guess what? I asked for *one meal*, for one person. Send one of your production assistants to buy a vegan meal within walking distance from here. It's not rocket science!" If she is playing the hurting people game, I can play too.

I see the anger simmering on her face. I used her own insecurities against her and I don't regret it. She came here accusing me of being a diva without making any effort to ask anything about me. I'm tired of being pushed around by someone who clearly has some prejudice about me. She's never even tried to understand my reasoning. She comes here shouting and accusing and never listening. I'm freaking tired.

"We all know you eat chicken! We all saw you eating it. Today it was the chicken, but guess what? You demanded a vegan meal. You are not vegan! You are a spoiled movie star used to having everything served on a silver platter. You have a diva complex. You thrived for years in this sick Hollywood industry where they praise men like you and make women suck dick to have a fair chance at working. News flash, sweetheart. Not. On. My. Set."

So this is her problem with me. She thinks I had everything thrown at me without working for it. She's right, in part. I had an easier life than a woman, I can't deny that. But I'm not a spoiled brat who takes everything for granted. I didn't use my position as a white male to take what wasn't mine to have.

I turned down a lot of parts where they tried to whitewash the movie using my face to attract my fans. And I turned down a lot of brands when they asked me to be an influencer when the role would have been better filled by a woman. I never stole anything from anyone, and the only parts I accepted were ones I was sure I would do well on. I've always taken these things very seriously and I worked hard for every single part I got. I never left anything to chance, demanding a role I wasn't ready to play fully.

The anger simmers inside me, because she doesn't know me. Worst, she doesn't *want* to know me and I'm done trying to play nice.

"You want me to play the diva? Congratulations! You just used my lunch break to yell at me and now I have to finish eating before coming to the set, so I will be late. And I won't be on set tomorrow unless you guarantee I have a decent meal. I got your diva complex right here."

She says nothing, she just turns around and furiously slams the door behind her. I let out a low sigh, grab my salad and throw it away. My appetite and my concentration are gone for this afternoon's shoot.

A soft knock on the door makes me want to crawl out of the window and disappear from this set entirely. I don't want to see anyone right now.

"I'm coming, just give me a minute," I answer without much conviction.

"It's Viola, can I come in?" Her voice is soft, not the usual chirpy tone.

What can I say? No? Go away because I don't want to see anyone?

"Come in," I finally say.

She steps into the trailer and lingers a long moment before closing the door. She studies me with her sweet green eyes and then walks toward me, sitting on the other side of the table and giving me the space I need.

"Are you okay?"

"Yes." I smile, but I can feel it's forced.

She frowns. "I'm going to repeat the question and you are going to avoid the bullshit. Are you okay?"

I can't stop a sincere smile spreading across my face. It's small and uncertain, but it's there. "Why do you want an answer, if you already know everything?"

"Because I don't need to hear that answer, *you* do."

I'm taken aback by her words but decide to humor her. "No, I'm not okay," I say out loud and surprisingly I feel a weight leave my chest.

I snap my gaze on her and she smiles. "Do you feel better?"

Surprisingly, my answer this time is yes and I don't need to lie about it.

"Everybody already knows what happened, right?" I want to know.

She nods "It was impossible not to hear you two shouting. And it's not like you're on good terms," she admits, and I'm not surprised to hear that.

"Do people think I'm a diva?" There is no other way around this. The sooner I take off the band-aid, the better.

She shrugs and thinks a bit about it. "Not exactly. They know you're used to much higher-budget movies, but they don't think you're spoiled. You're funny and easy to work with. I think they don't know why you and Sierra are on such bad terms. I think they're taking bets about when you'll have sex or when one of you gives up and walks away." She giggles and I admire her being so genuinely a happy person.

"No way am I going to have sex her. I'd rather stab my dick with a pencil than stick it in any part of her." I scoff.

"Idiot."

"I'm serious. She is one of the hottest women I have ever worked with, but I can't even stand the idea of having sex with her. I hate her so much I just can't," I explain.

"Geez. Thank you for not even considering me on your hot-ness list!" she jokes.

"You're like my little sister. I couldn't make a move on you," I say honestly. She's so sweet I would run over her like a bull-dozer.

"That is the most unflattering thing a man could say to a woman." She raises a scolding eyebrow at me.

"Sorry, girl, but I'm just being honest. I'm not used to flirting with women I'm not interested in, not if it's not clear for both of us that it's just a game. Especially if I have to work with them."

She stares a me for a long moment, studying my face like it's a piece of art.

"You know, Harrison?" she asks. "You are a rare gem. Don't ever let this industry change you." She stands up and walks to the door. "I'll wait for you on set. Take your time," she adds before slipping out of my trailer and closing the door behind her.

It was the strangest conversation I ever had on set, but surprisingly refreshing, dampening my anger.

***

The afternoon flies by surprisingly smoothly and the scene goes down without any hiccups. I'm so happy when Sienna calls it a day, sending us off early, I almost run to my trailer to get changed.

When I hear a knock at the door, I answer with a smile thinking it's Viola.

"Come in!" I holler while I put on my sweatshirt.

I'm surprised when I finally put my head through the neckline to find Sienna looking at me.

"What do you want?" I ask a bit more bitterly than intended.

"Here. I sent my assistant to grab you some pasta. She told me it's vegan, like you asked." She hands me the paper bag.

"Thanks," I murmur not knowing what to say.

She seems to hesitate for a second, but then she says nothing. Her dark, almost black eyes struggle to find mine. I don't know if she's ashamed, but I doubt she knows what that emotion is.

"Well, see you tomorrow. I'll make sure you have your lunch," she murmurs before turning around and walking out of the trailer.

I have no idea what just happened, if that was her way of apologizing. I appreciate the effort, though. Not sure where this box of pasta leaves us, but I suppose in a better place than where today's salad left us.

CHAPTER 8
Sienna

"He's not here," Ronan announces when I let him in the trailer.

"What?" My head snaps in his direction from the note on the script in front of me.

"He called in sick five minutes ago," he explains a bit nervously.

"Are you fucking kidding me? It's the third day in a row he's called in sick." I punch the couch in frustration and the production assistant flinches.

I take a deep breath, trying to calm down. It's not this guy's fault. I can't vent my frustration on him. He's fidgeting, waiting for me to make a decision, and right now, I hope I don't throw up. I'm so nervous and tired from this constant fighting with Harrison I'm not sure my stomach will hold the breakfast I ate half an hour ago.

"We have to send everyone home," I breathe out.

"What? We can film something else," he suggests.

I know he's trying to be supportive but I can't deal with him right now. It's already humiliating that Harrison is doing whatever he wants on this set, including calling at six in the morning to tell me he's not coming. I don't have the strength to share Ronan's optimistic view of this day.

"No. In the last two days we've filmed all the scenes where his presence wasn't required and we don't have any left. We'll have to change location if we want to film other scenes where he's not involved. It's too late to do anything right now," I explain, keeping my composure.

He seems defeated and I can't shake the feeling that I let him down. I let everyone down. I should have gone to Harrison's house the first day he called in sick and demanded he come back. He threw a tantrum about eating vegan and the day after, he called in sick. I don't believe in coincidences. He is clearly punishing me for the fight we had.

"I'm going to talk to Ellen and then let you know the new schedule, okay?" I put on a smile on my face but I feel furious inside.

He nods as he opens the door and we both slip out of the trailer. It's still dark outside. It's barely six a.m. and the sun won't rise for another fifty minutes. Everyone is here doing their job, waking up before dawn, not even having the time to see their kids before they go to school, and he just spits on our job and time because he's a diva.

I'm so furious with him I even forgot to knock before opening the door of the trailer. Ellen is sipping her cup of coffee, sleepy eyes and a tired face.

"Let me guess, he's sick" She rolls her eyes from behind the cup.

"How'd you guess?" I grit out of my teeth.

She smiles. "Your face says everything."

"I'm so furious I can't even think right now." I sit down on the couch in front of her, on the other side of the table.

"You'll have all the time in the world to think because we have to send everyone home. We don't have other scenes to film here. Even if you use a stand-in, we'd have to reshoot the entire scene for all the close-ups," she points out.

I can hear the disappointment in her voice. We'll have to call Kevin about this delay in filming because it will cost us a good chunk of the budget. Considering we're a women's team he was reluctant to have on board, he'll probably be more harsh than usual in yelling at us. She's just setting her mind and heart up for the yelling that will come in the next half an hour.

"I'll send everyone home, then we do that call. We'll do it together," she says firmly.

I nod. I should be the one going out there and giving the news, but I honestly need a few minutes to calm down and gather the strength to have a conversation with the producer. He called me two days ago when I rearranged the schedule. He called me yesterday to ask if I have everything under control. I'm sure he'll call me as soon as he knows we had to send everyone home. It's better if I just call him and avoid pissing him off further.

Ellen comes back and sits down in front of me.

"Put him on speaker," she suggests, sitting in the same spot as before.

I put my phone on the table between us and hit the button next to Kevin's name. He answers on the second ring and it's not pleasant.

"What?" he barks.

I take a deep breath and Ellen gives me a reassuring smile.

"Harrison called in sick and we had to send everyone home," I spit out almost in a rush.

I kick myself for that. I should sound more confident with him but I can't help feeling small and scared. This is the first time I've had to deal with a production so big and I feel like everything is slipping from my hands.

"Oh, for fuck's sake!" he yells. "Is that your set or not? Who's running it? Because you clearly have no clue about how to be in charge."

Anger rises in my chest. Like it's my fault that a spoiled, unprofessional brat is driving me crazy. Making me look like a fool and reinforcing the idea that I'm not fit for a big role in Hollywood—it's making me simmer even more. I've been there once because of a man; I don't want to go back again.

"Harrison is the one creating problems, calling in sick for the third day in a row. I know we're behind schedule, but let me handle this the way I see fit," I say in a firmer tone.

He scoffs and I want to hang up on him.

"Handle it like you see it fit? Are you sure you're up to the job? Because it seems like I have to put a more experienced director on set to guide you. You have a problem with Harrison, that's the problem. You assured me we could save on hiring an experienced producer on set because you could flank the new guy you've already worked with and guide him in a job you've been doing your entire life. But here you are, calling the executive producer at six in the morning because you can't handle your beef with Harrison. What the fuck are you doing on that set?"

"I don't need anyone here. I'm more than capable of handling it. I called you because it's the right thing to do, not to dump the problem on you. And I want to remind you that I didn't want Harrison. You pushed him on me. If it was up to me, he'd be out the door since day one." At this point, I'm fuming.

"I did what I needed to get you the money to film this fucking movie. If you're so confident in solving the problem, did you go find out what this sickness is?" He mocks me, knowing Harrison stayed home after our fight.

He doesn't believe he's sick like everyone else here. I'm looking like a naive fool to feed him this lie. Maybe I'm really not fit for this job. Maybe it's too big for me and I don't have the experience to handle people—problems—like Harrison.

"I'm on my way there and to bring his ass on set," I grit out.

"We'll see," he murmurs before hanging up so abruptly I find myself blinking at the phone.

"Well, that was quite a conversation." Ellen looks at me like she wants to rip off his balls with her bare hands.

"I swear, I've never met a bigger prick, not even when I was trying to make it big in Hollywood. And I've met some shady producers." I let out a sigh.

"Are you going to see if Harrison is really sick?" she asks.

"I have to. I gave him three days to give us an explanation, I'm not waiting longer."

I arrive at Harrison's house on the Hollywood Crest—in the heart of the most exclusive neighborhood of Holmby Hills—almost an hour later. The house is nestled in with lush trees and greenery, giving it the privacy a Hollywood star like Harrison needs.

The gates open as soon as I'm in front of them, even before I figure out how to ring the bell. He probably has cameras on the entrance, letting him see who's about to disrupt his day. I drive along the driveway until I reach a fountain in the middle of a paved roundabout in front of the house.

"A freaking Tuscany-style villa?" I mutter to myself while turning off the car and walking up to the front door surrounded by what appear to be orange trees.

It always amazes me what rich people can afford and what they decide to buy with their money. Harrison didn't plant these trees, they look like they've been here since the eighties, probably since when this mansion was built, but what did he think when he saw it before buying it? "Damn, I love orange juice, let's buy a freaking mansion with orange trees!"

Maybe it's because I come from a middle-class family, but I'm not used to Hollywood extravagance.

The door in front of me swings open and a disheveled Harrison scowls at me. I didn't expect him to be so…imperfect. His hair is sticking out all over his head like it's been days since he washed it. He's wearing a white crumpled t-shirt with gray sweatpants and looks like he's been to hell and back.

I frown as I enter when he steps aside to let me in.

"I thought you'd come when I called in sick the first day," he mumbles as he guides me into his house made of arches, stucco, raw wood and stone.

We reach a country style kitchen and he beckons me to sit on one of the stools at the counter while he pours two cups of coffees, fishing a bottle of honey from a cabinet and putting it in front of me. He knows how I take my coffee and I don't know how to feel about that.

"What happened to you?" I ask when he doesn't offer any explanation about his clearly distressed status.

He shrugs. "I almost died three days ago." He peeks from behind his cup to gauge my reaction.

"You what?" It takes me a few seconds to register what he said and process the information.

"You know the pasta you gave me on set the other day? Well, turns out it wasn't vegan after all."

"What does that have to do with you almost dying?" I don't understand what he's talking about.

"There was butter and mozzarella in it and I can't eat them," he explains.

"Are you lactose intolerant or something? Did you get diarrhea?" I know sometimes people get it really bad and have terrible cramps.

He sighs and shakes his head like he's had this conversation too many times. "No, I'm not intolerant to milk proteins, I am allergic to milk. It's so bad I have to walk around with an EpiPen in case I accidentally ingest some."

I feel the blood drain from my face. "Are you serious right now? Because if this is a joke it's not funny. I'm not laughing."

"The pasta wasn't vegan. Someone just picked out the bigger chunk of mozzarella, thinking that was enough. But they obviously didn't squeeze the pieces from inside the pasta, and when I came home and ate it, I start to swell up like a balloon, including my throat."

I'm staring at him, baffled, unable to process that I almost killed him.

"Fortunately, my publicist was here and gave me the shot immediately before bringing me straight to the emergency room without calling an ambulance. I would have been all over the gossip magazines and their theories about a drug overdose or whatever."

"Are you fucking serious? Why didn't you tell me? I roasted your ass for the vegan food and then I gave you pasta and didn't even bother to check if it was really vegan. I almost killed you! Isn't that something you should tell people you work with?" I burst out indignantly.

He smiles and sips his coffee. "Yes and no. Sometimes it's more dangerous if I tell people I'm allergic because they don't understand the difference between allergic and intolerant and, like you said before, they think I'll eventually just shit in my pants. When you tell someone you're allergic to nuts, for example, they check a million times before giving you something because they know you'll drop dead if they don't pay attention. Milk allergy is quite rare in adults, usually you find it in kids but they outgrow it. It's why nobody pays attention to it."

I feel stupid. I thought he was throwing a tantrum and I preferred to listen to the rumors instead of asking him why he needs to eat vegan. Something sounded off when they told me he wanted something vegan but he ate chicken before. It didn't fit with the perfect image Harrison is so careful to project on the outside. But I preferred the easy way, the rumors I needed to confirm my theory that he's a difficult actor to work with.

"So you'd rather be considered a diva for your absurd requests than tell people the truth?"

He shrugs again and stares out the window toward the luscious garden behind it. "They think I'm some lightweight Hollywood star anyway, so why put so much effort into trying to contradict people if I can't change their minds anyway?"

I think about all the movies he starred in. They all have the same characteristics: high budget, they want him naked, they break the record for higher grossing income every single time. They're made to make money. Except one, the one that earned him the Oscar. It's like there are two Harrisons. One before the Oscar and one after it.

"Why did you want to make this movie so badly? Why do you put so much effort into making it perfect? You're starring in it, you'll be successful no matter what."

"Isn't it obvious?" He raises a challenging eyebrow.

"Because you want to break the cycle," I murmur more for myself than answering him.

He nods. "I want to show people I'm the same actor that won that Oscar, that I didn't disappear or change. I'm stuck in this cycle where they offer me only roles that make them money, and the more of those movie I make, the more I get offered the same old shit."

I nod, seeing his point. The moment he succeeded they took away his ability to choose to showcase his skills. If he doesn't stay in that cycle he's stuck in making money, they forget about him, unless he shows them he's capable of more. That he can make money with serious movies too. But nobody will offer him a chance because they forgot the guy that won the Oscar.

He has to remind them of *that guy* and this movie is his chance to shout out loud to everyone that he's a damn good actor.

And to think I almost killed him.

CHAPTER 9
Harrison

I'm standing in in the middle of the set, trying to figure out how to approach this scene. It's crucial for the movie that I get this right. This will set the credibility of the character. If I don't win the hearts of the audience here, I won't get another chance. They won't trust me.

"Are you ready for this scene?" Sienna approaches me while people work around us to get the set ready.

I'm surprised by her approach as I was surprised this morning when she smiled and greeted me. It's the first time since we started filming that has happened. Something shifted yesterday during our conversation at my house. She seems more willing to avoid a fight and I'm more relaxed around her too.

"I'm not sure," I admit.

I take a look at the script in my hand as if it can give me some clue. Strangely, this is the page where I have the least notes of all. When I learn and rehearse a scene, I fill it with notes reminding me about ideas I had of how to approach it. Not this time.

"How are you thinking you'll do it?" she asks and my head snaps toward her.

She has a relaxed face, not the usual scowl, and she actually seems to want to listen to what I have to say. It takes me a few seconds longer to give her an answer.

"I usually have a clear vision of how I want to do it. I *feel* how I have to do it. But this time the only thing that comes to my mind is to shout and scream, and that doesn't seem right to me." I look at her and she's frowning.

I can see she agrees with me that there is something not working with that, but she doesn't point it out.

"What do you think. How would you approach it?" I ask her and she seems a bit surprised by my question, but she recovers immediately, pouting a bit like she does when she's focused on something important.

"I think my first reaction would be a complete lack of reaction. I think I wouldn't move, do anything, I don't think I would even breath. My usual response would probably be to process the information, the reasoning, the why. I would have a million questions but I couldn't voice them out loud. I don't know if I would cry. I'm a person who cries when I get overly emotional, when I get angry, but in this case, I would probably be too numb to cry."

I can somehow relate to that. I go back to the only time I had to deal with death and find some similarities to her reaction. I try to dig deep into the emotion of that day, even if it hurts, even if it makes my heart ache in my chest.

"You found it," she says quietly and smiles. "I can see that you found what hold on to in the scene."

And I smile too because I can feel in my gut this is the right direction. I raise my face to the ceiling and when I lower it, I take a glimpse of the set. They're all staring at us like we're some kind of strange animals. I smile, understanding their stupor. We've been fighting nonstop until yesterday, and if it's strange for me—this new interaction between Sienna and I—I can't imagine how it looks for the others. The extra playing the part of the doctor looks like he's going to faint.

"Do you think we can try it without a rehearsal?" I ask Sienna and she seems a bit hesitant. I'm so convinced that she doesn't question me, and I feel comfortable insisting. "Just this time, I promise. If I have to dig deep into my emotions, I don't know how many times I can do it without draining everything I have," I explain and she thinks about it.

She looks around and waves at the actor, the extra who will be in the scene with me, Ellen, and the director of photography, Christoph.

"Okay, but if it doesn't work, we go over it until we fix it. This scene is the most crucial one in the entire movie. Your character's grief is the emotional core of the script, you have to make the audience believe you, your pain. They have to see your heart shatter in front of the camera," she says firmly.

"I promise. If I can't pull it off, we go back to rehearsing it." I nod and see out of the corner of my eye the four people approaching us cautiously.

Ellen studies me like she's trying to figure out if I drugged Sienna, considering we're not tearing out each other's eyes.

"Can you do the scene without rehearsing?" she asks the other actor. "Just follow Harrison's cues. He has one line in this scene, but you still have to manage not looking like a cold fish when he breaks down."

He nods. "Yes. I just need to go through my entrance and position in the room, then I'm fine with the rest. I don't have to walk out, right? The scene cuts with me still in the room." He sounds confident and I don't think he'll have a problem.

Sienna looks at Christoph. "You have to help me out with this. Do you think you can give me all the cameras covering this in one take?"

"You aiming at a one-take wonder?" He grins and I feel the pressure of this moment dawning on me.

Doing the scene right in one take is one of those rare occurrences during filming. It's not just a matter of being prepared, trying the scene, and being perfectly coordinated with the person interacting with you in the scene, you also have to count on a bit of luck. And that you can't rehearse.

"It's worth a try. It's a particularly emotional scene. It's challenging to pull off more than one great performance to cover all the angles. I don't want to risk having a weak scene in the editing because the angles have a different impact," she says firmly, and I can see the excitement bubbling up while she speaks.

She believes we can do this and I feel my heart squeeze in my chest. I don't know what changed from how she saw me yesterday, but I can't shake the feeling that something massive happened. It's electrifying to work with her when we aren't constantly fighting. Our ideas mingle in a way I didn't think possible and it's mind-blowing. She's actually letting me try this, express myself, my heart, my skills. It's exciting and terrifying at the same time because if I can't pull it off, I'll let everyone down.

"Well, you have an Oscar-winning actor here. If anyone can do it, it's him," Ellen says winking at me.

I blush. I actually blush like a little girl at her compliment. She's always on Sienna's side and this concession is a pleasant surprise. I think she's trying to keep the mood light between everyone, avoiding pissing me or Sienna off. Everyone is so thrown off by us not fighting, they're walking on eggshells around us to not shatter the precarious peace.

"Can you rehearse the position on set while you dive into your character?" Sienna asks me and I nod.

We spend the next hour rehearsing the positions while operators set up the additional cameras and I dive deep down into the corner of my heart I locked away years ago because it was hurting too much.

When Sienna calls rolling and we start filming, I feel the pain already settling in my chest. I'm not Harrison anymore, I'm a father who got into a car accident and his daughter is in surgery suffering the consequences of his actions. I'm a man replaying in his head every decision he made that lead to that moment, in that hospital.

When the doctor comes into the scene, I stand up but the only thing I hear is, "I'm sorry."

"What? How? She was just talking to me!" I choke on my lines. My throat is clogged with emotion that feels too real, too painful in my chest.

I'm transported to the moment when Raphael came to my home one sunny afternoon more than fifteen years ago. I remember him choking while telling me Alba was gone. *How? Why? I was texting her not even an hour ago.* I feel the numbness as he explains and my legs giving up under me.

This time I flop onto a plastic chair in a fake hospital, not the front stairs of my childhood home, but it doesn't matter. The numbness is the same, the disbelief festering in my thoughts with questions I can't answer. Doubts I can't voice.

Then the realization hits. Hard. Relentless. Pain invades my chest like a wave. No, not a wave, like the rumble of the earth just before an earthquake hits. That low, deep sound that enters your bones and spikes your fear. You know it's coming, and you can't hide, run, or avoid it. It hits you hard like the earth shaking under your feet. It knocks you off your feet and you are powerless.

The first sob hits me like that first hit of the earthquake. Powerful, merciless, scarring. The second one hits when I'm trying to recover from the first and the third is the one that knocks the air out of my lungs.

A guttural sound rises in my throat, trying to free the pain in my chest, but when it comes out it's like opening a dam. All the pain I bottled up during those past years comes out without any chance of stopping it. It's so violent it doesn't let me breathe. I bend over, clutching my gut, and I feel the tears streaming down my face, neck, soaking the neckline of my t-shirt.

It's no ordinary acting I'm doing here. It's as raw, honest, ugly as the pain I'm feeling. I'm not the pretty boy everyone loves now, this is the real me, with my beautiful and ugly faces. It's the essence of who I am.

I'm brought back to reality when a hand rests on my shoulder. I open my eyes and realize Sienna is crouched next to me with a worried expression and eyes shining with tears. Sobs shake my chest but I have the strength to straighten a bit and dry the tears from my eyes. I look around and can't find a single dry eye in the room. They're all looking at me, some with their hands over their mouth, others with pained expressions.

I didn't even hear her call *Cut*.

"Are you okay?" she asks and I hear the concern in her voice.

"Yes." I sob. "This is why I wasn't sure about the rehearsals and everything. Makeup will hate me for this." I half-smile, pointing at my face.

She lets out a sound halfway between a laugh and a huff.

She stands up and turns toward the crew in front of us. "Good first take, folks. It was fantastic. Good job, everyone!" she shouts and, after a momentary pause where there is no sound, a collective cheer rises on the set.

I take a deep breath and try to get my shit together when the actor playing the doctor puts a hand on my shoulder.

"That was an outstanding performance," he says and my chest expands with happiness. "You made me wake up at six for two hours of work, but it was worth it," he adds, grinning.

I let out a laugh. "Thank you."

I stand up and walk toward my chair where I put my stuff. When I pass by Sienna chatting with Ellen, she turns to me and stops me, grabbing my hand.

"Take the time you need before the next scene," she says and I just nod.

I'm emptied. I put my feelings away about that day years ago because it was impossible to survive Alba's death. I had to cope somehow with her absence and I pushed down the pain in a place in my heart I couldn't reach. Today, when I opened that part of my heart, all the feelings poured out, leaving me empty and spent. I need to be alone for a minute, to understand how to deal with what I awakened today.

* * *

I just finish changing when a soft knock comes from the door. "Come on in."

Sienna's black mane peeks in as soon as the door opens. She seems unsure whether to come in but then steps a foot inside. She closes the door behind her but doesn't come closer to the couch where I'm seated.

"I wanted to tell you that your performance today was exceptional," she says in a soft voice, as though not knowing how to approach me anymore. We always shout at each other and it sounds strange to talk without fighting.

"Thank you."

"I wanted you to know that I appreciate that you dug into those emotions. I know it wasn't easy for you."

I can't stop a smile curling my lips. I lower my gaze to my hands, not sure what to say. This is the most honest appreciation

I've ever received on set and I don't know how to deal with it. It's difficult for me to talk about that day. It's like stepping into a room that suddenly becomes hot and suffocating. You can feel the oxygen is running out, but you can't do anything to avoid it. When you turn around the door you came in disappeared and you are trapped in your own thoughts.

"Was it someone you loved?" Her voice is almost a whisper but it tears through my thoughts like a shout.

"She was my best friend. The sister of the person who's like a brother. She died in a car accident when she was barely nineteen and she ripped a piece of my heart in the process. I haven't dug into those feelings for more than fifteen years and it was quite… frightening," I admit for the first time out loud.

She tilts her head and studies me for a long moment. I can't read what she's thinking but she doesn't seem angry with me.

"Thank you for sharing those feeling with us on set. I really appreciate that you put all your suffering in that scene. I know it wasn't easy for you," she repeats, surprising me.

It's my turn to study her. I want to say a lot of things but just one comes out of my mouth.

"Thank you for trusting me in not rehearsing the scene. It really helped me to put everything I had in that one take and it paid off."

She smiles and nods, lowering her eyes to her shoes.

"Will it always be this awkward between us?" I ask, chuckling.

"Probably." She shrugs, smiling. "Have a good night, Harrison," she adds after a long silence.

"You too," I say before she disappears behind the door.

I don't know what happened yesterday, but I'm happy that we finally got to bury the hatchet. I prefer awkward a million times over the tension between us.

CHAPTER 10
Sienna

Breathe. I have to remember to breathe. It's been ten days since the epic scene where Harrison nailed one of the best performances of his life and things finally started to run smoothly on set. Too smoothly, to be honest, and this is the moment I was dreading and anticipating at the same time.

We can't get this scene done.

It's the seventh take and it feels like we're drowning. It's June sixth, Los Angeles is melting under a wave of exceptional heat and we are miserable on set today. Nobody talks much, we just wave paper in front of our faces and move as little as possible to not sweat too much. I feel the sweat coating my upper lip and forehead. My t-shirt is a mess, sticking to my skin, and I'm sweating on my scalp under this messy bun on my head.

This is a nightmare.

The air conditioning is running at full force, driving the sound engineer crazy because they have to mask the buzzing sound in the background. But it's not enough. Cameras, lighting, and all the equipment are still generating heat. We're dying slowly, cooking in this building.

The light on set falters mid-scene and I have to call the cut.

"Are you kidding me?" I shout, exasperated, and a general groan rises from people exhausted from this day. And it's just noon. "What happened?" I ask walking to the technician tampering with the light. Next to me, Ellen seems to want to scream.

The guy crouched next to a bunch of cable hisses, retracting his hand quickly and shaking it. "It's too hot. The equipment is overheating and not working properly," he explains and I feel my stomach sink.

"Is there a way to get around it?" I ask when he stands up after turning off the light.

He shrugs, looking down at the culprit as if for a solution. "Not really. It's not like we can put ice on it to cool it down. It's way too hot today and the air conditioning can't keep up. We can try to use the fans to cool it, but I think the sound engineer is going to have my ass if I add other background noise in the scene."

I nod and rub a hand over my face. When I look up, I find Harrison next to me.

"It seems like we have to call it a day," he says.

"Don't even say it. We don't have time or money to waste this day." I point a finger at his face and he grins.

"I think he's right," Ellen chips in. "We can't even move without sweating or fainting. There's a heat advisory today telling people to stay at home. We can't risk someone having a heatstroke and ending up in the hospital."

She points out something I was already worried about. I'm mostly concerned about the technicians carrying out tasks that are already challenging. It's not safe for people working in these conditions and I can't risk someone getting sick—or worse.

"And we risk the equipment overheating and catching on fire, burning down the set," the guy in front of me remarks and I shiver. I don't need the fire department here trying to put out a fire that will burn down half of Los Angeles with these temperatures and Santa Ana winds picking up strength, even out of season.

"And I'm sweating so much I have streams of sweat running down my asscrack," Harrison adds.

"Geez. That's disgusting." I scrunch up my nose.

He laughs. "I know, but it's true. I can't work like this. My shirt's sticking to my chest like I'm a sweaty pig." He points at the fabric plastered to his abs and pecks, outlining his perfect, defined body.

I hate to admit it, but they're right. We don't even have a good shot from today's work because it's impossible to work in these conditions. I hope Kevin won't have my head because I'm sending them home.

"Listen, everybody. It's way too hot today and we risk burning down this place or someone ending up in the hospital with a heatstroke. Go home, cool down and see you tomorrow!" I shout and everybody groans in relief. They don't even have the strength to cheer. "Please, be sure that nothing catches fire," I say to the guy handling the lights.

"Don't worry, I'll turn off the breakers and just leave the air conditioning on," he assures me and I feel a bit relieved.

After not even half an hour, the set is completely empty, with just Harrison and I left. I don't know exactly why he's still here, but when I close the door behind me, he's right next to me.

"I forgot my backpack," he says, showing me the blue culprit on his shoulder.

I nod and smile. "Have a good day," I say, turning around and walking toward my trailer.

"You're going home, right?" Harrison calls out.

I turn around and shake my head. "I'm going to take advantage of the air conditioning in my trailer."

He frowns. "How so?"

I let out a sigh. I'm embarrassed to talk about this with him. He lives in a huge mansion in Hollywood, while I'm just a step away from being homeless.

"Our air conditioning is not working and the landlord refuses to fix it. If I go home, I'll melt on the couch," I explain.

He strolls toward me, pulling up the backpack on his shoulder, his biceps bulging in the process. Even with his hair flopping down on his forehead with sweat, he's still gorgeous.

"So you're going to stay in that trailer until the heat wave goes away? You're crazy."

"I don't have any other choice. It's not like I can afford to go to a hotel," I point out, a bit annoyed.

It's easy for him to talk. He lives in a huge mansion surrounded by lush trees. I, on the other hand, don't have the money to buy a popsicle, let alone pay for a room with air conditioning.

"What if they turn off the air conditioning because the set is empty?" He raises an eyebrow challenging me.

I thought about this possibility and I don't want to make a plan unless it happens. "I'll die in there, I suppose."

"You're coming home with me," he states, beckoning with his head toward the parking lot.

"What? No!" I almost squeal.

"Yes, you are! You have a roommate, right? Ask her to come too if you don't want to be alone with the big bad guy." He points a finger at his chest.

I roll my eyes. "It's not that. And she's at her mom's this week, so she's not at home, luckily."

"Good, so you don't have any excuse. Come on. I'm sweating out here."

"I'm not coming!" I insist stubbornly, even if the idea of air conditioning is tempting.

"Why not?" he asks, exasperated.

I open my mouth to say something, but the truth is I don't have a good reason to refuse his offer.

"That's what I thought. Stop being a stubborn ass and accept that sometimes people just want to help you," he says, turning around, and this time I follow him.

"It's not that. The problem is when they ask you something in return for their favors," I mumble as I keep up with his long strides.

He throws a quick glance in my direction. "If they ask for something in return, they are not favors, they are services and you should be able to choose from whom you want those ser- vices."

I think about his words and, somehow, they make more sense than any other part of the argument. If the price is to suck a dick, at least I get to choose which dick to suck. Not that I'd ever do something like that, but it's a good reminder to take back the power that men want us to give up.

"No Ferrari today?" I struggle to hide a smile when we reach a black SUV in the parking lot.

"Too flashy. I use it only when I want to show off." He grins.

I sit down on the leather seat and feel my skin stick to the material. "This heatwave is terrible," I murmur more to myself than to him.

"I know. I can't even put my hands on the steering wheel. We have to wait until the air conditioning is working before we go home." He turns on the air conditioning and a bit of fresh air comes out in front of me.

After Harrison is finally able to put his hands on the wheel, we hit the Los Angeles traffic without saying too much. It's strange to be in a car with him. Under normal circumstances, I would have gone out with the actors since we began filming. The bond you create on set during filming is a long-lasting one that often ends in lifelong friendship.

With Harrison things didn't start that way. That's partly my fault. I should have given him more credit and not judged him based on rumors and preconceived ideas I had of him. On the other hand, he didn't make it easy for me, pointing out my every fault. The result is that this drive to his house is a bit awkward.

When we finally park in his garage, I walk out of the car and take a deep breath. It's already less suffocating here. Walking into his house, I'm pleasantly greeted by a cooling breeze, but not too cold like some places can be. Sometimes the shock is so sudden I feel sick. Not in this house. Everything is tasteful and balanced, from the furniture to the temperature, and I'm not surprised. After getting to know Harrison a bit, I find that a lot of his extroverted image is a facade for the public, while in private he's a very balanced and calm man.

"I have water, soda, or iced tea. I'm not offering you alcohol, considering the temperature," he offers, peeking into his fridge.

"Iced tea is perfect, thank you."

He points at a cabinet and I open it and grab couple of glasses while he put the pitcher with the tea on the counter. He grabs a lemon, cuts a couple of slices, then gets ice from the freezer and puts it in the glasses, before pouring the tea and topping it with the lemon.

He grabs the pitcher and walks out of the kitchen toward the patio, crosses it and goes down a pathway in the garden surrounded by low bushes and some sparse tall trees until we reach the swimming pool. I follow him with the two glasses.

"Put it there." He points to the low table between two deck chairs and then motions for me to follow him.

The swimming pool is surrounded by tall trees and, this time of day, they cast a shade over the water. It's hot, but not hot like the inside of the warehouse where we work.

We enter in the pool house with its generous living space with couches, a table, and a small kitchen, and walk straight to a bedroom.

"You can find guest swimsuits in there. Choose what you want, there should be enough sizes to find something that fits you," he says pointing at a dresser under the window.

Of course he has swimsuits for his guests. I wonder how many women wore them before me. I don't say it out loud. He's kind enough to lend me a bikini, I'm not spitting on his offer.

I open the first drawer and take a look at what's inside. Everything is brand new, with the tags still on, and I feel guilty for assuming I had to wear something other women used before me. I appreciate the fact that there are one-pieces in every size, not assuming every woman feels comfortable in skimpy bikinis. But I choose a skimpy one because it's way too hot to cover my skin, and because I've never had a problem with showing my body.

When I walk out in my red outfit, I find him pushing up from the edge of the swimming pool to get out after taking a dive. The rivulets of water run down his muscular back, disappearing into the waistband of his blue swim trunks. His broad shoulders and trim waist are a vision. I've always found him attractive, utterly irritating, but attractive nonetheless. But discovering that he's not the bad guy I thought he was, and in fact has quite an appealing personality, adds something to the turmoil rising in my stomach. It's becoming more and more difficult to find reasons to hate him.

He pushes himself up and rubs a hand through his hair to shake off some water. His arms bend, making his biceps bulge. I bite my lip and squeeze my thighs.

Damn! He is drool-worthy. I want to lick every single inch of that glorious body.

As soon as this thought crosses my mind, I recoil. He is Harrison Bates, not someone I should consider sharing bodily fluids with. No matter how drool-worthy he is.

I walk around the swimming pool and reach him at the deck chair.

"The water is amazing, you should try it," he says, and I don't miss him checking me out in this red bikini.

I take a sip of the ice tea to try and calm my hormones. His gaze leaves a scorching trail over my naked skin. He bites his lower lip and for a moment I'm tempted to taste his mouth too. Would it be soft, rough, hot? How would it feel on my flesh? And his tongue? It takes me an unnecessary long time to divert my mind from the dirty thoughts my brain is conjuring.

"Are you coming in too?" I ask putting down the glass on the table.

He doesn't answer, at least not using words. He laces his strong arms around my waist and rushes to the swimming pool, dragging both of us into it. I let out a shriek before closing my eyes and pinching my nose.

I can feel the bubbles tickling my skin and his strong body against mine. I can't tell what's up and what's down and feel the panic kicking in. I frantically try to swim to the surface, but suddenly he's dragging me up. When I'm finally able to breathe again, I throw my arms around Harrison's neck, my legs around his waist, and cling to him for dear life. I mold my body to his, my heart beating so fast I'm sure he can feel it trying to jump out of my chest.

I stare at him, wide-eyed, trying to take in more air I can to calm down my racing heart. He's staring at me with a small perplexed smile and I don't fail to notice his hands gripping my ass. I don't know if he realized where he put them. His fingers are scorching hot against my skin.

"You can swim, right?" He chuckles, puzzled.

I tighten my grip on him. "Barely. I'm not comfortable when I don't know if I can touch the bottom," I confess, tightening my grip around his waist.

His chest molds perfectly to mine and I'm surprised by how much I like his skin against mine. How his perfect, toned body is quite pleasant to touch.

Damn, he fits perfectly between my thighs! Stop your thoughts there, you pervert!

He laughs and slips his arms around my waist, maybe realizing his grip was a bit inappropriate for the professional relationship we have. Not that my legs clenching around his waist is any better, but I'm the one panicking here! Though I'm not completely sure I'm doing it for safety reasons. The feeling of having him so close is inebriating.

"Sorry about that. I promise you can touch the bottom everywhere in here." He apologizes and I put a tentative tiptoe on the ground. The water reaches my shoulder and I sigh in relief. Or at least I try, because my arms are still around Harrison's neck and his are around my waist. His handsomeness is intoxicating.

I find myself staring into his blue eyes and I'm so close I notice a few bits of gold inside the ocean of his irises. His dark blond lashes are long, the pearly drops of water trapped between them making his eyes stand out even more.

I don't realize I'm staring at him until he clears his throat and walks toward the pool edge, helping me out. When I'm finally on the deck chair again, I sigh in relief.

"Thank you for letting me stay here. I really appreciate your help," I say taking a sip of the tea.

Harrison studies me for a long moment. "It's you that have a problem with me, not the other way around. I'll always be there for someone I'm working with."

And just like that, Harrison proves he's not the bad person I made him out to be in my head. I feel guilty for treating him like shit and making his experience on my set a nightmare. Something I promised I would never do.

I lower my gaze, unable to look him in the eye. I feel like a shitty person and I can't shake this feeling in my chest. "Sorry about that. I don't have any excuses for how I treated you," I mumble way too low to sound convincing.

His fingers graze my chin and force me to look him the eye. I can only describe his expression as a mixture of concern and wisdom. Why can't he just be a pretty-boy star? It would be easy, but I suspect nothing is easy with him.

"Don't beat you up for that. We got over it. Just enjoy the rest of the filming and put everything you have into this movie," he says in a serious tone.

I smile. "You really like your job, don't you?"

"I love it. I don't think I could live without it." He looks almost dreamy as he answers.

I think Harrison and I have a lot more in common than I thought, and the realization is scary enough to make me want to run away from his house.

CHAPTER 11
Harrison

A soft knock at the door startles me.

"Come on in," I say, looking out the window and barely making out Sienna's outline. It's pitch-black, what time is it?

"Thank God, you're alive. What are you doing here? It's almost ten." She looks a bit worried.

I rub a couple of fingers over my eyes and sigh. "Sorry. I lost track of the time."

"What are you doing?" she asks, coming closer.

"I was going over tomorrow's scenes. I can't get this one right." I point at the script.

She turns her head as though to leave, but then seems to give up and sits next to me. Her long hair is tied up in a messy bun. After yesterday, when she walked out of my pool house with that red bikini, I can't stop thinking about her glorious curves in my arms. I know we had our disagreements. Okay, maybe disagreements is putting it mildly. We ripped each other's throats out, but the truth is she's an intriguing person wrapped up in an unbelievably amazing body. She's smart, she's funny when she relaxes a bit, and she has those luscious pouty lips I want to kiss.

"Is it a problem that Viola isn't here to run lines with you?" she asks.

"No, it's not like that. I know she has her little girl to take care of."

"If you want, I can run lines with you. I don't mind," she insists.

"Sienna. I'm fine, really," I reassure her with a smile.

"Doesn't it bother you that she can't ever rehearse with you off set because she has to run home?" she flat-out asks.

I know she's a perfectionist and the fact that Viola can't be here twenty-four-seven freaks her out. There's no such a thing as personal life in her vocabulary, and while she doesn't blame her or make her stay longer, she doesn't understand how an actress can live like that. It's a foreign concept for her. She breathes, *lives* for her job. I'm the same way, but only when I'm focused on a project. I enjoy my life when I take time off between movies.

I shrug. "No, not really. I'm used to working with different costars and I don't find it difficult to adapt to different lifestyles. At the end of the day, I'm the single one with a more flexible schedule. She's a single mother who has to juggle her job with having a five-year-old. I can adapt and help her out."

She looks at me for a long moment, those dark gorgeous eyes scrutinizing me with an intensity I'm drawn to. She's one of the most gorgeous women I have ever had the chance to meet and I want to kiss those lips. I really, *really*, want to. My gaze flickers lower on that pout and it's difficult for me to divert it. And when they part a bit, I almost give in.

"You're not what I expected," she says, dragging me out of my daze.

"What? Rich and spoiled? I am rich. You were right about that." I grin and wink at her.

She bumps her shoulder against mine. "Spoiled. I thought you were a brat throwing tantrums but you're not."

I know what she thought about me and that's why I wanted to prove her wrong. "Sorry to disappoint." I laugh.

She is silent for a long moment. "You're a perfectionist, aren't you?"

I nod. "I like to plan in advance so I can improvise without feeling weird when I'm on set," I explain.

She studies me again and I start to squirm in my seat a bit. I'm not used to such scrutiny, not by a director I'm working with, at least.

"Explain. It's an interesting theory."

"It's not rocket science. I have anxiety, so knowing what happens next helps me to be comfortable in my own skin. When I study a scene and feel confident with it, it's like muscle memory, I can do it without thinking about it. Then I can pay attention to my surroundings, the other actors in the scene with me, pick up some nuances of their performance and adapt to it. I can't do that if I have to focus on my acting, my lines, how to move in the space I have."

She nods and seems fascinated by my explanation. It's who I am: I'm an anxious person dealing with a job that requires me to be under scrutiny every day of my life. It's stressful; it requires me to pull off high-level performances, but I love it and would never change anything about my life.

"What is it that bothers you about tomorrow?" she finally asks, looking down at the drawing the production assistant made for me.

"The problem is, I haven't seen the location."

She frowns but waits for me to clarify.

"On the set in here," I point to the building outside the trailer. "I got comfortable. I know it like the back of my hand because we filmed half the movie in there. But tomorrow is new. We're in a house and not a set our people built, there are different spaces, you can't bring down walls to fit a camera or anything like that. I feel trapped when I don't have enough time to prepare myself."

She grabs the piece of paper in front of me and points a finger at different lines, the floor plan for tomorrow.

"You should have told me you wanted to see the location. We went there the other day to scout it and decided where to put the camera and everything," she points out and I shrug.

The truth is, I don't know how far I can go with my demands when it comes to her. I'm someone who always finds a way to interact with the director even before we start filming, to get the pulse of the situation, get comfortable around them, try to get a clue about what I can ask and what pisses them off. The problem here is that everything pisses her off because we started a war that ruined our relationship from the beginning.

I blame myself partly for that. I could have stopped long before my emergency room visit, but I decided to be a child and fuel her anger instead to find a peaceful solution.

"I didn't want to bother you." I shrug.

She seems to want to point out something but then gives up and looks down at the paper.

"There will be cameras here, here and here." She points and I get closer to take a good look.

"If I walk from here to here," I point at the floor plan, "is this glass door open or do you have a problem with the reflection of the cameras? I'll have papers to go through, but I can have them on the coffee table here instead of the kitchen counter on the other side of the room. So we can avoid moving the camera in front of the glass door."

I get excited discussing these things with her. I can feel the anxiety slowing down and easing the grip on my stomach. I can finally relax a bit.

"We talked about that, and we think we should be fine with the right lighting and everything, keeping the door closed. It's a cabin in the woods. We won't have a problem with traffic noises, but the birds in that place are freaking loud." She laughs for the first time since we've had some time alone and the sound is like magic.

"I know. They're an inch high and sound like they have the lungs of an opera singer, right?" I grin as she laughs even more.

"Exactly." She shakes her head.

"So what do you think? Do we keep the paper on the coffee table?"

She frowns and pouts and I want to bite and suck those lips. "I'm not sure. There will be three people in the living room. With the couch here and the TV here, I think it's way too cramped if all three of you stay on this side of the room. I need you to walk over here and give me some breadth in the scene. We need the lake in the background anyway because we have to bring it to the audience's attention, so don't worry. Walk to the kitchen counter and leave the rest to me to worry about," she reassures me and I definitely feel more comfortable.

I watch her raise her eyes to me and flicker her gaze briefly on my lips. Our hips are touching, our shoulders too. We were so focused on our brainstorming that I didn't notice we got so close.

"Thank you," I whisper, my voice barely audible.

She lowers her gaze to my lips again and hers part in response. She is attracted to me, I can tell, but I don't know what she would do if I kissed her. There's only one way to find out, and when I slowly close the distance between us her eyes widen and she stands up abruptly.

I flinch. I'm a freaking idiot. I shouldn't have pushed my luck, especially because I risk messing up the fragile truce we built.

My heart thunders in my chest and I can't tell if it's because I anticipated that kiss way too much or because I'm terrified I ruined everything. Both scenarios are equally stressing me out.

She looks uncomfortable and I feel guilty. I clear my throat and smile.

"Thank you. I really needed to hear this, you helped me out a lot." I stumble a bit on my words. It's awkward and I'm not used to this kind of tension with people. This is new for me and I'm not sure how to act.

She nods but stays silent.

"Did you already eat? Because I didn't have dinner and we can grab something together, if you want," I blurt out when the silence between us become a bit embarrassing.

The question seems to shake her out of the awkwardness we fell into. She stiffens her spine, schools her face into a neutral expression and looks me straight in the eye.

"I'm happy we figured out your doubt and addressed it, but I think we should keep our relationship strictly professional. I don't think we should hang out outside the set," she says firmly and I feel the defeat seeping into my chest.

I ruined the only step forward we made because I couldn't resist kissing those lips. I'm an idiot and I should just be grateful she didn't kick my ass for even trying, but I feel my heart sink instead.

"Yes, sure. No problem," I say with a way-too-fake smile.

"You should go home. It's late and tomorrow we have an early shoot," she says, walking to the door and opening it.

"Give me five minutes and I'll pack my things. Goodnight, Sienna."

"Goodnight, Harrison." She steps out of the trailer and closes the door behind her.

I lean back on the couch and sigh. The problem with what just happened is not that she dodged my kiss. It's what would I have done if she hadn't. I didn't have any plan except the kiss. I don't know if I wanted it to go on or stop at that. It was an impulse reaction to my attraction to her, and I was going to fuck up everything for I don't know what.

I can honestly say that this time I reasoned with my dick, and I can confirm that my dick makes really bad decisions. Every time I screwed up with a woman it was because I gave in at my attraction for someone instead of taking a step back, a deep breath, and a cold shower.

I can't fuck up my relationship with Sienna and jeopardize my career in the process. My cock twitches in my pants, reminding me it will give me hell for this decision.

CHAPTER 12
Sienna

"I can do this," I mumble to myself staring at Harrison's trailer.

Yesterday I was in front of this same trailer, but at a different location, and I didn't know I was going to spend the night awake thinking about an almost kiss. Because he was totally going to kiss me. I have no doubt about that.

I freaked out, bad. I didn't know what to do so I just bolted. That's not like me. I face my problems and tackle them until they're behind me like a slight inconvenience in my life. Not this time, because I don't even know if a kiss is a problem. I mean, it's a huge screw-up, but at the same time, I wanted to taste those luscious lips. From a professional point of view, it's an undeniable mistake, but from a personal point of view, it's been so long since I've had a man in my life that even Harrison would do for a kiss. He is gorgeous, I can't argue that.

I take a deep breath, snap out of my indecision, and knock on his door.

"Come on in!"

I open the door, step in, and find Harrison scribbling something down on his script. I'm always amazed by how much he prepares for his part. He obviously knows his lines, but it's not just that. While most actors run their lines, he goes over and over the scene, making it his. It's like he is *living* the scene, not just playing it.

I was massively mistaken in judging his work ethic before even knowing him, assuming he was shallow based only on rumors and his social life. And I regret it, because I contributed to creating a toxic workplace for him and for everyone dealing with our fights. Normally I'm not like that, but I let my personal experience with toxic men take the reins of my decisions.

When he looks up from the page, he smiles at me. "Sorry, I needed to get this down before I forget it."

I sit in front of him, avoiding the awkwardness of yesterday's closeness. "Do you need help with it?"

He shakes his head. "I'm basically done. I was about to go home."

"Can I ask why you stay here in your trailer when you have a fabulous mansion to go back to? Not that this is a problem. I'm just curious." I lean back in the couch, studying his face.

He shrugs. "I feel lonely at home, I guess. Not that I don't like it, but it's huge and empty. Here, I can see someone walking around through the window and I feel like there are other humans on earth. Up there it's me and the freaking loud birds." He chuckles.

I didn't expect this answer. I always assumed Harrison is surrounded by hordes of adoring fans and people who want to be near him. I let my judgement be fooled by the party and social network images of him always surrounded by people. Another of my misjudgments about this man.

I nod, not sure what to say at that confession.

"Listen, I want to apologize about yesterday when I turned down your suggestion to go out for dinner. I freaked out because

I'm not used to Hollywood high-class places and I feel uncomfortable in those situations." That's at least a half-truth. I was thrown off by the almost kiss, but I also hate those places where you have to watch your every move because someone is ready to put a picture of you online if you do something weird. And being seen with Harrison Bates puts me front and center of every gossip website on earth.

He studies me with an interested expression and a small smile curving his lips. I don't know if he is amused or just curious, but he seems to believe my explanation.

He nods. "Fair enough. I wasn't suggesting one of those fancy restaurants, but I understand your point."

"Not one of those fancy restaurants? So, you famous people hang out in normal places like us mere mortals?" I joke but there's a bit of truth in my words. "I always wondered where celebrities go when they don't want to be photographed like animals at the zoo."

He laughs. A full, belly laugh that makes me smile. Sometimes his sunny attitude is as contagious as his dark moments. If there's one thing I know about Harrison, it's that he is someone who doesn't just blend into the scenery. Even his silence is deafening sometimes.

"We have our places where we don't attract attention."

"You mean, like, places where all the celebrities hang out together but in secret?" I make fun of him.

"No, that's called rehab and the food sucks there."

This time it's my turn to laugh. "Did you already eat or do you want to show me one of those places?"

I don't even know where my proposal comes from, but I find myself nervously waiting for his answer. If he turns me down, I'll probably be disappointed. The realization makes my stomach quiver in a nervous grip.

Harrison seems as surprised by my suggestion as I am. A smile spreads across his face and I'm glad he says yes.

"I'm driving." He grabs his keys and stands up.

"I have my car here." I don't want him to feel forced to give me a ride.

"I'll bring you back to pick it up later. It's a bit tricky reaching this place if you lose me following my car." He motions for me to follow him to his car and I decide to humor him.

When he stops in front of a big red muscle car, I roll my eyes. "A Camaro? Really? It's very bad boy. Congratulations." I grin.

He leans with his elbows on the top of the car and smirks at me. "It's a Z28, sweetheart, not just a Camaro," he explains, like I know what he's talking about.

"And that's, what, something special?"

He looks at me with an are-you-serious-right-now look and unlocks it for us to jump in.

"It has a big engine and it's fast. That's all you need to know. If I start talking about this car you'd probably jump out that door while I'm driving." He winks at me and I squeeze my legs. My hormones are running all over the place.

When he turns on the car, it purrs with a deep low rumble, but when he puts his foot on the gas pedal, it roars to life, squishing me against the seat.

"Okay, now I get it," I admit.

He grins at me as we drive out of the almost empty parking lot.

The drive there is mostly silent and when we arrive, I'm surprised to discover it's not a fancy part of the city, but one of those neighborhoods where normal people live, ones who don't pay millions for a house but they're happy anyway. Harrison parks in a mostly empty parking lot, except for a few cars and a food truck where the pink neon sign says "Tacos." In front of it sit five round plastic tables and chairs.

We step out of the car and walk to where the food truck is parked. Three guys, two in their late twenties and one a bit older, grin when they spot Harrison.

"Mr. Oscar! What a pleasure to have you back." One of the two younger men greets him, pushing off the counter he's leaning on.

There's no one around and I watch with amusement as they take their time with Harrison.

"Shut up, Diego. You saw me last week." He laughs and I smile at the confidence they have.

It's clear they know each other and I can't stop wondering how someone like Harrison ended up befriending them. I'm sure there's an interesting story behind that.

They all laugh and when it dies down a bit, their curious gazes land on me.

"Who is this beautiful woman and why is she hanging out with your ugly face?" The older one chuckles.

"She's my boss. Don't get me fired, Santiago." Harrison winks at me and I smile.

"Hi, I'm Sienna. And I'll pay whatever you want if you have something embarrassing to tell me about him"

They all burst out laughing and Harrison smiles. One of those gorgeous smiles that show off his dimples. One of those that melt panties. Not mine, of course.

"One time he came here with a chick that didn't like meat, cheese, or anything with gluten. She ended up eating a cup of salad and chopped tomatoes while bitching at him for half an hour until he stood up, came over here, and told us to please kill him. She heard that and dumped her salad all over his head. He had tomatoes running down his face. It was the first and last time he brought a girl here," Diego says.

"Hey! Not cool, man. You can't talk to a chick he's dating about another chick. Bro code, man." The other young guy slaps Diego on the back of the neck.

I laugh and wave my hand. "We're not dating, so we're cool. And I eat meat. How's your carne asada?"

"The best. You can't find any better in Los Angeles," Santiago assures me.

"Can you make me a quesadilla with Carne asada?"

"Queso Oaxaca?" He grins at me.

"Is there any other cheese for a quesadilla?" I raise an eyebrow, daring him to contradict me.

He puffs out his chest and looks proudly at Harrison. "Keep this one. She knows. She knows."

I laugh and shake my head while Harrison smiles at me and shrugs like he doesn't know what to do with them.

"You're not planning to kiss him tonight, right? Because he drops dead if you kiss him after eating cheese." Diego seems worried.

I hesitate for a second. I didn't think about this possibility, but I'm not planning to kiss him, right?

"Can we stop talking about my non-existent romantic relationship with Sienna, please? Did you miss the part where I told you she's my boss?" Harrison chuckles, a bit exasperated by the turn of this conversation.

"You never kissed your boss?" Diego asks raising an eyebrow at him.

Harrison thinks about it. "Honestly, no. They all had beards. It gives me a rash." He chuckles and we all laugh.

Santiago hands us our food and the other guy whose name I don't know gives us a bottle of water. Harrison pays and we sit at one of the tables.

"How do they know what you want?" I just notice he never ordered his tacos.

"I come here so often they know what I like. And removing the milk from the equation, I don't have many alternatives."

I bite into my quesadilla and moan. I turn around toward the food truck. "Hey, Santiago! You were right about the carne asada. This is the best I've ever had in Los Angeles."

The man beams and slaps Diego on the shoulder. "I told you!"

Harrison chuckles and looks at me while he bites into his dinner.

"How do you know about this place?"

He sips the water, swallowing his bite. "Five years ago, I stumbled into this parking lot so drunk I couldn't even walk straight." He starts to explain and I put down my food, focusing my attention on him.

"Nobody knows how I arrived and who dropped me here. I was at a party and I got carried away with the open bar. I threw up on the back of the truck and after Santiago made me clean up my mess, he sat me down at one at the tables and fed me tacos until I sobered up. The only thing I could say was 'Milk allergy. I die.' So fortunately, they avoided putting any dairy in it, just to be safe."

"Thank God you said that or you could have died!" I marvel at his presence of mind even under the influence.

He nods. "It's something so ingrained in my head that no matter how much I drink, that's the first thing I say when someone offers me something to eat."

"So then someone came to pick you up?"

He shakes his head. "I hung out with them all night until I sobered up and had the strength to call a taxi. Santiago packed me something to eat at home and the day after I came back here to pay them. Since then, I come here any time I can."

Even in this story about his life, there's nothing about friends or family that helped him out in a difficult moment. The more time I spend with him, the more I realize we're not so different after all. I only have Harper to count on, and sometimes she can't be there for me.

"Thank you for bringing me here. I like this place way more than the Hollywood flashy restaurants," I confess.

"To be honest, me too. I can sit here without the need to look perfect and in shape. I can eat whatever I want without someone counting the calories and putting them online. You know that there's a website that records every public meal I eat and counts how many calories I have to burn to be in shape for the next movie? They call it the Bates Diet and I can't do anything to take it down. It's dangerous for people who feel insecure about their bodies and they try this 'diet' and exercise."

"Are you serious?" My quesadilla hovers in front of my mouth as I try to figure out if he's bullshitting me.

"I swear. I lost the case and had to pay their lawyer fees because the judge ruled that it clearly states on the website that it's not medical advice and they should talk to a doctor before trying it. And it also states that the website isn't in any way affiliated with me." He finishes his last bite and cleans his hands on the paper towel.

"That is nuts!" I blurt out and understand even more the necessity he feels to do this movie. This is the first time in his career he won't take off his shirt on set except in one scene, one we still have to shoot.

"All finished? Do you mind if I bring you home? I'm starting to get tired." He smiles at me while I swallow the last bit.

"Yes, sure, but my car is back at the parking lot. I don't know how I'll get to work tomorrow morning."

"I'll pick you up," he casually drops and I feel my cheeks go up in flames.

"Aren't you worried about what people could think about it?" I wave at the guys in the truck while we walk toward his car.

"Why should I worry about it? There could be a million reasons we arrive together, after how we started our work relationship, nobody will think we're sleeping together." He winks at me when we sit in his car.

I hope he's right because I don't want to deal with the gossip that will stir if word gets out. But in all honesty, I'm tired too. It was a long day and I could use some hours of sleep before getting up at five tomorrow.

An hour later, Harrison parks in front of my house and I'm glad I didn't pick up the car. I'm way too tired and I need to go to bed.

"So, five-thirty tomorrow morning," I say when he walks me to my door.

I didn't expect him to walk me to the door and the realization makes me nervous. Does he expect me to let him in? Or will he try to kiss me here at the door? Damn! I ate cheese. Am I really hoping he makes a move?

I'm so caught up in my thoughts that I don't notice I'm at my front door and I should look for my keys in my backpack. I raise my gaze and find Harrison staring at me. Under the dim light of my apartment, he seems even more mysterious than usual. It's difficult to read him because he's always smiling, friendly, positive, but now I know that's a facade to hide his true emotions. You will never catch Harrison less the perfect in public, but now we're not in front of an audience. *What are you thinking, Harrison?*

I can see the hesitation in his eyes. He's conflicted about what to do, but I don't know what choices he's evaluating in his head.

Does he want me to invite him in? Kiss me and risk ending up in the hospital? Maybe he's just thinking about telling me to call a taxi tomorrow morning for all I know. Or maybe he's thinking about the quesadilla and the cheese I ate. I feel my stomach clench in a nervous grip when his eyes lower on my lips. His tongue peeks out to wet his, like he's trying to imagine what my mouth taste like.

We stare at each other for a long moment. I'm so close to him I can feel the heat radiating from his body. My keys, I should grab my keys and walk inside, with or without him, but I stay here, staring at those perfect lips, that gorgeous face, and do nothing. It's like I'm completely paralyzed when it comes to interacting with him. What's wrong with me? Why am I acting like a fifteen-year-old with a crush? I seriously should do something besides thinking about his glorious mouth.

Harrison takes a step back, breaking the spell I'm under, and smiles at me. "See you tomorrow, Sienna," he says before turning around and walking to his car.

I watch him hop in and start it without a glance in my direction, and when I walk into my apartment and close the door behind me, I can't stop wondering if he would have kissed me if I had eaten something different. Disappointment settles in my gut and I don't know if it's for the non-kiss or because I would have totally let him kiss me this time. I'm probably more disappointed with myself for wanting him.

"Damn quesadilla!" I mutter as I walk to my room and collapse on my bed, knowing I ruined my chance to know how his lips taste.

CHAPTER 13

Harrison

I walk to Sienna's trailer and knock on the door.

"Come on in!" she hollers from inside.

I walk in to find her bent over her table with a bunch of papers in front of her. The crazy thing is, I knew I'd find her like this. This woman is worse than me when it comes to working extra hours.

The more time I spend with her, the more I understand she doesn't have boundaries when it comes to her work life. I doubt she even has a personal one when she walks off of this set. At this point in the filming, after months of working side by side, I usually know a lot of personal stuff about my coworkers. Sienna is still a mystery to me. I know the bare minimum, and not because she's opened up to me, but because of what I've caught from talking to other people on set.

"What are you still doing here? We finished early, you should be home," she says without looking up from her papers and writing something down in the margins.

"I should be asking the same question." I raise my eyebrow when she finally looks up at me.

She smiles, drops the pencil on the table, and leans back in the couch she's siting on. I feel a bit awkward standing here, to be honest. After we had dinner together the other night, I don't know what to expect from our relationship. Are we colleagues? Friends? More? I would have totally kissed her at front of her door if I was sure she wouldn't freak out. I want to taste those pouty lips so badly I dream about them.

"I have some work to finish," she says, waving her hand and inviting me to sit down.

"Something you need to do for tomorrow morning? We don't work weekends. Do you *have* to work or are you just a workaholic that can't stop even on a Friday night?" I sit in front of her.

She smiles shyly and blushes, lowering her gaze and avoiding eye contact with me. I got it right. She's not behind schedule, she's just reluctant to go home. I wonder if she feels her home is empty the same way I do.

"We're going to a party," I say after she doesn't answer my question.

Her eyes snaps on mine. She blinks twice, surprised by my words, then shakes her head. "No, we are not."

"Yes, we are. There's a producer hosting a party for his birthday, I have a plus one, you're coming with me."

"I don't even know who he is!" she blurts out. "I'm so out of this circle I didn't know someone was having a party."

I roll my eyes. "Yet another reason to come with me. We all know these parties have nothing to do with birthdays and everything to do with networking. I'll introduce you to him and a bunch of other people."

She shakes her head even more vigorously than before. "You are completely crazy. I'm not crashing a Hollywood party. There's a reason I wasn't invited." She crosses her arms over her chest, giving me that I-know-better attitude I'm getting used to.

I grin. "First, you're my plus one. You're not crashing anything. Second, you're not invited because nobody knows you exist outside a set. They think you come with the furniture because they never see you around. We need to change that!"

She stays silent for a while because she knows I'm right. I can see from the expression on her face she's debating about what to say next.

"I don't have a dress. I can't come wearing jean cutoffs and a tank top," she protests, but her defense is weak. She's losing the battle with her own logic.

I raise my hand with the clothing I was hiding. "Suzy from costumes gave me this. She said it's perfect for the party but don't tell our boss, you, that she gave it to me. You have to keep your mouth shut and don't ruin the dress."

She snorts and I grin.

"You are an asshole. You know that?" she says with a smile. I don't know if she's referring to what Suzy told me or if she's giving up and coming, but I'm slightly optimistic it's the latter.

"Is that a yes?" I raise an expectant brow.

"Give me that dress. I already know I'll regret it five minutes after we get there." She reaches out her hand to grab the dark green fabric.

"Give me some credit! I promise if you don't like it, I'll bring you home."

I stand up and walk out to give her some privacy to change.

∗∗∗

One hour later we're passing through the gates of a mansion in Bel Air. There are a few paparazzi outside taking pictures of the cars but nothing major. The neighborhood here is a bit strict about celebrity privacy and when it comes to the photographers, they don't tolerate a mob of intruders in front of someone's house. They'll call the cops if it gets out of control. It doesn't matter that the owner of this place called them to shine a spot-light on the party. No one cares about a celebrity birthday party unless there's some kind of promise of a scandal.

I drive through the gates and Sienna looks down at her lap. I don't know if she's trying to protect herself from the paparazzi or just embarrassed to be seen with me.

I drive to the back of the house where a bodyguard helps me find a spot to park in. When we step out and Sienna notices there's no one taking pictures of us, she seems relieved.

"You knew there were paparazzi, didn't you?" she asks with a knowing smile.

"Yes, why?"

"You drove the Ferrari to the set. You never come with this one. You use it just to show off your status." There's no judgement in her voice, just a simple observation.

I chuckle. "Guilty. I knew about the party and I needed to be on my best appearance."

"Why? They all know who you are here." Her voice is laced with curiosity while she waves in the direction of the mansion.

"I'm making an indie movie. I have to remind them that I'm still the king of the jungle or they'll forget that I can still make them money. A lot of money," I explain and she stops in her tracks.

"Really?"

"This party is as useful for you as it is for me. Every move is monitored in Hollywood, and it's easy for someone to spread the rumor that I accepted an indie movie because I'm at the end of my career," I explain as we head toward the front door.

She seems worried. "I never thought this could be a problem for you. I always assumed you can do whatever you want when-ever you want."

I shrug. "There are non-written rules in Hollywood that everyone follows. If you step out of line, you need to have a really good and convincing reason unless you want to see your career crumble."

"The more you describe Hollywood, the more I want to stay away," she murmurs with an adorable pout on her lips.

I laugh. "It's not that bad, and fortunately you have the most amazing captain to navigate these waters."

She rolls her eyes. "The most cocky and annoying too."

"Admit that you like me." I wink at her with a grin.

She scoffs. "I tolerate you. Don't fool yourself."

"I can work with that," I say while I put a hand on the small of her back and guide her inside.

The place is packed with people and it's easy for me to introduce Sienna to the most influential ones in the room. At first, I almost want to hug her and tell her that everything will be fine. She's so tense she barely moves her lips to speak with people. But when she starts to relax, she becomes the perfect compliment to every conversation.

"Why an indie movie? It's a peculiar choice for you," Alan, one of the producers that terrifies almost everyone in Hollywood with his blatant honesty in telling you that you suck, asks me.

"Should we tell him?" Sienna asks me with a knowing smile that piques Alan's attention. His eyes widen just for a second, but the curiosity is plastered all over his face.

I make a scene of thinking about it. "Okay, just because it's you," I say, looking around to be sure there isn't someone eavesdropping over the loud music.

I look at Sienna and she nods. Then I lean closer to his ear. "A friend tipped me off that there was this great script around but it was tied to a director that was really picky about the casting." I nod toward Sienna and Allan takes in her presence with more interest. "She couldn't find the male lead because she wanted specific acting skills. She's the terror of the indie industry. She's known for making people walk out crying after their auditions." This last part makes Alan smirk in approval at her.

"But you didn't cry. You put on your Oscar pants and nailed the audition. It was a closed-door process, I didn't want anyone to know that *pretty boy* here auditioned for the part. I have a certain reputation to maintain," she chips in and Alan laughs.

"Long story short, I got the part and I'm going to star in one of the best movies of the year," I finish and Alan makes an outraged face.

"Well, we'll see about that. I have a couple of projects that are pretty good and a budget bigger than yours," he challenges. He's known for not wanting to lose, ever.

"Sure, you have a big studio that supports you. But do you have an Oscar-worthy movie to produce?" Sienna smirks, raising her brow, challenging him to step up the game.

She's so convincing that Alan smiles and turns his body toward her. He's captured. She has his attention and I'm happy for her. He's one of those people that could make her career take off.

"Well, you're pretty confident about what you have in your hands."

"Because I *am* sure this is an award-winning movie. I'm not bullshitting around like a rookie. I have ten years of experience as a director and I know when I have a good script in my hands, or an Oscar-worthy one." She smiles at him and he chuckles.

He grabs his phone and gives it to her. "Put your number in here, I may have something to discuss with you."

Sienna's hand is firm when she grabs his phone, but I know she is about to snap from the tension because her shoulders stiffen. She's not one to give away her feelings, but I've learned that when she stiffens her shoulders, she's a step away from freaking out. It's time for me to take her away from him.

"Sorry to interrupt this lovely conversation, but I have to steal your director here and drag her to meet Aaron, or he'll kill me," I say to Alan grabbing Sienna's elbow delicately.

"Damn, that bastard always has the best at his side. Don't let her sign an exclusive contract with him or I will personally kick your ass," the man says, pointing a finger at me and winking at Sienna.

I laugh while I pull her stiff body away. When we reach the bar, she lets out a shaky breath.

"Thank you. I was going to freak out any minute," she says as I wave down the bartender.

We order a Cosmo for her and a soda for me. I take my time while the guy prepares our orders to take her in. She's gorgeous in this green dress that hugs her in all the right places.

"I know, this is why I dragged you away." I wink leaning on the counter.

"Where's Aaron?" She looks around.

"At home, I think. It was an excuse to end the conversation." I sip my soda when the guy puts it in front of me.

She smiles shyly. "Thank you. I can't believe Alan Leery asked for my number. He's like the God of producers."

I chuckle. "See? It wasn't so bad. After two hours of networking you have the number of at least three important people. Oh, don't answer if Cain calls you. He's known for asking girls to suck his cock."

She grimaces. "Thank you for the tip. He gave me creepy vibes. He looks like an old dude lurking around high schools."

"He is." I nod.

I look around at the almost hundred people crowding this place. They're dancing, sweating, grinding way too inappropriately for a public place. I'm sure I got a glimpse of a bare ass in there.

"Do you want to step out for a minute to breathe some fresh air? It's suffocating in here," I ask Sienna and she nods, appreciating my suggestion.

We reach a part of the garden hidden by low trees and I peek around the corner to avoid walking in on someone having sex out here. Considering the tone of this party, I wouldn't be surprised.

"What are you doing?" Sienna asks before I drag her around the hedge.

"Making sure there isn't someone fucking out here."

"Out in the open?" she asks incredulously.

I raise a brow. "This is Hollywood. Normal decency doesn't apply here."

"Go figure." She snorts.

I take in the spectacle of the lights of the city, the downtown skyline reaching high in the middle of the sea of lights.

"It's beautiful out here," she murmurs, taking in the view.

"Soon you'll be able to afford to live in a place like this too." I study her out of the corner of my eye.

She frowns, like she's surprised by my statement. Sometimes I can't understand how pessimistic she is. She's a great director, I know she can go far in Hollywood, make money, make a name for herself, but I suppose that after ten years barely surviving at your job, you don't dare to hope anymore.

"You don't believe that?" I ask when she remains silent.

She shrugs. "It's difficult to believe something like that when for years you struggle to make ends meet. I know this movie is great, but I don't know how great because I've never had something like this in my hands. It's like, in a few years maybe I'll look back at this moment and realize it's one of those life-changing turning points, but right now I don't recognize it."

I nod. "I know what you mean."

She turns toward me. "Have you had one of those moment too?"

"When I won the Oscar. Only in that moment I realized I delivered a performance that completely changed my life. Before that, like you said, I was just a pretty face. I didn't know I had something more than my physical appearance." I smile at her.

"You know I only said that to Leery back there because I was following your lead, right? I don't think you're just a pretty boy, now."

She's cute when she's worried and I can't stop from smiling. *Since when do I think a woman is cute?*

"Oh, I know what you thought about me. You were really vocal about it the first time we met," I tease.

She groans. "Can we not talk about that? I was really out of line that night and I still feel embarrassed for how I treated you."

I put a hand on her cheek and gently guide her to look me in the eye. She tilts her head up and her eyes widen a bit. We're so close if I take a step forward my chest would touch hers.

"I know you don't think that anymore. Don't beat yourself up for a mistake I already forgave." My voice comes out raspy and deep. I almost don't recognize myself.

Her skin is so soft against my hand I can't resist brushing my thumb over her chin, just a breath away from her lower lip. She quivers under my touch and her eyelids drop slightly, showing me a glimpse of the lust she's trying to hide. The sight is so appealing my breath catches in my throat and my heart awakens in my chest.

"Okay," she whispers and her lips stay parted after the word rolled out of her tongue.

I lower my gaze on that luscious pout and *that* is my mistake. I can't resist the temptation to taste her, to finally savor the woman that makes my blood boil for a thousand different reasons. I close the distance, slipping my fingers into her hair, fisting it, my other hand on her waist pulling her to me. I crush my lips on hers and heaven falls down to earth, making my heart hammer in my chest.

She's perfect in every sense, and she molds between my arms like lava flowing between rocks, burning her way under my skin. She fists my shirt and stands on her tiptoes as though wanting to climb me, craving me closer. I tighten my grip around her body and mold her curves to my chest. Heaven and Hell, this is how she feels.

I swipe my tongue over her lower lip and she opens for me, granting me access to her sweet taste, intoxicating me. I can't get enough of her. I can't stop from groaning when she presses her hips against my raging erection. She is the fiercest woman I have ever met and every stroke of her tongue is a reminder that I may have initiated this kiss, but she is guiding it, dictating the rhythm, guiding me in a sensual dance I can't stop. Her fingers slip from my shirt to my hair, gripping it tight, making me shiver in pleasure.

She moans in disapproval when I pull back to take a breath and lightly bites my lower lip, sending a jolt down my spine. I'm so gone I would fuck her here in the open, forgetting the people just a few steps from us. My hand slips down from her waist to her butt and I squeeze firmly and press her against my body. She whimpers in response like she can't get enough of me in the same way I can't get enough of her. I need her. I need to explore with my tongue every single inch of her perfect body.

When I look down into her eyes, I try to figure out what she's thinking. I find only lust and surprise, like she didn't expect this move from me. But what crosses her mind, the real thoughts that swim in her brilliant brain, is a mystery to me. Everything about this woman is intriguing and mysterious. And it scares the hell out of me.

I release my grip on her body, slipping my hand up to the more appropriate place that is her back.

"Well, this time you didn't run away or kick me in the balls. I call that a victory," I murmur against her lips and then peck them.

She giggles. A feminine sweet sound, rare coming from her. "I still have time for that."

I smile and stare into her dark eyes. I have no idea how to move from here, but I don't regret taking this step. I just hope it won't lead to burning and the world crashing down on the precarious relationship we have built.

CHAPTER 14
Sienna

I yawn for the hundredth time this morning and rub my eyes. I didn't have the courage last night to tell Harrison that I needed to be on set on a Saturday morning to film some scenes he's not in. They weren't planned, but we needed more shots and we decided to come here over the weekend instead of delaying the regular shooting.

The point is that I was looking forward to going out with him again. After we had dinner together at the taco place, I realized he's fun outside the set. And that kiss. I was dying to finally have those perfect lips on mine. And he delivered. Damn! He delivered big time. If I swipe my tongue over my lips, I can still feel the lingering tingle on my skin.

"You look like someone punched you in the face. The circles around your eyes are so dark you look bruised." Ellen smiles sympathetically at me.

I yawn again and straighten in my chair. "I went to a party last night and I haven't slept much."

And I haven't slept much because I was thinking about that kiss. I tossed and turned trying to find an explanation for that scorching moment, but the truth is, there is none. I'm attracted to him in more than a physical way and I gave in, taking what I want. There's no doubt he's equally drawn to me, so it was almost predictable what happened. That erection doesn't lie and my drenched panties don't either.

She looks at me with wide eyes. "You were at a party? Is that a joke?"

I chuckle. "No, it's not. Harrison asked me to go with him to a birthday party in Hollywood. I didn't want to, but it was a good chance to make connections. Walking with him into a party is like opening every single door to producers and giving your number to people you wouldn't even dream of."

"You went with Harrison? I see." She tries to hide a smug smile but fails.

I decide to pretend not to notice it and the implication of that knowing gaze. She's clearly fishing for gossip and my lips are sealed. She became a friend filming this project, but I don't want to put my personal life out there with someone I've known for barely a few months. I didn't even tell Harper about it. *And why not?*

"Yes, and now Alan Leery has my number." The smile on my face is so big it distracts her from every thought she had about Harrison and me.

"Shut up!" She gawks at me.

"Yes. He also texted to be sure I gave him the right number and I got his. I think we impressed him." I beam.

"Impressed who?" Harrison's voice startles me.

I turn around and find him handing Ellen and me cups of coffee. He looks a bit tired but he's gorgeous anyway. How does he look so perfect every single damn time? My stomach clenches in a pleasant squeeze when he winks at me. I am so fucked.

"What are you doing here? You're not schedule to shoot today," I ask, puzzled.

He grabs a chair from a few feet away and puts it next to me, plopping down and giving me the side eye. "No, I'm not, and you didn't tell me you were working today. I would have brought you home early last night," he says in a half-joking, half-scolding tone.

I shrug. "It's not like you forced me to stay up late. I can sleep in tomorrow morning." I feel a bit guilty for not telling him. "But the question still stands. What are you doing here?"

"I saw some colleagues posting on social media from the set and found out you lied to me. So I decided to come here to keep you company and suffer with you, considering it's my fault you look like you're falling asleep on that chair," he explains and I almost "aw" in response like a teenager.

I feel my cheeks warm up a bit and shake my head. "You should go home and relax. You have a tight schedule Monday."

"Spending the Saturday on a deck chair by my swimming pool when I can be here with all my favorite people? Never!" He winks at me again and I almost squeal. Almost. I'm not *that* desperate after the kiss.

But I have to admit I'm a bit flattered that he's here with me. I'm not delusional—I know he's not here *for* me, but I indulge the thought that he's not totally disinterested about what happened last night between us. After months of working together, I know Harrison enough to think that he wouldn't risk messing up an entire movie, or at least the friendly atmosphere on set, for a kiss. He doesn't strike me as the careless type.

And this is why I'm freaking out. Why is he here and what does he want from us? Maybe he *is* here for me. To *talk*. God, I hate these kind of interactions, and not dating for almost five years doesn't help me in handling this game.

"You never told me who you impressed," he asks, sipping his coffee.

"Alan texted me this morning to be sure I gave him the right number." My smile is so big it almost hurts.

"Are you serious? I knew it! I freaking knew you had him wrapped around your finger!" He laughs like this is the best news ever. He seems genuinely happy for me.

"You have to take the credit. You were the one pushing him my way."

He shakes his head. "It was team work. You worked the magic as much as I did." He winks at me. Again. I almost squeal. Again.

Ellen clears her throat and I'm suddenly dragged back to reality. For a moment I forgot she was here and when I look at her, I feel my cheeks going up in flames of embarrassment at her smug smile. I blame my lack of sleep for my poor control over my emotions because I'm scared to admit that Harrison affects me in ways I shouldn't be affected by a colleague. To be fair, I don't randomly kiss colleagues, so this messes with my head.

It takes all my strength to straighten my spine, focus back on my job, and try not to think about the fact that Harrison is here, for no apparent reason, watching my every move while I try to act like his presence doesn't affect me.

***

It's a long day, filming and trying to get the best out of every take and, at some point, I forget Harrison is even here. I can see him in the background, following my every move with his eyes, but he doesn't intervene, unless I'm the one speaking first to him. His discrete presence is somehow almost comforting.

It's strange how he has something to say about almost every scene he's in, but he never volunteers his opinion when it comes to other people's scenes. I can see his face scrunching in puzzlement, sometime borderline disapproval, but he never offers his thoughts.

A couple of times I gave in to curiosity and asked for his opinion, and his response is always very supportive and diplomatic, but never downright negative.

"Why isn't this freaking scene coming along?" I mutter under my breath.

Ellen is on set talking to a couple of extras and changing their position for what seems like the millionth time today.

"Are you okay?" Harrison asks with concern on his face.

"I see it in my mind," I blurt out, exasperated.

He frowns, staring intently at me.

"The scene," I explain. "I have it all in my mind. I know exactly what should happen. And we're doing exactly how I imagined it, but on screen it just falls flat. I can't put my finger on what we're doing wrong."

"Explain it to me, maybe saying it out loud will help to clear your mind," he suggests, and I know he has something in mind but he doesn't want to tell me.

"This is a chaotic sequence in the ER, people coming and going, people fighting for their lives, doctors, nurses, paramedics. It should be chaos, and Justin's over there looking for someone to help him with a toddler bleeding out in his arms. It should look dramatic, but the truth is that he gets lost." I don't even know how to explain what is wrong.

"Gets lost in what?" he asks, sipping his third cup of coffee since he walked onto the set this morning.

I look at the set in front of me, the front desk bustling with nurses, the fake doctors chatting with one another.

"He gets lost in the chaos. He should make a dramatic entrance but he doesn't stand out in the chaos," I murmur more to myself than as an answer to Harrison.

A half-idea is forming in my mind but I can't grasp it until Harrison speaks.

"So, remove the chaos," he says, and when I turn toward him, I'm sure this is what he was thinking since the beginning but he wanted me to make the call to change it.

I stand up and march on set, almost buzzing with excitement.

"Okay, folks. Listen up. Everybody off this set unless you have a line. I want to try something different for this take. Justin, you walk in from the doorway slowly. Try not to look panicked, but rather numb, confused. Go slow, okay? Madison, you're the only one in here in the beginning, I want you to look confused when he asks you for help. Don't look at him, pretend you didn't see him until he's a foot from you. When you realize what's happening, call for help and everyone in the scene rushes in then. I want chaos after you realize this kid is dying. Before that, I want calm, almost peaceful. Okay?" I say when I have everyone's attention.

Justin, Madison, and everyone else nods at me and I hope they understood what I meant. It's a completely different approach from what we filmed today and I'm not sure they get the gist of it.

"Do you need to rehearse the scene?" I ask Justin and Madison. She shakes her head and smiles at me.

Justin shakes his head too. "No, I think I got what you want from it." He appears sure, and I don't push for going over the scene again.

I sit back in my chair, Ellen taking her place next to me, and I pray that I made the right call. When the scene unfolds before us, I smile from ear to ear. The close-up on Justin's shocked face is perfect, that bit of blood on his forehead making you pause to figure out what's happening, especially when you see his face

completely void of emotion. When he drops the line, whispering, "I think I need help," my heart jolts in my chest like it wants
to reach him on the screen.

I move my eyes to the other screen with Madison's face and I
can see the confusion in her eyes before taking in a deep breath
when realization sets in. When she shouts for help, the chaos
explodes around them and it's absolute perfection. That's it. This
is the scene I wanted, the drama of a father trying to save his son.
I look at Ellen and she's grinning back at me. I turn to Harrison
on my other side and see him smiling, watching the scene. He
knew this was a better take but he didn't say anything, he waited
for me to figure it out.

He would make a really great director. The realization hits
me in the chest, but contrary to how I would have felt at the beginning of this project, I'm not annoyed by it. I'm almost proud,
and curious to know how it would be to work with him in a
different way than directing him. I think he has great ideas and
I'm pretty sure he has a strong opinion about how he wants his
movie done.

Harrison has years of experience on set behind him. He's
worked with major director and actors during his career. And
he is damn smart. I'm sure he's learned a lot from every movie.
I misjudged him so badly I'm ashamed about what I thought of
him.

***

"Why didn't you suggest removing everyone from the set
when you saw that the scene wasn't working? I would have listened to you. The scene was perfect after that," I say when we
finally walk out of the set and call it a day.

He shrugs and smiles almost shyly. "It wasn't my call. You have a precise idea about what you want and it's not my place to say something about your creative vision."

"Yes, but you could have hinted something. It was clear after the tenth take that something was wrong and you already figured out it. You're pretty vocal when it's one of your scenes." It's not an accusation but mere curiosity.

"Because those are *my* scene and I know how I can perform better. This is the movie that will reshape my career, taking it in a different direction, and I want to be perfect in it. I know my skills, I know where I perform better and where I'm lacking. That's my call."

We walk toward the parking lot.

"You didn't want to make me look like I don't know what I'm doing. Did you?" I raise my eyebrow.

"Yes, that's also a reason. But not because I think you need guidance, but because I have my vision and you have yours. In a creative job like this one, there is no right or wrong, just different approaches, different angles."

I nod and realize we're already at my car. He stands in front of me, a couple of feet away at a safe distance. He doesn't do anything that makes me think he wants something from me. A dinner, another kiss, something more. I find myself wondering where we are, what we're doing with this thing between us.

We're more than colleagues; I would dare to say friends. But friends don't kiss and they sure don't feel the attraction I feel for him. This is the first time in my life I don't know what to do with a man. There were always two options: fuck them, hate them. No in-between.

With Harrison it's confusing. We're almost at the end of the filming, if we dip our toes in a relationship it wouldn't be a scandal, they wouldn't say one of us got the job because of who we fucked. But here we are. Yesterday he kissed me and today he keeps a couple of feet between us.

Does he want me or not? I would be more than happy to explore that physical attraction that consumed us last night. But when he says goodbye, turning around and walking toward his car, I'm left wondering if maybe he's regretting what happened.

CHAPTER 15

Harrison

There's something strange about preparing for a sex scene. You have to be believable for the public to get into it, but you also have to disconnect your brain to not get too excited about the situation or your counterpart will end up with an unwanted boner against her intimate parts. You have to be passionate, but you also have to repeat the scene so many times you lose sight of what you're doing. It's like making out for so long you end up not even reaching the sex part.

Having sex, with or without feelings involved, is all about instinct, sexual tension that builds up, and then explodes in one bomb of a moment that makes you switch off your brain. The exact opposite of when you have three cameras and microphones pointed at you to catch the best angle, the best light, every kiss, whimper, and moan. Even the breathing has to be artfully controlled to not sound like you're dying on screen.

"Are you nervous about tomorrow's scene?" Sienna's voice comes from the open door of the bedroom on set.

I turn around and take her in. It's quiet right now, everyone is already home, and we probably are the last ones on set. She undid her ponytail and the waves cascade down her shoulders.

I can still feel the pleasure run down my spine from six days ago when I put my fingers into that silky hair and kissed the hell out of her. Damn. That was an exceptional kiss. It's a shame we didn't have the chance to replicate it.

Or rather, we had it, but we didn't discuss if it's a good idea to dive into something we can't quite explain.

"No, I'm fine, but I need to prepare for it."

"Do you want me to explain where the cameras go?" she asks, pushing off the door jamb she was leaning on and walking closer.

"Christopher already explained what you're going to do. I think I have a good idea about how to move into the scene. I was just going through my head about how to toss my clothes." I smile, but she doesn't mirror my gesture. She studies me for a long moment and I'm pretty sure she's worried about something, but I don't know what it is.

The set is ready for tomorrow morning, the bed is in front of us like a suffocating presence that holds a meaning neither of us wants to acknowledge. I wanted this scene to be raw and real, this movie deserves that, but that also means it requires me to put a part of me out there. Something I've never done, something that will change my future for the better or the worse.

"Are you worried about the full-frontal nude? Are you regretting agreeing to do it?"

We went over this point until we were almost going crazy. My penis will be on screens all over the world for everyone to see and I'm sure it will stay online forever for everyone to judge. I'm confident enough to not feel threatened about showing that part of my body. But still, it worries me.

"Regretting, no. Absolutely not. I came up with the idea because this movie needs it. And not in a sexual way." I smile at her.

She thought I was crazy the first time I suggested it. She went through the pros and cons a million times and then she agreed with me that delivering my lines partially naked or fully naked would make a difference. The sex part is not the main focus of this scene. My character's vulnerability is. My emotion poured into the camera for everyone to see, feel,…judge.

"I know, but I don't want to put pressure on you about showing your body. I know how you feel about being naked on set before and I don't want you to feel forced to do it," she says firmly.

In the beginning, I would have thought her intention was to avoid a possible lawsuit from me, but after months spent side by side, I understand she really cares about my well-being. She's smart, she understood why I wanted this project so badly, and she knows my insecurities. She's worried she's treating me like everyone else in this industry did.

"This is different. In the other movies I had no reason to be naked besides dragging audiences into the theaters. They exploited my body to reach my fans. The plot didn't require me to show my abs, but they know if I do it, it helps with the gross income during the release. I knew the reason behind it. They didn't trick me into doing it, but it doesn't mean I liked it."

She nods, softening her gaze.

I continue. "This is another story. There's no flirting, no un-called-for sex, no sexual innuendos. This is a father who lost everything. They ripped off his family, his freedom, his credibility, his life. They stole from him the ability to love someone, and him being naked like this is exactly that. He's depriving himself of the last layer that makes him human. He's so defeated, he becomes vulnerable in every possible way, physically and emotionally."

She smiles softly and nods. She knows where I'm coming from with this, the need I have to show what I'm capable of. I want to pull off a performance that overshadows my nakedness, my penis, for everyone to see.

"Are you worried about what people will think about it?" She leans her thigh on the bed .

I think for a moment about it. It's something I turned over in my mind for days, maybe weeks. I didn't even tell my manager because I knew he'd flip over something like that.

"Not people in general. I'll lose fans and gain others. That's not a problem. I'm more worried how the industry will take it. I'll probably lose a lot of blockbuster movies—that's a good thing—and my manager will lose his shit for it."

"Are you worried you'll have difficulty finding other jobs?"

I've thought about it, a lot, but it's not something I would consider a problem. Not where I am right now.

"I'm a billionaire. I can stop working today and not have to worry about my finances. I was wise with my money, I didn't squander it. I invested, I diversified my income, I used it wisely. I do this work because I love it, not because I need it. But that doesn't mean I'm not worried about what might happen. I'll probably have more time on my hands to find projects I really like with people who want to give me a chance to show them I'm not just a pretty face."

She smiles and nods. "Or you can write and produce your own movies."

I'm surprised by her suggestion. It's a big deal to create something from scratch. It takes a lot of trust in my skills beyond acting. Being a good actor and putting a fantastic story on screen are completely different from actually *writing* that story.

"Do you really think I can pull off something like that?" There's a shade of insecurity in my voice. Nobody has ever believed I could do something so massive.

"I'm pretty sure you can pull off anything you want. When I didn't know you, I thought you were a spoiled rich dude who has everything he wants. And I'm ashamed about that. I shouldn't have judged, because it turned out you're damn good at everything. And not because you're magically gifted, but because you work for it. And you work hard. I've never known anyone more dedicated than me on set," she confesses with a firmness in her voice I don't know how to answer.

It's the most genuine compliment I have ever received and, coming from her, there's another level of pride that expands in my chest. I never really knew how much her opinion means to me until now.

There's a tension between us I can't explain. Should I thank her? Yes. But I can't open my mouth without ruining this perfect moment. Her lips parts slightly when our eyes lock. There is an underlying sexual tension I can't ignore, but that's not what makes my stomach clench with a nervousness I've never experienced before.

She believes in me. She *sees* me in a way nobody has. She's giving me credit to do what everyone else dismisses because they think I'm just good at taking off my shirt. I can't squash the feeling that she makes me feel proud of myself and *invincible*. I've never felt invincible in my entire life.

"How do you want to approach the scene?" she asks, taking me out of my misery of how to thank her for the compliment.

Her voice is a bit raspy, as if her mouth is dry.

"Is there anything you don't want to see? Side boobs or nipples are okay? I know Viola gave you the green light for boobs and everything, but if you don't want to show it, we need to figure out how to put her on the bed without making it awkward."

She smiles at my question. "Considering you will be flaunting your junk in the same scene, I don't think nipples will be the problem."

I chuckle.

"Okay, I'm joking right now, but you were right. We need a sex scene that's raw. I don't want to put out porn, but I want it to feel real and desperate and something you didn't see coming but that makes you squeeze your legs in the theatre while you watch it," she explains and I nod. "How would you approach a woman who lived next to you for months and experienced you at your worst, but you'd never been intimate with her?" She asks the last question in a slightly lower voice.

I don't know if we're talking about the movie or us. Sure, we've had our intimate moments, but we're definitely far from exploring the full range of this attraction. We're so desperate around each other I don't know if we're not acting on our attraction because we're trying to preserve a bit of professionalism or because we're just dumb.

I take a step closer to her and realize we weren't far apart at all. Like every time I'm around Sienna, I physically gravitate toward her like I'm craving contact but rationally restraining myself.

"I don't know. I would probably approach her slowly, almost mesmerized to realize how beautiful she is." I look down at her and her head tilts up a bit to look me straight in the eyes.

She lowers her gaze to my lips and her eyes widen for a second. It's the push I need to reach out my hand.

"I would probably cup her face, and lower to kiss her," I whisper, doing exactly that.

As soon as our lips lock, I feel like everything makes sense. I reach out to grab her waist and she slips her hands behind my neck, sinking her fingers into my hair.

I wrap my arms around her, pulling her closer as our tongues intertwine in a fiery dance. The soft curves of her body are like heaven against me, and I know that I want her more than anything else in the world.

I nibble at her lower lip and get lost in her soft moan. Her grip tightens in my hair, making me shiver in pleasure. I nip, kiss, lick my way down to her neck, making it my mission to pull the sexy groans from her throat.

Her skin is soft under my lips and I take my time tasting her goosebumps forming under my tongue. There is nothing more intoxicating than a woman molding her body against mine trying to find relief for the ache between her legs.

Sienna grinds slightly against my hardening erection and I don't even realize I'm guiding her on the bed behind her. I nestle between her thighs, pushing my hips against hers, swallowing her whimpers when she matches my slow movement.

I love the taste of the mints she consumes in massive quantities on set, and I love the way her tongue swipes against mine in a frenetic dance that borders on a fight. She's fierce at her job and the kiss tells me she's fierce between the sheets too.

I hold my weight on one elbow as I lower my hand to graze her soft body. I brush my thumb against the tank top covering her breast and she moans in response. I dare more, brushing it against the hardening nipple and she arches her back silently, demanding more. I grant her wish and pinch it lightly, making her moan against my lips.

She raises one of her legs over my thigh, giving me access to her sensitive clit. I push my hips against hers and I know I've found the bundle of nerves when she lets out a small cry. I rise up on my elbow and admire her perfect face, her eyes closed, breathing hard. I thrust my hips again and her lips parts in a perfect O that makes her look even more beautiful. We're fully clothed and I've never felt so connected to a person like I am right now with her.

I crush my lips on hers and frantically grind against her jeans.

A loud clunk startles us. My heart is hammering in my chest and I don't know if it's because of our searing kiss or the noise hitting us like an ice-cold bucket of water on our heads.

I look up and smile. "It's the broom that was leaning against the bed. They left it here to sweep the floor tomorrow before the shoot," I explain when I see her frozen and wide-eyed.

"Fuck," she finally breathes.

We got so carried away we almost had sex in a public space. The set is deserted, but still, we can't afford to have someone walking in on us for any reason or, worse, filming or taking pictures of us in a compromising position. Quite literally, in this case.

"We should go home," I murmur as I stand up and help her stand too. She's all flustered and sexy, with sex-tousled hair. We almost fucked up big time. When it comes to her, all my good judgement goes out the window. Fighting or fucking, I can't think straight when I give in to my emotions with her.

"Yes. We should. Separately. Each to our respective homes," she says, looking down at her shoes.

I chuckle. "Yes, I get it. Don't worry."

She nods and scurries off the set like it's on fire. I take a moment to recompose myself, let my cock take the hint that there will be no action tonight, and finally step off the set.

When I walk out, I find Sienna waiting to close the place with her keys. She doesn't say a word, but I can see the nervous smile she gives me. We walk silently toward our cars and a sense of discomfort settles in my stomach when neither of us stops to say anything.

Shouldn't we be talking about the fact that we just lost our minds and risked giving a peep show to anyone walking into the set? Or do we just pretend nothing happened? To be fair, we're good at pretending we're not attracted to each other, or that we just kissed and groped like teenagers on their parents' bed.

This is the first time I'm not sure how to act with a woman, and when I watch her start her car and drive away, I feel like a part of me is missing. A big part of me.

CHAPTER 16
Sienna

This is the first time since I set foot on a set years ago that I'm dreading going to work. I stare at the front door, almost tempted to turn around and call in sick. But you can't lie to your boss if you *are* the boss. Even if you know you spent the night thinking about making out on set with the lead actor of your production. What a cliché.

The problem is, I can't find a single reason I should regret what I did. I was honest with him yesterday when I said I discovered a Harrison I hadn't even imagined could be under that pretty face. And when I find a person with my same work ethic and the same maniacal attention to details, I can't resist. Harrison is not just a pretty face, he's a pretty brain too, and the combination is lethal to my resolve to stay away from him.

"Are you going to come in or will you stare at the door all morning?" Ellen's voice startles me.

"Sorry, I'm just a bit sleepy this morning," I murmur an excuse she didn't even asked for.

Her brows tug together and she studies me while she grabs the door handle and pulls it open.

"Are you sure you're okay? You look like you need a day off," she insists when I yawn for the third time in front of her.

"Yes. I just need this day to be over soon," I mumble, feeling the anxiety churning in my stomach.

She smirks. "Can't wait to see Harrison's package? Because I sure can't."

I glare at her like she just told me to take off my clothes and walk naked onto the set. The desire to rip her head off is almost overwhelming and the reaction is so sudden it's like a slap in the face.

"Okay. No joking," she murmurs.

"It's completely inappropriate. I don't know why everybody has to see, touch, or say things about his body. It's utterly disgusting," I spit out a bit too harshly and I regret it immediately.

She raises her eyebrows and studies me for a long moment. I've never talked to her like that and she seems almost offended by my words.

"I don't know what got into you this morning, but it wasn't anything sexual. I mean, I made a joke, but I wasn't going to harass him for that. It was something innocent between us and it would have never reached him. It's not like I'm going to jump him," she points out fiercely.

Her remark hits me square in the chest. I jumped him at the first chance I got, even if he was more than consenting, and I feel a bit guilty for what I did last night on that same bed we're looking at right now.

"Sorry, but I find it highly inappropriate, even if it is between us. And also, I'm a bit concerned about this scene and my lack of sleep is making me grumpy," I murmur.

"More than usual?" She chuckles.

"I don't want to mess up this one." And it's true. Harrison's entire career is riding on this movie, and this scene is problematic, to say the least. The weight I feel on my shoulders right now is almost unbearable.

"So, grab a coffee and get your head in it." She winks at me.

I nod and walk to the table where we keep the coffee, pour a cup and turn around and watch the set to find the will to be professional like every other day. When my eyes land on Harrison and Viola laughing on set, her hand resting on his arm, the feeling churning in my stomach is anything but professional. The desire to rip her hand off his body is so sudden it almost scares me. *What the hell is wrong with me? First Ellen, now Viola, am I becoming some kind of serial killer?* The idea of being off today puts me in a foul mood.

"Okay folks, just start to rehearse this scene and be sure everything is perfect before leaving the set. As you already know, this is a closed-door scene and anyone not strictly necessary have to clear the set before the cameras start to roll," I say when I reach the set.

I'm so nervous about something I can't pinpoint that I don't even look at Harrison. Okay, maybe I know *who* is making me nervous, but admitting it to myself is harder than expected.

"Do you want me to take over the explanation for this scene?" Ellen mumbles in my ear.

"Why?" I frown at her.

"Maybe because you barked that last statement like you were ordering some freaking military subordinates?" She raises an eyebrow, challenging me to contradict her.

Did I? I turn around and see the puzzled faces staring at me like I'm a wild animal who needs to be contained. Even Harrison seems to have lost his smile and I feel a pang of guilt in my chest.

"Sorry, I only got a few hours' sleep last night and I'm a bit drained this morning. I didn't mean to be rude. Ellen is taking over with the explanation before I bite someone's head off and we have to clean up the bloodstains," I say with a smile and people chuckle and go back to what they were doing before I barked at them.

I venture a glance in Harrison's direction and see a mixture of amusement and something else I can't pinpoint. I can't say he is worried, but he looks like he wants to ask me something but he thinks twice about it. Maybe because it's painfully obvious, at least for him, that I'm avoiding his closeness. Heck, I didn't even greet him this morning when I arrived later than usual on set.

I turn around and go back to my chair, putting on my headphones to give everyone surrounding me the idea that, if it's not strictly a life-or-death matter, nobody can disturb me. This is a perk of being the highest in command on a set. Nobody will bother you if you put down clear rules at the beginning of filming.

I take my time sipping my coffee and studying what is happening on set. Harrison resumes rehearsing with Viola, laughing and touching like it's vital for them to do so, and it's difficult to remind myself this is a freaking sex scene, they're supposed to do this. Not the laughing, but they have to make it believable for the public and I should be happy that it is, indeed, believable. They have to be comfortable around each other and that's exactly what they're doing.

Jealous. I'm utterly jealous about what Viola will taste in a few minutes. His lips. Something I tasted last night and I can't shake off my skin, my flesh, my bones. Harrison got so deep inside me, I can't get rid of him and his taste even if I wanted to.

Fuck.

When Ellen finally comes back to sit next to me after we clear the set and only a few remain, I realize the worst is yet to come. I'll see what Harrison looks like without his clothes on, I'll have to endure Viola kissing him, touching his body, she will have his utterly naked body against her, for fuck's sake.

When Ellen signals the cameras to roll, Harrison starts with his monologue, stripping off layer after layer of clothing. Pieces of fabric lay on the floor like he's taking off his armor; his interpretation is absolute perfection.

He's a very good actor, but his skill for creating dramatic scenes is utter madness. He is so good at it, I've learned to have all cameras on him at every angle to avoid repeating the scene. Especially in this one where he's the only one speaking, he commands the scene like a master puppeteer. Viola could mess up big time and the scene would still be good enough to not do another take. He's raw, honest, emotional, and so damn beautiful it hurts.

When his cock comes out, I struggle to hide a shiver running down my spine. Even naked, he is the emblem of perfection.

He pushes Viola down on the bed and she lands with a soft thud. I wait for him to take off her clothes, piece after piece, before calling the cut, and for every layer of fabric he takes off, a disgusting acid taste rises in my mouth. I watch the scene, transfixed, like looking at a horror movie with the morbid fascination of seeing someone getting brutally murdered on screen.

I'm so disgusted that when I stop the scene, my voice comes out raspy and barely audible in the open space.

"Well, that was hot," Ellen murmurs while staring at Harrison and Viola, now dressed in fluffy white robes.

Yes, it was. It was perfect because I know how Harrison acts when he pushes you on the bed and he did the exact same thing with Viola. He looked at her like she was the only person on earth and I know exactly how it feels being on the receiving end of that look.

The memories of last night are so vivid I feel the tingling in my lower belly, like I'm still on that bed with his erection pressed against my throbbing clit. I'm so focused on my feelings I don't even notice Harrison and Viola approaching me.

He clears his throat to grab my attention and when I look up, I see the embarrassment on his face. It's the first time I've seen him look so insecure and I'm a bit taken aback.

"What?" I bark and regret my tone as soon as he flinches.

"I have to put on the cock sock," he states.

"I know," I say slowly, not knowing where he's going with this.

"I need fifteen minutes or so," he adds, and I'm more lost than before.

I squeeze my eyes trying to figure out what the heck he is talking about. "Why do you need all that time? Do you want me to call someone from the costume department? I don't know if they're comfortable fondling your private parts." I frown and he seems mortified by my statement.

Viola giggles beside him, while Ellen lets out a chuckle.

"No! Please, don't. I…can't fit in the sock right now," he tries to explain and I stay silent, lost to his point.

"He has an erection, Sienna. He needs a moment to cool down," Ellen explains like I'm a teenager who's never met a man in her life and I'm utterly mortified.

I snap my eyes on him and he's smiling. Not the usual grin he wears. It's almost shy, I would dare to say guilty. Viola, giggling next to him, is the proverbial cold bucket of water on my head. He had an erection filming with her. *Of course* he did. She's gorgeous and he's a man who likes women.

The punch in the gut that follows the realization that I'm not so special after all makes me almost bend over. What was I thinking? That I'm the only one making him hot for sex? He's used to actresses and supermodels. I'm just a willing pussy coming his way.

"Of course, no problem, really. Take your time. I'm taking five minutes in my trailer if you need me," I say in a hurry, standing up and walking as fast as I can out of this place.

I can't breathe. I can't even think as I open the door of my trailer and step in, feeling stupid to be jealous of something like that. There's nothing between us and there's nothing preventing him looking to fuck someone else. I let out a half-laugh, half-scoff. We didn't even sleep together.

I'm so frustrated by my lack of control this morning I don't hear Harrison coming in. When I turn around, I see him bare-chested and wearing a pair of jeans, flip-flops on his feet. His eyes have an anxiousness I didn't expect to see.

"What happened between last night and this morning? Because you look like you want to rip somebody's heart from their chest," he asks me.

"Nothing. Nothing happened, especially between us. Forget about last night!" I blurt out and I feel my chest constrict with every word that leaves my lips.

He looks hurt. There's no other word to describe the expression on his face. He seems gutted by my request and my heart squeezes painfully.

"Forget about last night? Are you serious? I don't want to forget about it!" he says firmly.

"You just had a fucking erection for another woman!" I point out with more venom than I expected from a person who shouldn't care about a fling that goes wrong.

He frowns like I just spoke a language he doesn't understand. There's a long silence where I don't know if he'll say something or just turn around and walk out of this tiny space. And I don't know what will make me more disappointed.

"Are you jealous? Is that why you're so moody today?" he asks in disbelief.

I scoff, crossing my arms over my chest. "I'm not jealous."

I can't convince even myself that this isn't the reason behind my grumpiness. I spent the entire night thinking about being forced to see Harrison kissing another woman over and over again. This is why I'm so on edge today. Deep down I knew it would be awful to see it and I can't hide it anymore.

Harrison messed with my head so bad I didn't even realize it. I thought I was just seeing him in another light but it's so much more than that. I like him. I really like him, and it's increasingly difficult to keep this relationship on a professional level. I never fully understood what it would be like for an actor's partner, to watch them making out on screen with a costar. I thought they'd be able to analyze it from a work point of view, but now I know that's bullshit. You're jealous, period. And I'm not even his partner.

"Yes, you are!" he counters.

"Well, sorry if I thought we shared something special and then you have a boner for someone else," I scoff.

He half-laughs. "Are you freaking serious right now? Do you know why I have an erection? Because to get in the mood, I was thinking about you sprawled on that bed with my cock buried deep inside you. Well, I got too much in the mood!" he spits, grabbing his awakening erection through his pants.

I'm speechless. I had no idea I was the reason behind his arousal. My chest expands with a warm feeling and I feel ridiculous, reacting like a rejected teenager. I close the distance between us and crush my lips on his, lacing my arms behind his neck.

His response is immediate, wrapping his arms around my waist and kissing me back. He licks my lower lip and I open for him. His tongue dances with mine in a frantic kiss. I moan into his mouth when he reaches down and grabs a handful of my ass.

He licks and bites my lower lip, moving his expert mouth over my jaw, my neck, the naked skin of my shoulder. I'm happy to oblige when he pushes me against the trailer's table and makes me sit on it, slipping his narrow waist between my legs.

Heaven. This is heaven and I'm dirtying it with my impure thoughts. Because right now, the only thing I want is to have Harrison fuck me senseless on this table. To hell the movie, the scene, and the people waiting for us to move forward with our job.

I slip my hands inside his jeans and find he's not wearing underwear. His stiff, throbbing cock leaks from the tip and, when I run my thumb over it, Harrison lets out a low groan into my mouth. I squeeze him tighter and repeat my gesture. This time he lets out a curse through gritted teeth and fists my hair, forcing me to lean back. His face is a mask of lust and need. I've never seen *perfect Harrison* so out of control. He's like an animal ready to make me his mate and I find it extremely exciting.

He looks like he could fuck me into the next day and leave me begging for more.

"Are you still convinced I don't like you? That I would get my cock hard for another woman?" he growls and my pussy quivers in response.

"No." I let out a breathless response.

"Good, because I'm going to fuck you so hard I'll cancel any doubt about it."

He underlines his words by grabbing the straps of my tank top and bra and pulling them down my arms and freeing my breasts. His eyes light up with flames of lust and anticipation, almost making me come.

He dives his head onto my nipples like a starving man over a banquet and he bites, licks, sucks me into paradise. I arch my back and fist his hair, keeping him exactly there, sending shivers of pleasure down my spine straight to my core. I'm a mess of moans, whimpers, and dirty words.

"You are perfect," he whispers almost to himself, biting his way down to the button of my cutoff jeans.

He looks up with a mischievous smirk, asking my permission to go all the way.

"Fuck me, Harrison. Please," I whimper when he stares at me way too long for my taste.

He lets out a groan, unbuttons my jeans and tears them off my legs so hard, my ass flies over the table. I squeal in surprise as he throws my clothes on the other side of the trailer. He stares at my bare pussy like he can't believe it's there, at his mercy.

"Fuck," he curses, dropping on his knees between my legs. I'm sprawled on this table like a meal ready to be devoured. And Harrison does just that. Bites my inner thigh hard enough to make me squirm and then licks the length of my wet pussy all the way up to my clit.

"Jesus Christ," I let out, breathless.

He repeats the gestures, this time slowly, taking his time to savor my most intimate parts. He prods his tongue between my folds, toying with me, making me beg for more.

"Please, Harrison. You are going to kill me." I raise my head to look down between my thighs.

His response is classic Bates. He grabs my waist, brings me to the edge of the table, moves his hands behind my knees pushing them high and spread, baring my pussy to his assault. His eyes never leave mine as he grins and seals his lips over my clit, sucking hard. I come so fast my head spins like a merry-go-around.

"Holy shit!" I cry out, throwing my head back while I ride my pleasure, wave after wave, as Harrison keeps licking and sucking, prolonging my orgasm until I can't catch my breath.

He stands up and I don't have time to recover because he's already grabbing a condom from his wallet and pushing the jeans down his legs. I watch him pumping his cock a couple of times and his big hand wrapped around his stiff shaft is a sight to die for. I thought he was gorgeous during the scene on set, but I knew nothing. He is so intoxicatingly sexy I can't tear my eyes from from his hands rolling the condom in place. When I finally raise my gaze to his face, he grins at me and I realize my mouth is slightly open. I'm shamelessly drooling over him and he knows that. And he enjoys every single second of it.

He positions his cock at my entrance, putting my calves over his shoulders, and then lowers himself on me, kissing me sense-less. I can taste my arousal on his tongue when he swipes it over mine, swallowing my groan when he thrusts his hips, burying himself in one long stroke deep inside me. He's still for a mo-ment, giving me time to adjust to his size. With my legs in this position, he can go so deep that I feel him everywhere inside me. I've never felt so full in my entire life.

His hips press against mine, causing a delicious friction against my sensitive clit. I moan and push against his firm body, needing more. He leans on his elbows over me and looks straight into my eyes when he slips almost completely out of me and then thrusts hard again. My pussy clenches around his demand-ing cock. The table creaks a bit under his force.

He slowly pulls out again and then thrusts hard and fast. I close my eyes and arch my back in pleasure.

"Look at me, Sienna. I want to watch you while you come around my cock." His rough order is like a shot of lust straight into my veins.

My blood sings with desire. I open my eyes and I'm taken aback by Harrison's gaze on my face. He looks at me like he's never seen a woman so beautiful. My heart runs fast in my chest trying to escape through my throat. This is not just mere pleasure. I don't have time to overthink it because Harrison starts hammering me, fucking me so hard I forget my name.

The table creaks with every thrust, and I'm sure this entire trailer is shaking, but I don't have the will to care about it. The orgasm mounts so fast and so deep inside me that I go off like a rocket, squeezing my pussy around his throbbing cock.

He groans in response and dives deep inside me with such force that when he comes with one last powerful thrust, a loud crack echoes inside the trailer and I'm squealing, gripping my arms around Harrison's neck as the table collapses underneath us.

For one long moment, we stare at each other, wide-eyed and stunned speechless. Then we burst out laughing like two insane people, lying there on the floor with a destroyed table and papers scattered everywhere, sticking to our sweaty skin.

This is what it's like with Harrison. It doesn't matter if we're fighting, kissing, or fucking. We're so explosive, we literally shatter furniture.

I just hope we don't shatter our lives and careers too.

CHAPTER 17
Harrison

I study Sienna's face from afar. She's humming something while she put the remains of our small party on set into a trash bag. Everybody already went home, except the two of us, and she looks like she is finally relaxing after all these months. There's something carefree in her attitude tonight that wasn't there this morning.

We finished this movie. We had our last shoot today and we're allowed to go home and enjoy a bit of free time. At least I am. She still has the editing to supervise with the film editor and I'm a bit scared this is the end of everything between us. Because while four days ago we had the most explosive sex I've have ever had, after that, there was nothing. Not because I don't want to, but because we didn't have the time or the chance to talk about what happened in that trailer, and now we're stuck in this situation where I don't even know what to say. Are we dating? Keeping it casual? Nothing at all?

"So, that's a wrap!" I say when I come closer and grab the trash bag from her hands.

She looks up at me and smiles like there's nothing better in the world than being here with me during this happy time in her life. My heart flutters in my chest at her gaze. *What are we, Sienna? Please, spell it out to me because I feel like I might be falling but I'm the only one.*

"Can you believe it? A few months ago, I was terrified this movie would be the downfall of my career, but here we are." She walks to her chair and grabs her bag. The chair that has her name over the "director" printed on it. A chair that means a lot to her.

"Why would you think something like that?" It's the first time she confesses it to me to me. I'm not sure she told anyone else about it either. She doesn't strike me as someone who whines to people who aren't like family to her, and even with them, she wouldn't complain but rather whisper her fears.

She shrugs. "Because I had to find someone to invest money in it, and I'm terrible at networking and randomly asking for money. The night I insulted you at the party was me doing that." She smiles shyly, her cheeks becoming redder with every word out of her mouth.

I chuckle. "I admit you could work on your social skills. But you had a great script, people talk in this industry, it was only a matter of time before you found someone willing to chip in."

"Yes, I know, but then you came into the picture and I thought I was going to blow my only chance at making this movie great," she adds, wincing when she sees my hurt expression.

I have to remind myself that we've come a long way since when she thought I was just a sellout actor with zero skills. I've shown her time and time again that I can do my job and I'm not just a fluke. But it still hurts to hear that. She really made my life hard in the beginning. And I hers. I wasn't on my best behavior either.

"Lucky you, you discovered I'm good at what I do." I laugh.

We stop at the exit door, turn around, and take one last look at the set. It's always a bittersweet feeling stepping off of a set for the last time. Every good and bad memory, every early morning makeup call and late-night shoot rush to your mind, reminding you how hard this job is but, at the same time, how rewarding it is. When you film a movie it's an immersive experience in every sense of the word. You don't just dip your toes into the character, you *become* that person, and when the lights shut off for the last time, you have to remind yourself who you really are.

This is an emotional moment for me, and when I look at Sienna, I notice she's staring at that set too. I don't know how it is for her, maybe she's thinking of some scene that could be better, or something that could have been done differently, but at the end of the day, she has to release this project. She's such a perfectionist I have no doubt she would film for years, if it was an option.

She shuts off the lights one last time and locks the door behind us.

"You're not just good. You're great, and I didn't think a dramatic role would be your strong trait. You surprised me in so many ways I can't even start to count. I'm sorry I judged you without knowing you." She's so sincere I can't help but reach out my arm and drag her toward my chest.

"Stop thinking about it. I get it. I swear. I judged you as a bitch after our first encounter, so we're even," I say, kissing her head and basking in the feeling of her arms wrapped around me.

She half-laughs. "I *was* a bitch the first time we met."

I chuckle. "Yes, you were." I reluctantly let her go from the embrace. "Where's your car?"

She lets out a defeated sigh. "At the shop. It was making a weird noise the last couple of days and I had to suck it up and get it fixed."

"How did you get here?"

"Same way I'll go home: Uber."

I shake my head and grab her hand in mine. The feeling of her fingers wrapping around mine is something I didn't know I could crave. I'd never let her go, if it was up to me. She follows me silently to my SUV and smiles at me when I open the door for her.

"Like a true gentleman."

"I *am* a gentleman!" I point out.

"Well, I can't say that isn't true." She chuckles.

I turn around the car and can't hide a bit of nervousness gripping my stomach. I take a deep breath before jumping in.

"Listen, I saved a bottle of champagne to celebrate the wrap. Do you want to share it with me?" I blurt out when I start the car and drive off the parking lot so I have an excuse not to look her in the eye if she rejects my proposal.

"I though you billionaires drink champagne every day. Are you telling me you save it for special occasion like us commoners?" she says with a grin.

I chuckle, glancing at her. "I'm not that kind of billionaire."

"I noticed. I would love to celebrate with you," she adds, and my nervousness eases a bit.

I don't know where we are with this thing between us, but I decide I'll take a step at time. She's coming home with me and that's good enough for now.

***

I park in the garage and guide her through the lower level of the house, enjoying her puzzled face as I twist and turn a few times. This space made me dizzy too when I first bought the house.

"Of course, you have a wine cellar." She rolls her eyes and I can't hide a grin from my face.

"Where did you think I kept the wine?" I raise an eyebrow at her, but I'm genuinely curious.

I grew up in a very rich family, the wine cellar was the bare minimum of what my father looked for before buying a house. I'm a bit ashamed to admit that I don't know where people usually keep their wine.

"I don't know, I keep it in the fridge or in a cabinet near the sink." She giggles.

She doesn't giggle a lot, only when she's really comfortable with a person, and I'm glad she's doing it with me. There's a certain degree of satisfaction in making her feel like she can trust me. She's used to counting only on herself.

"It's the best way to ruin a good bottle."

"I can't afford good bottles, Harrison. I drink cheap wine from the supermarket," she says. There is no reproach in her tone. It's just a statement about her life and I can't figure out why she's so broke when she has the talent to become a millionaire. Or maybe I know the reason, but it's so unfair I can't believe there is not a way to make it right. At the very least, karma should do the thing.

I enter the room where I keep the white wines—because yes, I have separate rooms for red and white bottles—and I grab the champagne. Our walk to the upper level into the main living room is silent and I can't tell if she's nervous or just taking in my house.

I don't know what she expects from this night. Champagne and a good talk? Sex? Both? It's unnerving how much I can't read this woman. Usually, I know when I pick up my date how the night will end. It takes me one look—at how they act, how nervous they are, how they are dressed and where they want to go—to understand if sex is on the menu for the night.

Sienna isn't like any other woman I've met. She doesn't dress to impress, she's confident and sexy enough in her own skin to know she doesn't need to show off to get exactly what she wants. And she doesn't assume you're attracted to her. Her jealousy when I filmed with Viola was a clear enough sign that she doesn't expect me to choose her because she thinks she's better than other women.

I like this balanced part of her character: she's aware of her potential but doesn't let it tear other people down to get what she wants. Maybe that's why she didn't make a big splash in Hollywood right from the start. She's too honest and loyal to make it in this industry.

We reach my living room and I motion for her to sit on the couch while I grab a couple of flutes. I uncork the bottle and pour the wine into the two glasses.

"To this movie. Hoping it will have the success it deserves," I toast.

"To this movie," she echoes with a grin before sipping from her glass.

Now what? The silence that falls between us is the kind that follows the kind of sex nobody has the courage to address. After I sleep with a woman, I know what happens next. Either we see each other again or we agree that it's not working. I've never left things in limbo like this.

"Are we going to acknowledge the fact that we're attracted to each other? I mean, it was the best sex I've had in a long time, so we should talk about what happened in the trailer." Her words come out firm, but I glimpse a bit of uncertainty in her eyes. Maybe I'm not the only one thinking this situation is a bit awkward.

"Thank God you said something; I couldn't find the words," I admit, putting the glass on the coffee table at the same time Sienna does the same.

"Good."

"Are we going to repeat the experience?" I ask, trying to gauge her reaction.

There is a heartbeat where we stare into each other's eyes without saying a word. My heart hammers in my chest anticipating what I hope is a big, fat yes.

"God, yes! Please," she breathes out before rushing to straddle me.

Her lips frantically search for mine and when her tongue swipes over mine, everything clicks into place. I groan into the pleasure of this moment. I didn't realize how much I missed her body against mine until she started to grind against my growing erection.

I lower my hands on her firm ass and squeeze it through the jeans, dragging her hips closer. She moans into my mouth when I thrust my hips against her core.

I grab a fistful of her raven hair and force her head back. I miss her lips, but the taste of her skin, the softness of her neck, makes up for it. She quivers under my assault to the spot just below her ear.

She rises up on her knees and lowers down again on my crotch to chase that friction that makes both of us groan in pleasure. I open my eyes and stare into her deep dark irises. She is perfect, even in the dim light of this room. She reaches out a hand and puts it on my face. She cups my jaw, almost mesmerized by the sight. She follows the movement of her thumb brushing my lower lip and I enjoy the flash of lust crossing her gaze when I lick it and suck it into my mouth. Her lips part slightly and I can't resist.

I stand straighter on the couch and crush my mouth on hers, savoring every whimper she gifts me. Perfect, she is perfect.

And when she detaches from me, I'm almost disappointed. At least until she grabs the hem of my t-shirt and drags it over my head. She brushes her fingers over my belly.

"Oh, come on! You look like the cover of a magazine," she lets out incredulously.

"I'm actually on quite a few of covers," I smirk.

She rolls her eyes. "Yes, but I thought your abs were photoshopped." She raises an eyebrow.

I chuckle. "You saw me the other day in the trailer! Nothing changed," I point out.

"I know, but I was focused on other things." She smiles mischievously.

"Oh, really? Focused on what, exactly?" I raise an eyebrow, beaming a bit.

She says nothing but she swipes a coy gaze over my crotch and reaches out to unbutton my jeans. She stands up in front of me, grabs the waistband and drags them down with my boxer briefs.

"I was paying more attention to this." She grins, kneeling between my thighs and I catch my breath. Gone is the gloating smile on my face. All my focus is on her hands slowly caressing my inner thighs from my knees to my crotch, and when her long fingers grip my stiff shaft, I close my eyes and groan in pleasure. She pumps me slowly a couple of times, waiting for me to open my eyes.

When I do it, she smiles, never taking her eyes from mine, and licks my erection from base to tip. She repeats it agonizingly slowly and I can't breathe.

"Fuck!" The curse escapes my lips when she wraps her lips around my cock and sucks the tip, licking the bead of precum leaking from it.

If I thought Sienna was sexy before, I knew nothing. Watching her bobbing head over my dick, swallowing more and more every time she lowers herself on it, is a sight I can't resist. She's still dressed and I've never seen a woman so sexy. She is fucking deep-throating me, for fuck's sake! Seriously, can she be more perfect?

Apparently, the answer is yes.

She takes my cock out with a pop and smirks at me. "Are you going to fuck my mouth, or what?"

That's it. My brain is lost in those lust-filled thoughts. I grab a fistful of her hair and drag her toward my erection. She swallows it all, gagging a bit from my thrust but recovering like a champ. I guide her with my hands in her hair, and it takes a lot of restraint to not hammer her throat like I want to.

She goes up and down my erection, sucking, licking, gripping her lips around my meat like her life depends on it. When she reaches out her hands to fondle my balls, I almost lose it.

I relieve the grip on her hair so she can release me before I come into her mouth, but she doesn't move.

"If you don't move right now, I'll come in your mouth," I plead, putting a couple of fingers under her chin.

She looks up at me with a mischievous gleam in her eyes and she sucks harder, sending me over the edge. The orgasm hits me so hard every single muscle tenses and my hips thrust up. She doesn't even budge, milking every single drop I have and swallowing it all.

"Fuck!" I try to catch my breath.

I look at Sienna as she lets my cock out and smiles at me.

"Naked. Now!" I order and she smirks, standing up and discarding her clothes on the floor.

Her eyes never leave mine as she stands in front of me with her sinuous body in full display. She is so beautiful it hurts. Her perfect tits, with dark nipples and olive skin are to die for, but her raven hair cascading behind her shoulders is the icing on the cake.

A cake I want to taste badly. I reach out my hand and drag her to me, kissing her deeply and tasting myself on her tongue.

"Straddle my face," I order her and a flash of lust crosses her eyes.

She doesn't make me repeat it twice, and when her perfect pussy is hovering over my mouth, I rest my head on the back of the sofa and grip her hips firmly dragging her down on me.

I hear her catching her breath in surprise, but moan deeply when I finally lick my way over her wet folds. She is sweet and a bit salty, and aroused like she was waiting for me all this time.

I lick, nip, and use my tongue to explore her most intimate parts. But when I suck hard on her clit, she lets out a low, deep groan, gripping my hair with both hands and riding my face, chasing that orgasm she's craving. I open my eyes and stare, mesmerized, at her perfect tits bouncing while she reaches her peak and lets out a desperate cry.

The view is so erotic my cock is hard again.

"That was unbelievable," she says, crawling back to the couch and kissing me.

"Well, are you up for another?" I raise my eyebrow, pointing to my dick standing proud between us.

She smiles and reaches out her hand, palm up. "Condom," she orders.

"Wallet."

She scrambles to reach the pocket of my jeans and gives me my wallet. I fish out the condom and she rips it from my hands. I study her while she rips the golden foil with her teeth and wraps my hardened shaft with her long fingers. I love the fact that she's not shy about us fucking.

"Are you ready for a ride?" she whispers in my ear and bites my lobe.

"Fuck yes," I breath out when she lowers herself on my cock up to the brim and then starts to roll her hips, chasing the friction on her clit.

She rides me like she's trying to win a competition, and when I grip her ass and tease her hole with my finger, she goes off like a shooting star. I feel her wet, hot pussy clenching around my cock, and I start to thrust into her, chasing my own release.

When I come deep inside her, letting out a deep groan and wrapping my hand around her waist holding her tight, she caresses my hair and kisses my head, both of us trying to catch our breath.

Sex with Sienna is spectacular, but it's the ache of longing in my chest that makes my head spin.

Step one in our relationship: sex.

I'm comfortable saying we nailed it.

The other steps? Not so sure.

CHAPTER 18
Sienna

I open my eyes and the familiar sight of my lamp on the nightstand greets me. It's a familiar view, but nothing else about this morning is familiar. Harrison spent the night here, after five days locked in his home having mind-blowing sex after we celebrated the wrap of the movie. When Harper called me, worried about my wellbeing, I forced myself to come home, and he offered to accompany me…and we had explosive sex in my bedroom.

Which is why I now have his tantalizing scent on my pillow. I turn around, expecting to face a sleeping Harrison but I'm disappointed to find his half of the bed empty. After we spent five days rolling around naked in his bedroom…swimming pool… okay, every room in his house—even the wine cellar—I expected him to spend the night and not slip out early in the morning like a thief without even telling me. I know there's a good reason, but still, it's disappointing.

I walk into my bathroom and take a shower to look halfway presentable when I show my face to Harper. She was delighted when Harrison showed up yesterday and stayed for a movie night. It was a surreal moment, having a massive Hollywood star staying at our home, sitting on the twelve-year-old beat-up couch eating microwaved popcorn and discussing the photography of the movie we watched. Like stepping into an alternate reality where I have a glamorous life.

When I walk into the kitchen the sight in front of me is more confusing than waking up alone. Harrison is at the stove, shirtless, while Harper is on her computer at the kitchen counter, chatting with him and laughing. When she notices me, her smile turns into a grin.

"Here is she, Sleeping Beauty," she says, and Harrison turns around as I approach him at the stove.

He smiles at me, reaching out his hand and dragging me to his chest. A giggle escapes my lips. A giggle. I rarely do that but this man makes me do things I didn't know were possible. Like having hot sex with a Hollywood movie star.

"Good morning," he whispers, pecking my lips. "I'm making breakfast." He winks.

I smile so hard my face hurts and I say nothing. Like a fifteen-year-old nerd who snatched the high school quarterback from the popular cheerleader, I feel like this is a dream.

"Oh, come on! Have a bit of compassion for a single woman," Harper complains.

We turn around and I raise an eyebrow watching her half-pouting. She waves her hands toward us like that's enough to explain.

"What?" I ask her.

"Seriously? How can I find a man if you set the bar so high? He's all sweet and funny and hot. And he's making breakfast. Shirtless. After he blew your mind with incredible sex. Don't think I didn't hear you trying to scream into your pillow." She raises an eyebrow, challenging me to contradict her.

Harrison chuckles and I want to disappear. I hide my face in the crook of his shoulder and grin like a fool. I thought the pillow was enough to muffle the toe-curling orgasm that made my core explode like fireworks. Twice.

"So, eggs, bacon and English muffin. Is that good for you?" I don't miss Harrison's attempt to divert the attention from a topic that makes me uncomfortable.

As much as Harper is my best friend, I'm not someone who talks about her intimate life with someone else. I find it difficult even to talk with my doctor about it.

"English muffin? Where did you find those?" I raise my gaze to his.

"I made them," he answers a bit shyly. Is he embarrassed?

"You made them? How?" My eyes are as wide as saucers.

He tries to downplay it. "You have the ingredients, I just put them together. Minus the milk, for obvious reasons. Not a big deal. I wasn't sure you had yeast, but I found it."

"We have yeast?" I ask Harper who shakes her head like she has no clue how he found it.

"Yes, in the cabinet next to the fridge." He chuckles.

I go to where he's pointing, open the door, and grab the box. I turn around. "Did you know that?" I ask Harper.

She shakes her head and giggles.

"I...I...I don't even know what to say." This is the first time I've found a man who can cook and actually do something more elaborate than boiling eggs. And I find it extremely attractive. Someone who doesn't need to be fed like a toddler, and who can actually spoil me with a meal from time to time, is high on my list.

I'm a busy woman, most days the only time I have to make a meal is spent opening my phone and ordering delivery. Having a man who can actually cook something while I do my job is something I didn't know I could even have.

I move my gaze to Harper and she's looking at me with a smug smile, as if to say, "See? The complete package!"

I have to agree with her, Harrison is really the complete package and I don't know how scared I should be about it.

Harrison drops me off in front of the studio and I take a deep breath before opening the door and marching toward the room where Nolan, the film editor, is working today. When I open the door, I find three pair of eyes staring at me. Christopher and Ellen look more grim than ever.

"Your text sounded like a funeral announcement. What's happening?" I ask Nolan.

When I saw the message during breakfast saying I needed to come here ASAP because there was an emergency, all the happiness I've felt during these five days with Harrison dropped into my stomach and sent a sour taste into my mouth.

I dared to live in a bubble for five long days, where work crossed my mind a few times, but it wasn't the center of my attention like it's always been. I have the feeling this happiness has an expiration date and my heart sinks a bit. It was refreshing to not to think about work for longer than I ever have before. Scary, too—I'm not used to not working for so long—but relaxing. It gave me the chance to enjoy small things like waking up at almost noon, something I didn't do even when I was in high school.

I tried the glamorous life and apparently it didn't last long.

"We need to reshoot a bunch of scenes," Nolan says with a firmness that dries my mouth.

I'm not even able to ask how many or why. I grab a chair and drop into it, taking a deep long breath. The silence that follows is unnerving. Not even Ellen with her normally positive attitude is saying anything to cheer me up. It must be bad.

"Can I see what you have?" I ask and he just nods, playing the chunk of the movie he edited and moving his chair aside to make space for me to see.

For twenty-four minutes, I stare at the screen in silence, taking in the mess unfolding in front of my eyes. It's not ugly. Those twenty-four minutes are pretty great, actually, but I can clearly see at least three parts where the movie doesn't work. It's like that for a few minutes, changing the angle, so we're watching what seems like a different movie. And you can clearly see it. There's no way it could pass for an artistic choice we made.

I feel defeated and guilty. I should have stayed here instead of acting like a teenager with her first crush, even if I rationally know I couldn't have done anything in this room while Nolan worked.

"You're sure there are no other usable shots?" I ask Christopher, but my hope dies when he shakes his head before answering.

"We sifted through hours of material but, for some reason or another, it doesn't work," he confirms.

I have to bite my tongue to keep from asking to see them personally. I have to remind myself that I hired people to do this job. I wanted the best and I got the best. I don't have to do everything like in my previous movie, but rather let them do their jobs. But it's difficult. It's so damn difficult to delegate to someone else and trust what they're doing.

I trusted someone once, because he told me he was more experienced, and I had to let him do the job. He screwed me over so badly that I swore I wouldn't let anyone else use me in that way.

"Okay." I rub my hand over my face, trying to erase the disappointment before it pisses them off. "We're out of budget by a long shot. I need to ask Kevin for more money for the reshoots or we won't have any budget for the promotion. But I want to ask him all at once, so, if there are other scenes to reshoot, I need to know," I say firmly.

I already have to mentally prepare for this. I don't want to go through the process of being insulted twice.

"I can put together a rough sequence up until the end and then tell you which ones we need," Nolan suggests, and it doesn't escape me that he didn't use "if" in his sentence. He's sure there will be others and I dread the moment when he shows me the list.

"I'm okay with that, are you?" I ask Christopher and Ellen.

"Yes, sure." They answer in unison.

I grab my phone from my pocket. "Okay, I'll cancel my lunch and stay here with you, so if you need something I can help you right away."

"Oh, no. Absolutely not!" The firmness in Nolan's voice makes me stop immediately. I turn toward him with a raised eyebrow in a silent request for an explanation.

He looks like he's trying to not physically throw us out of the room. He's a middle-aged man with nothing remarkable about his appearance—not his dull sandy hair or his pale blue eyes. He is not an ugly person, but definitely someone who blends into the background. What does make me look at him twice is there's something off about him. If I saw his face on the news with "serial killer" in bold letters under his mugshot, I'd definitely think, "Oh, yeah. I saw that coming!"

"I chose this job because I can stay in a room alone without anyone breathing down my neck. I hate people. I don't want to deal with them any more than necessary and you are definitely not needed here. I will call you when I have something to give you." He blurts it all out with a vehemence that leaves us speechless.

Well, you can't say he isn't honest!

"Okay," I say, dragging out the word, trying to figure out if he'll snap if I say something else.

Ellen snorts. I stand up, not sure if we're dismissed or not, but I see Christopher and Ellen doing the same and I don't breathe until we're safe out of the room with the door closed between us. As we walk away, we hear the unmistakable click of a lock shutting us out for good measure.

"What do you think he does in there?" Ellen chuckles.

"I don't want to know. As long as the job gets done, I don't want to dig deeper into his life," I confess and we walk out fast before he decides to shoot at us.

I step out of the Uber in front of the "Jail," a glamours restaurant I've seen on the cover of magazines but never even driven by the place, let alone have a meal here. But Harrison wanted to meet here, apparently the chef and co-owner is a friend and he loves to come. He says this is the best restaurant in Los Angeles, maybe even in the United States. I think he just loves his friend and wants an excuse to come here as often as he can.

I take one look at the sleek black metal door and know I'm way underdressed for this place. My skinny jeans, vans, and tank top definitely don't belong in a place like this. I put aside my discomfort and walk into the total black, modern reception area. The blond behind the counter smiles at me, though I can see the questions in her eyes. She's probably wondering what I'm doing here.

"Hi, there's a reservation for Harrison Bates. Is he already here?" I get straight to the point, making it clear that I'm not here by mistake, despite my appearance not exactly fitting into this place.

Her smile never wavers, but I see the doubt in her eyes. Anyone seeing Harrison come in could take a chance and pretend they're here for him. Fans would do anything for a few seconds in his presence.

"Your name, please?" she asks.

"Sienna."

She looks at her iPad and nods. "Mr. Harrison is waiting at the table. Please, come with me."

If she thinks it's weird for someone like me to hang out with someone like Harrison, she's good at hiding it. We walk into the dimly lit restaurant, even though it's noon on a sunny day in Los Angeles. The tinted windows help to keep prying eyes on the street from getting a peek into the lives of famous guests.

The place is a modern classic, minimalist in its decor. It's classy without being pretentious and I have the feeling that people who can afford this place are the type who wear thousand-dollar-or-more watches you don't even notice unless you're rich yourself.

"I'll spend all my income from this movie on a meal in this restaurant," I say when I reach the table.

Harrison raises his eyes from his phone and smiles at me. He stands up and kisses me on the cheek before pulling out my chair like a real gentleman. I'm not used to guys that do that, I've always considered it way too old-fashioned, but I admit, sometime it's nice. Especially coming from someone like Harrison, it doesn't seem forced, just good manners.

"Can you let me gift you this lunch? I know you're all for splitting the bills and everything, but I really want to try their new fish tacos. Sady bragged for a month about how perfect they are and I want to verify myself if it's true," he pleads, almost pouting.

I chuckle. "Okay, just this once. Only because it's already been a hard day and I don't want to fight you on that."

I regret the words spilling out of my mouth when he frowns, ruining the light atmosphere we had until a few seconds ago.

"What happened?" he asks.

"I don't want to bother you. Just work stuff." I try to escape his inquisition but it's hard to get away with a work-related argument when you actually work together.

"I *want* to know. We're in a relationship and if we don't talk about this stuff, what do we do? I mean, sex is great, but we aren't going anywhere if we don't talk," he points out, not noticing my stunned face.

Are we in a relationship? And are we *going* somewhere with that?

I take a deep breath and try not to focus on the implication of his speech and bring my mind to the actual point of the conversation.

"We need to reshoot a few scenes and we're already out of budget. I dread the moment I have to ask Kevin for more funds." I feel my chest deflate with my confession.

I feel ashamed. Working with tight budgets made me an expert in containing costs, but it's clear that when I have a bigger project, I need to learn a lot. It's kind of a personal defeat.

He seems to struggle with what to say. He frowns, fidgets with the glass of wine, then takes a deep breath and exhales slowly. I've never seen Harrison so restrained in saying something. He's always pretty vocal about his suggestions.

"Spit it out!" I finally say, sipping my water.

"I can give you the money. You don't need to beg Kevin to find it," he finally blurts out.

"Absolutely not," I say firmly.

The defeat expanding in my chest is overwhelming. I don't want his money. I don't want him to save me from my misery.

I'm perfectly capable of doing my job without a man rescuing me, throwing money at me and taking all the credit.

"I knew you would say that, but can you at least listen to me?" he pleads. So this is why he was fidgeting. He already knew I was going to refuse his offer. So why do it in the first place?

"Why should I listen? I won't accept your money, why bother to explain?" I can feel my anger boiling inside me.

"You're stubborn, you know that? Why don't you want to accept my help? Why Kevin and not me? It seems like you have a lot of preconceptions about me and you don't want me to step out of the box you put me in." He sounds almost hurt and I feel guilty about it.

"I apologized for that. Either forgive me or not, but don't bring it up every time you see fit," I spit and it sounds mean even to my own ears.

He scoffs. "Wow. Talk about low blows."

"I'm sorry," I mutter.

"Yeah, sure, but this doesn't change that you're not letting me help you. You won't even let me talk about it."

"Do you know how that would look?" I raise my voice and immediately regret it. Fortunately, the tables are quite far apart and the background music helped to cover my outburst.

Harrison doesn't seem to care about other people eavesdropping on our conversation. He seems more focused on trying to understand what I'm talking about.

"I'll look like a woman who got her big chance because she slept with the Hollywood star," I explain.

"Why would they say that? They don't need to know who put up the money," he says, sounding offended.

"How do you plan to keep it secret? This is Hollywood, Harrison, they'll dig up every bit of dirt for everyone to see and judge." I exhale, defeated.

"I really don't see a problem with being one of the investors in this movie. I think it's a damn good project, I believe in it, it's normal for people in this industry to invest in their own movies. I think you just have a problem with me and I don't know why." He sips at his wine, lowering his gaze and cutting this conversation short.

I don't answer because, in part, he's right. I have a problem with him and his money. I can't play this game and feel like we're equal. He'll always have that advantage over me and the fact that I can't contribute in the same way makes me feel like I'm a leech sucking at his money. He's comfortable with sharing it, but I'm *not* comfortable with taking it.

And then there's the fact that I trusted a man once to help me out in this industry and that backfired big time. I know Harrison is not my ex, but it's hard to put my future in another man's hands and hope this time it will turn out right.

I'm not so lucky when I mix my work and my personal life.

CHAPTER 19
Harrison

Stubborn. She is freaking stubborn and it drives me crazy! I suggested helping her with the movie, not pushing her down a cliff, for Pete's sake!

The sweat is running down my forehead while I push the leg press for the umpteenth time. I should count how many reps I'm doing, but every time I start to focus, my mind goes back to the lunch I had with Sienna a few hours ago.

"Are you sure you don't want to stop?" Leonard's voice drags me back to reality.

When I finally put my feet on the ground, I can feel the ache in my leg muscles. I look around the Hunting Club gym and notice how many people have changed since I first came in here today. How long have I been exercising today?

I look up at my friend and can't avoid his puzzled and maybe a bit worried face. He is one of the calmest people I know. Running his billion-dollar empire, he learned how to hide his emotions. I must look crazy if he's staring at me like that.

"Yes, I probably should," I say, exhaling slowly.

Now that my frustration toward Sienna has lessened a bit, I realize how tired I am.

"Do you want to talk about it?" he asks and I think about it.

Leonard isn't someone who asks that just to have a conversation. He means to hear you out. And probably try to help you with a solution. He's usually the practical one. If there's a problem, he tackles it head on.

"I had a fight with Sienna," I explain as he sits on the bench next to me.

"You always fight with her. You didn't have a good start," he points out matter-of-factly.

"Yes, but then we slept together and we solved our disagreements."

He chuckles and shakes his head. He's in a good mood today, usually he doesn't so much as smile. "So, what's the problem?"

"We need to reshoot some scenes and we've run out of budget. I suggested covering the costs and she went batshit crazy."

He frowns. "Why doesn't she want your money? She knows you're rich, right?"

I roll my eyes. Only Leonard would ask something like that.

"Yes, she knows. She says it would look like she slept with me to make this movie."

"That would probably happen, yes," he states, and sometimes I wonder how he got so far being so blunt with people. Maybe because he's a tech genius and they overlook his peculiar ways.

"So what? There will always be someone talking shit about her because she achieved what they can't even dream. Their opinion doesn't count and I definitely don't believe those things. Nobody with any real influence in Hollywood believe those things," I blurt out angrily.

Leonard tilts his head and watches me with an almost-smile on his lips.

"Are you pissed because she doesn't want your money or because you already gave it to her and she doesn't know?" He raises an eyebrow in a silent challenge.

"Aaron should really keep his mouth shut," I mumble, a bit pissed about him talking about my situation to other people.

"Aaron is just worried that you'll fuck things up and end up hurt," he states and I'm taken aback.

I know they all care about me, as much as I care about them, but I didn't know they talk about me when they're worried about my wellbeing.

"I…it's just…I don't know why she's so against Hollywood money. I understand being an indie director and not wanting the big production companies to push you in a direction you don't want just for the sake of the gross income. But this isn't the case."

"Have you tried to ask her why she hates that money so much?"

His question is so easy and so complicated to answer. I feel guilty about my decision to keep quiet about the funding with Sienna, but I know this is a topic that will rip us apart and I'm not ready to let her go yet.

"It's complicated."

Leonard shakes his head, almost disappointed. "You should really talk with her about it. Maybe she'll understand your position."

"I know. But if she doesn't, I don't think we can come back from that."

This time Leonard doesn't say anything. He seems to think about it, but then drops the topic. I like that about him. He knows when to not press for more.

"But you could help me," I blurt out after a long silence.

He looks at me, puzzled, his dark eyebrows knitted.

"You could help me to dig in Sienna's past to understand why she's so reluctant about my help. So I know how I can help her," I explain to clear his confusion.

His serious expression turns into a scowl. "You can't violate someone's privacy like that!" he scolds.

I roll my eyes. "I'm not asking you to dig up her Social Security number or her private emails. I'm just asking you to help with some research online. Public records, not the dark web or anything."

"You have no idea what the dark web is, do you?"

I shrug.

"Besides, it's not like in the movies, where you can magically find an explanation for your existential crisis. There are no videos to dig up or secret documents to uncover that will miraculously answer your questions. It doesn't work like that."

"I'm asking you for help with a Google search, not to involve the FBI for a background check on her!" I point out.

"You know how a computer works, why do you want to drag me into this mess? If she discovers I helped you she'll be pissed with me too," he complains, but I can see he's giving in.

***

I've been in Leonard's home I don't know how many times, but I've never been in his private office. This place is not what I expected from him. I imagined a room full of computers and everything tech, not classic furniture and a desk with two big, curved monitors and a laptop.

"That's it? This is your office?" I blurt out.

He turns around frowning. "How should it be?"

"I don't know. I expected something with all those closet-size computers with no monitors and blinking lights." I sit in a chair he dragged behind his desk next to his.

He chuckles. "A server? Why should I keep something like that in my house?"

"I don't know, you're the tech guy. I don't know how you use it."

"You know about the cloud and everything that's going on right now on the web, right? We're not in the nineties. I don't need to have a server. Hell, I don't even have them for my company, I use a third-party data center to do basically everything."

"Really? You trust them with the security?" I thought someone like him would have kept everything where he can have total control. This is the guy who doesn't want to use smart appliances because they have security problems.

"Believe me, if the governments trusts a third party to store their data, my company can too," he mumbles.

I don't ask for further explanation about how the security of our country is in someone's non-military hands, but this is a wild concept to me. Don't they watch movies where the guy blows up entire cities? How difficult is it to set ablaze a data center, or worse, sneak in and steal the data?

I sip the beer I stole from his fridge and stare at the computer while he inputs the password and everything lights up. There's a pale blue screen with one single folder on it. A series of codes identify the folder and everything else.

"You know this could be the computer of a serial killer, right?" I frown and he shakes his head like he doesn't even know how to answer that.

"I like order. I hate a desktop full of useless icons that make you waste an insane amount of time."

"I guess you don't have any games on this, do you?" I grin when he looks at me like I'm an annoying bug.

"So, where do we start?"

Leonard clicks on something I can't see a couple of times and a search bar pops up. It's definitely not Google. I want to laugh. That's probably way too mainstream for him.

"We start by searching her name." He types into the search bar and a second later the pages populate with links and descriptions.

The page is elegant and very well organized, even for my inexperienced eyes.

"What is this page?" I ask him.

"Something we're working on. I'm testing it," he explains, clicking on another part I can't see and a black page with some coding comes up for a few seconds before he hides it again.

"I know nothing about it, but it looks great," I say, feeling stupid. It's not exactly the brightest conversation I've ever had.

"I should make you sign a non-disclosure agreement," he mumbles like it's an afterthought.

I laugh. "Do you really think I can describe to someone what I'm seeing? Like, 'it has these cute little buttons instead of the plain links.' Very helpful to your competitors."

The corner of his mouth bends upwards. "Do you see anything interesting here?" he asks.

I take a good look at the page and the only things that come up are projects she worked on in the past, awards she's won, nothing I don't already know. Information well-crafted by a publicist but nothing major about her personal life. I think her Instagram and TikTok accounts are handled by Harper. Sienna doesn't do social.

"Nothing interesting. Just standard info from IMDB or similar websites," I admit, defeated.

He tries other combinations of Sienna's name and words, like finance, or projects, or movies, but nothing comes up. I want to ask it *Why doesn't she want my money?* but I don't think it will have an answer.

"This is a major waste of time, you know that, right?" Leonard tells me after his search comes up empty.

"I guess so." I can hear the disappointment in my voice.

He turns around and faces me. "Why is it so important for you to give her that money?"

I shrug, playing with the label on my beer bottle.

"I want this movie to do great. This is my chance to finally shine in something that has some value and I don't want to screw up this chance. I won't have another chance like this if this movie flops," I confess.

He frowns. "What does your manager think about it? He can find you other movies like this one. It's not like they don't make any indie movies."

I smile sadly. "He completely freaked out when I told him I was starring in this movie. He went batshit because I wouldn't make enough money. He tried to renegotiate my percentage but I cut him off. As soon as I finished filming this one, he gave me a script where I have to be naked half of the time. Back to square one." I can feel the bitter taste rise in my mouth. I hate how he thinks I can't do anything better.

"You know you should fire him, right?" He asks like he can't understand why I haven't already done it.

And I can't remember why either. In the beginning I felt honored to be his client, he was the best in his field, but along the way his only interest switched from finding good movies to making more and more money. I'm starting to wonder if this was his agenda since the beginning and I was too naive to figure it out.

"I know, but now I can think about it. Until a few years ago, the only thing I could do to be famous was star in a blockbuster movie or end up in the gossip magazines with some scandal."

An idea forms in my head as soon as the words leaves my mouth. "Gossip. Damn! Gossip," I blurt out.

"I'm not following," Leonard says, puzzled.

"We should search for gossip about Sienna. She's been in this field for a while. She's probably linked to someone who can give us new information."

"Are you serious right now?" he scolds.

"Do you have a better idea?" I challenge him.

He lets out a big sigh and then turns to the computer, typing Sienna's name and the word boyfriend. I hold my breath, hoping I don't come up in the research, not because I don't want to be associated with her like that, but because it will become impossible to find something useful with my name in the equation.

A few links come up, but nothing with my name. What surprises me is the name Glen Seymour. I stare at the screen with my mouth hanging open.

"Well, this is a surprise," Leonard says, clicking on the link.

This is *the* Glen Seymour, the most famous director in recent Hollywood history. I've worked with him countless times because he makes blockbuster movies. And she was fed up with me even before knowing me? After dating this douche? Well, that explains a few things, actually.

"So, this is why she had a beef with you," Leonard smirks, as though reading my mind.

"I don't get it. She can't possibly have dated that guy. I mean, she's the queen of indie movies, he's the king of…anything but indies." I can't explain how uncomfortable this information makes me.

"This article says they broke up after the release of *Humans*. Isn't that an award-winning movie?" He frowns.

I nod, still trying to put together the pieces. "Yes. It's actually what launched him into stardom and the only really great movie he's directed."

Leonard clicks on a few more links and reads through pages. I can't make myself read anything after this news.

"She was in that movie too. She was credited as a production assistant," he says, comparing two pages, one with Sienna's works and another one with Glen's.

"What? Are you sure about that?"

He nods, clicking a few more things and his software shrinks, leaving only one column on the two pages.

"They actually worked on quite a few projects together. They basically did everything together up until they split up. Everything except Sienna's first two movies." He keeps comparing the two careers.

"How is she credited in those two movies?" Something starts to click.

"Director," he answers slowly like he is putting the pieces together too.

"And the others?"

"Production assistant. Glen is the director."

"Piece of shit," I whisper.

"What are you thinking?" Leonard asks me, but I think he just wants confirmation.

"I think Glen used Sienna because she has a terrific eye for outstanding movies. I don't know if he dated her to get those projects, but he sure as hell convinced her to put his name as the director, probably because it's easier to sell in Hollywood if you're a man," I explain through gritted teeth.

"Do you think she directed those movies?"

"I can't say for sure, but did you notice that before he dumped her all the movies are great, and after they split up they're just blockbusters with a lot of explosions, tits, naked men, and very little plot? I don't think that's a coincidence. In fact, she kept doing great movies."

He takes a deep breath and crosses his hands behind his neck. "Now I get why she doesn't want your money, no matter how different your situation is. She won't let another man screw up her career like he did."

I feel all my hopes die, one by one. I know it's true and nothing could possibly change her mind about that.

***

When I get in my car to leave Leonard's house, I glance at my phone, almost hoping there's a call or message from Sienna. The only thing I find is a new text from my agent, asking me if I had a chance to look at the new script. The dread I feel is so intense I don't even think twice and call my lawyer.

"Hi. I know it's late, sorry about that, but I need to ask you a huge favor," I say as soon as he answers the phone.

"Yeah, no problem. What can I do for you?" He sounds almost happy to hear from me at ten in the night. I should definitely give him a huge gift next Christmas and maybe something for his birthday too.

"Can you look and see if there's anything that prevents me from firing my agent? I don't want him to sue me for breach of contract. I don't remember anything major, but I want to be sure," I say before I change my mind.

"Thank God you're taking this step. I don't remember any funny clause, but I'll look at it right away," he answers, sounding relieved.

"You don't need to do it right now. Don't stress." I start to wonder if I should have waited until tomorrow to call him.

"No. I'm doing it before you have time to chicken out," he rushes to answer.

I chuckle. "Why are you all so eager for me to fire him?"

It seems everyone is invested in my career.

"Because you're too patient and a good man, Harrison. That shark needed to go a long time ago," he points out, and I start to see a pattern in the suggestions, making me think I'm the only one who didn't see him for the shark he is.

"Thank you. I'll wait for your call."

I stare at the driveway in front of me, taking a moment to think about what's about to happen. My career will be completely turned upside down and, now more than ever, I need this movie to get the recognition it deserves. The problem is, I have no idea how to convince Sienna that she needs my help. We both need it.

CHAPTER 20
Sienna

A freaking private plane. Apparently when you fight with Harrison, he does everything to make it up to you. Including a private plane for a trip to Aruba for the weekend. I've never been outside California, except for a trip to Las Vegas once, let alone leaving the United States.

It's been ten days since our discussion about the money and we've had four dinners, five lunches, and countless make-up sex sessions. But I know this trip is not just to set the record straight about what we should do with the budget. He fired his manager, finally, and I'm sure this trip is to celebrate that too.

I've never seen Harrison so happy and relaxed about such a life-changing decision, and I'm happy for him. He deserves better than what that leech was giving him. His manager is one of the reasons that make me hate Hollywood: for him, everything is about money. He even threatened to sue Harrison for firing him.

"This private jet is a very bad idea. We should have used a commercial flight. Do you know how bad it is for the environment?" I ask Harrison while I finish chewing my lunch and sip from my glass.

He turns toward me and pins me to my seat with a challenging gaze. "They don't serve caviar and champagne on commercial flights, nor the salmon you moaned about fifteen minutes ago. Or the lemon tarts you just finished. Are you sure you want to fly commercial?"

I feel guilty because I have to admit, I really enjoyed my meal on this plane, and it didn't cross my mind that, maybe, I'm spitting on something that normal people don't have the chance to experience in their entire life. Still, this private flight makes me feel guilty for different reasons too. Or maybe it's not the flight at all that makes me feel uncomfortable.

"You're right," I murmur. "I think I'm just grumpy because I should be at the studio supervising the movie, not on a beach out of the country while other people do their jobs," I confess.

Harrison grabs my hand from the other side of the table in front of me and squeezes it. His smile is reassuring and the bit of tension I feel deep inside my stomach lessens its grip.

"It's for two days. They don't work weekends and you'll be back on Monday," he reasons.

"I know, but what if something happens and they need me?" Even my voice isn't convincing on this argument.

"Need you for what? Something life threatening? Because otherwise, there's no reason not to give them an answer on Monday. And if it's a life-or-death situation, literally, they should call 911, not you," he points out.

I know he's right, everything is going fine. I pay a film editor do this job, and he's a great one. He even told me to my face he doesn't want me there. So why am I feeling like I want to jump out of this plane and go back to LA?

"Do you know what the problem is, I think?" Harrison asks me after a long moment.

I shake my head and smile at him. I'm curious to hear his theory.

"I think that you're not used to taking a break, that you feel guilty for doing nothing a couple of days in your life. When was the last time you took a vacation?"

I frown because I have to think hard about it. "Never, I think. I don't remember going somewhere for an extended period of time." Not even staying at home doing nothing, for what it's worth.

Harrison seems surprised by my response but doesn't remark on my inability to take a break. "See? You need it. You have to get used to relaxing and recharging between jobs." He winks at me.

It's easy for him to say something like that. He doesn't have to worry about money like I do. Sometime the money I get from the movies is barely enough to survive until the next job a few weeks later. But I don't tell him that. He's genuinely trying to make me enjoy this gift and I don't want to spoil the mood more than I already have.

***

"Are you kidding me?" I ask and Harrison chuckles.

It's maybe the tenth time since we landed that I ask him this question. First, when he told me we were staying at the most exclusive resort—for privacy reasons, he said—then when a flock of pink flamingos strutted around us like they owned the world. I'm pretty sure those fancy-colored birds will conquer the world someday soon, with their I-don't-give-a-fuck-because-I'm-superior-than-any-of-you attitude. I'm in awe of every tiny luxurious detail I'm not used to.

Right now, I'm gushing about our bedroom, or rather, stilt house over the Caribbean Sea. The bedroom has a wall window that opens to a patio on the water. The color is so blue it looks painted.

I stare open-mouthed at the view, while Harrison tips the guy that brought our bags. I thought those pictures you see in the magazines were photoshopped to lure tourists to book their dream vacations. I couldn't be further from the truth. We even have the colorful bucket of flowers and fruit on the bed facing the sea. Basically, you wake up in the morning and stare at this blue paradise. I could get used to it.

"So, what do you think?" Harrison asks, wrapping his arms around my waist.

"I could live here. To hell with my job and the hot, stuffy apartment in Los Angeles," I blurt out.

Harrison barks out a laugh and tightens his grip.

"We should do it," he whispers in my ear, biting my lobe and making me shiver in pleasure. "We should stay here forever, naked all day, and fuck watching the blue sea," he adds, slipping a hand inside my shorts and cupping my mound over my panties.

"You sure know how to convince a woman." The words slip out breathlessly from my lips.

I close my eyes and bask in the pleasure his expert fingers are giving me, applying the right amount of pressure over my clit. I spent my flight here admiring Harrison's perfect face and the flirty looks the flight attendant gave him. Strangely, instead of being jealous, I was turned on. I can see how he has eyes only for me. He didn't even acknowledge the woman's attempt to get his attention. And there is something powerful in knowing that I have his undivided attention.

I am the one who shares a bed with him, not her, and all the eye-fucking she gave him did nothing to use up the lust he was reserving for *me*. That is a major turn-on. Like he can't survive without sinking between my thighs and it's a powerful feeling that fills my chest.

"Let's remove these short and see if I can convince you even better," he growls in my ear and I scramble to drop my pants and panties, followed by my tank top and bra.

I watch Harrison moving the fruit from the bed and taking off his shirt. He is absolute perfection and should be illegal. How can a woman think straight when he looks like he can give you the time of your life again and again and again? When he drops his shorts I move closer, ready to kneel in front of his raging erection, but he has other plans.

"On all fours on the bed, facing the window," he orders, and I feel my lower belly squeeze in a pleasant grip.

I do as I'm told and drop on my hands and knees watching the sea. I watch him grab a pack of condoms and throw it on the bed next to me and then kneel between my thighs.

"Eyes in front of you. Watch the sea, Sienna, enjoy the view." There is a smirk in his voice that teases my senses.

Watch the sea, is he serious? My vagina is pulsating with need, I don't want to watch the fucking fish right now!

The first moan escapes my lips when he laps my folds from clit to bum. Holy shit, this feels good. But it doesn't come a second time. I wriggle my ass, trying to tell him I want a second round of his tongue, but his hands fall hard on my butt-cheek, making me squeal.

"Don't be so greedy, sweetheart. We have all the time in the world," he whispers, biting lightly where he just slapped me. There is a mixture of pain and pleasure that runs up my spine and makes me arch my back and groan.

I lower my head and glimpse behind me. He's laid down on the bed, his head between my thighs. He smirks at me before grabbing my hips and dragging me down toward his mouth. The gesture is so sudden I don't have the time to say anything, I just groan when his tongue licks my clit with greed. He reaches out one hand while sucking on my clit, making my legs quiver in response, and grabs my nipple with a couple of fingers. He pinches hard enough to be painful but at the same time sends a shot between my thighs.

My pussy clenches, spasming with the impending orgasm, and when it hits me like a wave of the sea in front of me, I let out a low, long moan coming from the deep in my chest. I've never come so fast, but Harrison knows how to touch a woman.

I like that about him. He thinks of my pleasure first, then he takes his.

He releases my hips from his grip and I struggle to stay up. My legs can't handle my own weight after the wave of my orgasm shook me to the core.

I hear the distinctive sound of a condom foil opening, but I don't have the strength to look back. I feel Harrison's hand circling my waist, keeping me from falling, when he sinks between my thighs to fuck me from behind.

He plunges in with slow deliberate thrusts, filling me to the brim. I don't know if I can resist long. I need him to fuck me, to thrust into me like he wants to break me in two.

"Harder, Harrison, please," I whimper.

He lowers himself over my back, his hot chest pressed against my skin. I feel his hot breath on my ear when he whispers, "As you wish," before grabbing my hair with one hand and my waist with the other.

He hammers into me, slapping his hips against my ass. He plunges so deep I can feel him in my core, chasing that orgasm that's eluding him. He thrusts, slaps, pushes me to the bed. My legs give up under me and I end up face down on the mattress.

He doesn't stop. He keeps fucking me without rest, making me quiver with pleasure again, clenching my satisfied pussy around his hard shaft. I moan when he uses his knees to push my legs even farther apart and plunges deeper inside me like he's possessed.

He fucks me hard and good until he comes deep inside me, biting my shoulder hard enough to leave a mark. He completely lost it this time, indulging his instincts, removing every restraint he had and fucking like it's his last day on earth. And I loved it. I love when he completely gives himself to me, when *I* am the one who makes someone like him lose his mind.

He tries not to squish me under his weight, but at some point he has to roll onto his side, slipping his erection out of me. I feel the emptiness between my thighs, but I don't mind.

When I turn around and look at him, I see the smile plastering his face while he tries to catch his breath. As though feeling my eyes on him, he turns his head with a dreamy gaze and a smug smile.

"Was I hard enough for you?"

I laugh. A true belly laugh that makes happiness bubble in my chest. Only Harrison can make it like a challenge.

"I know you can do better," I tease.

"Oh, really?" There is a provocation in his voice.

I close the distance and peck him on the lips. "We can practice the entire weekend," I whisper and wink at his mischievous grin.

"I can do that. I will fuck you so hard you'll need crutches to walk next week."

I laugh again. How come I laugh so much when I'm with him? My cheeks hurt most of the time. A feeling I don't want to acknowledge warms my chest.

His smile fades a bit, replaced by a more serious expression. "Listen, I don't want to ruin this moment, but we should really talk about the money you need to reshoot those scenes."

I didn't expect this topic to come up again, at least not during a weekend vacation. But it seems like Harrison is almost more worried than me about this situation. Those two wrinkles between his eyebrows deepen when he's thinking hard.

"Yes, I guess we have to, at some point." As much as I don't want his money, I could use his connections to get what I need.

Kevin won't be happy with my request for new funds, but maybe he'll be more willing if I bring him a solution.

"I know you don't want my money. I get it, but let me help you find someone else," he almost pleads, and I'm surprised by his intensity.

I get it. He needs this movie to give him the recognition he deserves, but I didn't think it was so important to him. Maybe firing his manager was scarier than he let on.

"I could use your help with that. Thank you," I whisper, and I almost push him when I spot the surprise on his face. I'm not that bad when it comes to asking for help. Am I? Okay, maybe my first instinct is to say no, but then I'm not so unreasonable. I think.

"I can ask the company that funded the first time if they want to chip in again," he suggests.

I frown. I didn't know he was so close with them. I mean, they suggested him for the lead role, but I didn't know he had such a deep connection with them to feel comfortable asking for more funds. Who exactly are those people to him? I never asked Kevin for more details, and I don't know if I want to.

I nod at his suggestion but a strange feeling sneaks into my chest, like a bad disease I don't want to acknowledge. What exactly am I getting into?

CHAPTER 21

Harrison

Sienna didn't say no. It's a big step forward compared to what I got the last time I suggested giving her money. Now I just have to find a way to actually transfer my money to her without her suspecting anything. Easier said than done. When I called Edward this morning, after we landed yesterday from Aruba, to meet me for a chat, he was very suspicious.

I met him a few years ago when I was running near a location we were filming and his dog tripped me on the curb. He thought I was going to sue him, but it turned out I loved Pepper Jack, his Jack Russel, so much we had a great chat about dogs and dog food. By the end of the week, I invested in his company that makes healthy dog food to expand from his home kitchen to a more appropriate environment for a business.

That more or less sums up how a dog food company ended up investing in an indie movie. And it also explains why I'm in the parking lot of said company nervous about a meeting to ask for more money.

When I walk into the reception area, I'm greeted by the un-mistakable sound of dogs barking and playing. One thing I love about this company is that every employee absolutely lives for their dog. And everyone brings them to work. Hence, the day-care and play park where the furry friends can stay while their humans work at the establishment.

I greet Brenda at the reception desk and she points toward the hallway leading to the offices. "He's waiting for you in the Rottweiler conference room."

"Thank you." I wink at her and she blushes a bit. I love to flirt with her, especially after she gave me a homemade cookie while showing me pictures of her grandchildren.

I walk toward the room she pointed out and I smile. Everything in here is about dogs. They love them so much they name the rooms after the different breeds. When I walk into the room Edward's smile is almost blinding. He looks like a kid, though he's in his late twenties. His mop of black, unruly curls doesn't help him look more adult.

"Harrison! How are you doing?"

"Actually…great!" I say, realizing I haven't felt this happy in a long time.

"I'm glad to hear that. How's the movie coming?" His smile is genuine. I don't think he's following his investment in our production much. He's a good guy but his only focus is the dogs. Nothing else exists for him.

"Good, we finished filming a few weeks ago, now it's in post-production," I answer, not wanting to bring up money just now. I mean, I need to, but it makes me nervous. They did me a huge favor last time and I feel a bit guilty using them to solve my problems.

"That's fantastic!" The smile on his face never falters and I don't know how to bring up the topic.

I had this big speech in my head this morning but now I'm not sure what to say. I don't know if it's because I feel like I'm betraying Sienna or because I'm taking advantage of Edward and his kindness.

"You need more money, don't you?" he finally asks after a way-too-long silence.

I let out a low breath and nod. His grin never leaves his face, but I can see the answer in his eyes and it's not a good one for me.

"I'm sorry, Harrison, I would really like to help you. You know I love your movies, but I can't invest more money in that project."

Oddly, I feel partly defeated because I have to start all over searching for money, and partly relieved because it avoids putting me in an awkward position.

"I'd pay you. I wouldn't ask you to use your company's money," I point out, just to be clear I'm not here trying to scam him out of his funds.

He nods. "I know and that's exactly the problem. Our accountant said we can't play with sponsorship like that without raising a million red flags with the IRS," he explains.

"Oh. I didn't think about that," I admit.

Out of all the explanation he could have given me, this one didn't even cross my mind. Since when am I so careless about something as crucial as my finances?

"Yeah, I didn't think it was a problem either." He blushes shyly. He's a good guy and really doesn't like to be on the illegal side of the track.

"Did I put you at risk asking to finance the movie the first time?" My heart starts to hammer in my chest. I didn't want to put him in a bad spot. It was a request made in innocence, but my word doesn't count as proof against a tax fraud accusation.

"No, absolutely not." He scrambles to reassure me and I let out a sigh of relief. "I checked with them before proceeding, but still. They said that I can't do it anymore, not if I don't want to raise suspicion for the both of us. You're on the line too."

I lower my gaze, ashamed for not checking with my accountant before stepping into potential trouble. This movie has fried my brain since the beginning. I've never acted so recklessly before.

"Thank God. At least I didn't fuck up that one," I murmur and he chuckles.

"It's okay. I don't go blindly into those things. I would never agree if I'm not sure it's one hundred percent safe."

I don't feel better about it. I didn't become a billionaire by making reckless investments. I became one because I study the market and the companies, and I chose the right one to put my money into. And here I am. Feeling restless because I need to find another way to come up with the money. I have the distinct impression that I'm fucking this up on too many levels to even count.

"Do you want to see the dogs before you leave?" he asks with a smile when it's clear I've run out of time here.

"Yes, please. I love those dogs!" I stand up faster than ever and follow him into the daycare room. If there's one thing that puts a smile on my face, no matter what, it's playing with Pepper Jack and his friends.

***

"You have dog hair all over your pants and shirt." Leonard's face is almost comical. His disgusted expression makes it clear what he thinks of rolling around a dog park and laughing until your belly and cheeks hurt. Not his style, for sure.

"I know." I smile grabbing a cue stick while Aaron grins besides him.

"And you're okay with that?" he asks like it's the worst disease someone can get.

He's always so perfect, sometimes I wonder if he's even human. And sometimes I'm sad for him. His life revolves around his companies. He has so many I lost count. He loves to spend every waking moment glued to those computers or doing something that will help him to achieve another huge goal in his career.

He became a billionaire in his twenties, and not because he inherited a bunch of money from his family. He's one of those geniuses that drop out of college and succeed wildly just using their brain. College tried to put him in a box and he decided he didn't like it. Sometimes I wonder if he ever feels like he belongs to anything other than what he builds. It almost seems like he can't find anywhere to belong so he keeps building new companies.

"Do you want a hug?" I tease him and he hides his thousand-dollar shirt behind Aaron.

"Stay away from me," he spits out ominously.

I would tackle him to the ground if I wasn't so off balance about this whole situation. I don't want to joke around—a first for me.

"Did you ask Edward for more money?" Aaron gets straight to the point.

He probably figured it out because of the dog hair. He knows that's the only place I get it.

Leonard stops what he's doing and takes a good look at me, probably wondering if I dared to go to a business meeting looking so disheveled.

"I did."

Aaron shakes his head like a disappointed father at his kid's bad grades. Sometimes I feel like he *is* more of a father figure than mine. After I told my old man I wanted to become an actor, he didn't take much interest in my life.

"Are you going to stop with this insanity or what?" he asks sternly.

"Apparently I *have* to stop because they can't do anything or the IRS will start to freak out." I rub a hand over my face.

Leonard looks at me like I should be admitted to the psychiatric ward. "I really don't understand you. You'd prefer to risk a tax fraud accusation instead of going straight to Sienna and explaining why you need this movie more than anything."

I let out a breath and try not to get irritated by his reasoning. I know what I'm doing isn't mature. I know I should talk to her and explain why I want this movie to succeed. I don't need him to remind me of that.

"You know why I can't tell her. You were with me the other night. You know exactly what her reaction will be!" I spit out and Aaron looks at me, wide-eyed.

I've never acted like this with them. I guess I'm not the only one surprised by that. This is so out of character I don't even know how to explain it. Sometimes I feel weirded out when I finish a movie because I find it hard to step out of my character's shoes. But that's not what this is about. My outburst has nothing to do with me still being in character.

"You are not that douchebag!" Leonard points out, exasperated.

"I know, but she'll see it the same way. She was burned once and she won't give me a second chance." I feel the grip of anxiety tighten around my stomach.

This conversation is becoming more and more unsettling by the minute. I made a mistake coming here with them. I should have gone home and tried to think through a solution to this mess.

"Wrong. You don't know how she'll react because you won't talk to her. She's a grown woman, she's smart and can understand your position. It's not like you're suggesting you kill someone. It's a perfectly reasonable suggestion, what you're asking!" Leonard insists and Aaron frowns, not grasping the entire situation.

"You don't get it," I mutter.

Leonard scoffs. "Believe me, I get it. You're not willing to take a chance on talking, but you'll choose the easier, cowardly way instead."

"I don't want to take any chances because I'm afraid of losing her. I love her and I don't want to risk messing this up big time. That's why I don't want to talk to her. Because when she says no and walks away, there won't be a second chance to make this right!" I blurt out, practically shouting.

There, I said it out loud. Something I didn't want to admit even to myself. And instead of being relieved, I feel dread expanding in my stomach.

I've played it all wrong since the beginning. I've already made a mess and no matter what, I can't fix that. I screwed up when I first put myself into this movie. And the speechless faces in front of me confirm what I'm feeling. There is no coming back from this.

"Have you seen this?" Harper puts a gossip magazine in front of my breakfast.

I frown. "It's seven in the morning, when did you have time to go out and buy this?"

She shrugs. "Morning run. But don't avoid my question. Have you seen this?" she insists, her eyebrow raised, almost scolding me.

"See what?" I force myself to take a good look at the magazine.

I'm not someone who reads these magazines, so it takes me a while to understand what's going on with the cover. I usually skim over the screaming titles and blurred pictures of celebrities, but there's something familiar about this one.

"Is that Aruba?" I frown, remembering the blissful weekend that ended two days ago.

"Is that the only thing you recognize?" Harper asks me, dumbfounded.

I squeeze my eyes and see in the blur of water and pink flamingos, Harrison kissing someone. My back is to the camera, but I recognize my raven hair. I mean, I was there, I know I was kissing him. I move my eyes to the top of the cover where a red title screams *New Love for Harrison Bates!*

"Are there more pictures in it?" I ask, resuming my breakfast.

She looks at me, open-mouthed. "Is that all you care about? Aren't you curious about what the two-page article says?"

I shake my head. "Why should I? It's just a bunch of bullshit anyway. Why should I read what they say? I know what's happening in that picture. I was there."

She grins. "Okay, whatever you say. But to answer your question, yes, there are other pictures and we can see your face. By the way, you look fantastic in that red bikini."

I roll my eyes. "Is that the only thing you're interested in?"

"You're my friend! It's my responsibility to make sure you look stunning, especially when you have paparazzi following you everywhere." She scrunches her nose, like she doesn't know how I can take this novelty in my life.

I knew this was a possibility when I started sleeping with Harrison. He's world-famous, paparazzi have a field day with him. Does it bother me that I don't have any privacy when I'm out with him? Yes and no. I mean, I can't avoid them. They're part of the reason why Harrison is so famous and I can't complain about that. I'm benefitting from his fame—it creates a buzz around the movie. It's a necessary evil I can't avoid.

"I really don't care what they say about me in those magazines. As long as they don't come into our private spaces, I can't avoid them, but I can choose not to read what they write about me."

She sighs. "I wish I could be like you sometimes. I'd go over every article with a fine-tooth comb and cry over every flaw they point out."

"You should really consider forgetting about them, especially if you want to be an actress. You will screw up your mental health if you keep reading this shit," I point out.

Harper is the best friend I could have, but sometimes I want to shake her and make her understand that she's worth a million. She shouldn't let what other people think determine if she's good enough for this job or not. I know she's an amazing actress, no matter if the gossip mongers think she's too skinny or muscular or whatever they're pointing out in those pictures.

"What are you doing today?" she chirps like she always does when she wants to change the topic because she's uncomfortable talking about it.

I can't help the disgusted grimace forming on my face. "I have to go see Kevin to ask for more money."

She looks horrified. "That's horrible!"

"Tell me about it." The dread deep inside my stomach makes my legs week.

This is the moment I've dragged along for weeks but now I can't avoid it. I have a list of scenes we have to reshoot and I can't waste any more time.

***

I stare at Kevin's house like I can make it disappear if I wish it hard enough. I already know how this conversation will go, I should be prepared, but I find it impossible.

"Are you going to stay there for long?" Kevin's voice startles me.

I turn around and find him sweaty and breathing heavy, like he just came from a run, or a tennis match, considering the racket in his hand.

I stay silent, not sure what to say. He caught me standing like a creeper in front of his house, there's not much I can say to justify my behavior. He takes me out of my misery and beckons me to follow him through a side gate that leads to his backyard and swimming pool.

"I have a feeling I should take a shower after this conversation, to relax my nerves, am I right?" he says, drying his forehead with the sleeve of his t-shirt.

I can't fool him. He knows me enough to figure out I didn't come here for a friendly chat with him. We have nothing in common, he's just investing in my movie. We're not friends, this visit has only one purpose and he knows it.

"We have to reshoot some scenes and I need more money." Why beat around the bush when you can blurt your utter failure out in a rush?

There's a beat of stunned silence between us then he blows up. "Unbelievable. Un-fucking-believable! You have one job, to make sure the scenes you direct are flawless, and you fuck it up!" he shouts.

That's unfair. A lot of directors find themselves in this situation. Yes, you try to make sure that everything is perfect the first time, but sometimes things just don't work when you try to put them together.

I swallow my retort, grit my teeth and try to dampen the anger festering my stomach. He is an asshole, but he's also the one that has to put more money on the line.

"We can use the scenes we have and have a mediocre movie, or we can reshoot and make it great. There is no in-between. You don't want to put more money in? Okay, but don't expect to have the money you invested back, because it will flop." Maybe this is a bit of an exaggeration, but telling him it would go well anyway won't get me more funds.

"Not my problem. You're the one sinking your career, I'll survive just fine. For all I care, you can use the promotion budget to shoot the scenes," he scoffs.

"Are you seriously telling me you'd prefer to throw away a movie—and your money too—rather than find another investor?" I know he's right, but I'm desperate.

I messed up big time with this movie. I should have been more careful, checked the people dealing with the budget more closely and, most especially, put aside my preconceptions about Harrison sooner. That was my biggest mistake of all. All the scenes we have to reshoot are the ones Harrison and I didn't agree on.

But it's done. I can't go back. I can only fix what I messed up and go on. As Kevin said, this is my career on the line. Not his. I'm the one who fucked up my big chance when I had to deal with Hollywood.

"It's exactly what I'm saying. You want more money? *You* find it. I'm done saving your ass every time you fuck up."

I don't have anything to say. I don't know how to defend myself and how to ask him for another chance. He's right. I could find more money, use my connections, ask Harrison to bring me to other party and try that way. I feel like a beggar doing it, but I have to suck it up and grow up.

"You're fucking Harrison, right? Use that. Sell the story to some magazine and use that money to do whatever you want with your movie," he suggests.

I look at him, wide-eyed. He can't be serious. His scowl has softened a bit and I'm almost certain he means his words. It looks like he feels bad for me and he's offering me some sort of creepy solution.

"Are you serious right now?" My voice betrays a genuine curiosity about his solution.

"Why not? Talk with him about it, you don't have to do it behind his back." He frowns like he can't understand what's wrong with his proposal.

"You are completely out of your mind! I wouldn't sell my private life to make a few bucks," I scoff.

He looks at me with a pitiful smile face that makes me shiver, and not in a good way. "You don't understand, do you? By fucking him, you're already selling your private life to the masses. The only difference is you don't make any money off of it. Someone else is."

I stay silent. I don't like it, but he's right. My face is already plastered all over the gossip magazines, and I'm not seeing a dime for it. Shouldn't I be the one who decides if I want to use my image to make money? Why are other people profiting over my face, my body, my relationship with Harrison?

***

My discussion with Kevin dug a hole in my brain all afternoon and even now, as I'm waiting for Harrison to pick me up, the feeling of uneasiness is making me light-headed. In some twisted way, Kevin is right. Someone is making money with my life and I can't say anything. And I'm frustrated about that. I desperately need that money and someone else is getting it. It's not fair.

When Harrison pulls up in front of my apartment, my scowl is so deep that his smile dies on his face.

"What happened?" he asks me worriedly.

"Kevin happened," I mumble as he pecks my lips.

"Oh. That's something that would put anyone in a foul mood." He gifts me a smile that eases my nerves a bit.

"Where are we going?" I ask, trying to sound happy about it. He doesn't deserve to put up with my shitty day just because he's the one hanging out with me tonight.

"Are you up for sushi? I was thinking about Nobu," he suggests.

I'll spend a fortune, but at least the food is great there. And the location is fantastic with the ocean view and the easy vibe.

"Are you ready for the paparazzi? That place is crawling with them," I say when he slowly slips into the traffic.

He gives me a quick glance, assessing my reaction. After my conversation with Kevin, I don't even know how to react about it. I was never particularly aware of them, because I'm not famous enough to attract their attention. But it took just one weekend with Harrison to be thrown into the spotlight and now I have to deal with them.

"You saw the magazines today?" he asks.

I nod. "The cover, I didn't read the article."

He seems to think about my answer and how to lay out the next question. Is he worried that I'm freaked out about it?

"And what do you think? Are you uncomfortable about that?" His tone drips with uncertainty. I never saw Harrison be anything but confident and he's almost cute.

"I don't read those kinds of magazines, so I don't care what they say about me. If that's what you are worried about," I reassure him.

He nods. "Yes, but they'll take pictures of you and sometimes they can be quite annoying. I'm used to it, but I don't want you to be uncomfortable about that."

He thinks I'm going to leave him because I can't handle the pressure of being in the spotlight. I didn't think about our relationship, I haven't put a label on it, but it's quite clear that we are not fooling around. This is going somewhere and I've invested some feelings, even if I didn't plan to fall for him.

"I know how this industry works, Harrison. I'm not in the big Hollywood scene, but I was well aware when I started to date you that this is your reality. I'm not pissed about it," I state firmly.

He nods but he doesn't seem reassured. "Okay. Good. I'm happy to hear that. But? I feel there is a *but* in this story." He raises an eyebrow, glancing quickly toward me.

I take a deep breath, not sure how to say what's been bugging me since this morning.

"But there is something that Kevin told me, and I don't know how I feel about it," I blurt out.

"Okay…" He drags the word out, waiting for an explanation.

"He suggested talking to you and selling our story to a newspaper, or talk show, I don't even know what he was suggesting exactly." I hold my breath, trying to discern his reaction.

He is stunned silent for a heartbeat. "What?" He almost chokes on the word.

"I'm not saying I'm on board with it, but he has a point. Someone else is gaining from us, from our pictures, from living our life, and we don't have a say in it. I'm pissed about it. I mean, I'm okay playing the fame game, but why does someone else get to make money from my relationship, my body, my persona, and I'm here struggling to find funds for my movie? It's not fair." It sounds more like a rant than an explanation, but I can't express all the reasoning I went through today in a decent way.

"So—what? You want to sell us out like we're some kind of entertainment?" he shouts.

He's angry, furious. I shouldn't have said anything.

"They're already selling us out for anyone's pleasure and getting money from it. Aren't you even a little bit pissed about that?" I shout back.

He scoffs and shakes his head. "It's the deal of being famous. I gain popularity, they gain money. But selling my private life for cash? That is a new low for me. Are you that desperate to whore yourself out?"

His words sting because they go straight to the point. Willingly giving up that part of my life for money is exactly like selling my body for sex. There is no difference, in both cases I sell a part of me that should be private.

"Easy for you to say. You're a billionaire," I mumble.

"I offered you a solution and you spat on it. You have no right to complain," he says before taking the first exit and entering the freeway going the other direction. I assume we're not having sushi tonight, and I'm not sure we still have a relationship either.

CHAPTER 23

Sienna

"I fucked up," I blurt out as soon as Harrison opens the front door.

After he dropped me off yesterday evening after our fight, he told me he needed to cool down a bit. I haven't heard from him since, but I can't wait anymore to tell him how sorry I am.

I also realized how much I care about him. I knew I was liking him more and more, but it turned out I'm actually scared to lose him. This is not just some random hookup that I want to give up at the first sign of trouble. I don't want to give up on him.

"I know you told me you need to cool down, and I'm going away as soon as I tell you that I'm sorry. I really am. It wasn't my intention to tell you to sell our story. I was frustrated because someone is actually selling it and profiting from it. I find that difficult to get over. I always thought that the problem was the violation of someone's privacy, but it turned out I'm even more pissed about them making money from it." I take a deep breath and look at him in the eye.

It's impossible to know what he's thinking. He doesn't seem angry like last night, but he is silent. He needs time, as he asked me, and this is my clue to turn around and leave.

"Sienna, wait," he calls out after a few steps.

I turn and look at him. His hands are deep in the front pocket of his sweatpants and he looks at me with a mixture of longing and sadness in his eyes. I really did a number on him yesterday. I touched the only subject that would put a stain on the integrity of his career. He struggled hard to become what he is and I suggested taking a shortcut to reach my goal.

I walk back to him and he steps aside to let me in. We settle at the kitchen counter and he offers me a cup of coffee.

"Are you going to say something?" I finally ask.

I don't know what he wants me to say, at this point. I don't even know how to rephrase my apologies, what to add if what I said wasn't enough for him to forgive me. I'm not so good at groveling.

"I don't know what to say, honestly. I know you were serious when you suggested those things, but still, sometimes I don't know what to do with you," he candidly confesses.

I take a deep breath and try to figure out how to say what I'm about to say without sounding like a fool.

"I don't know if you know who my ex is, but let's just say he's big in Hollywood right now. He was nobody like me when we met. He was sweet, he used the right words, he convinced me that we were the perfect team and that everybody would recognize my talent even when he was the one putting his name on my projects, because, you know, Hollywood likes powerful career-driven men. They sell more, he said."

It hurts to think back to those days, but Harrison stays silent, giving me time to regroup before continuing with my story.

"It turns out that men actually sell more than women in Hollywood, and when he got his big breakthrough, he dumped me like the old worn-out couch in his parent's basement. He didn't give a shit about me, he just wanted my projects, my creativity, my art to get where he wanted to be. That day I promised myself I wouldn't accept any more help, partnership or anything from anyone. I promised myself that I would do everything on my own to avoid someone stealing what's mine."

I look at him and he lower his gaze, nodding.

"I suspected something like that happened to you. When you refused to take my money, I looked you up and found your relationship with him…odd. I figured something happened. I didn't know those were your projects," he confesses and I'm not surprised. Harrison is smart, I knew he figured something out but waited for me to elaborate.

"Yeah, those were my movies." It comes out like a whisper. I'm tired reliving those years.

"Did you direct them?" he asks.

"I found them, directed them, and did the editing for most of them, especially in the beginning. He just put his name on it. I was young, inexperienced, and in love. It was easy to fool me." I still feel the humiliation burning my chest and cheeks.

"Why didn't you tell someone?" He frowns.

"Would they believe me or the new Hollywood genius?" I raise an eyebrow, challenging him to contradict me.

He opens his mouth once, twice, and then shakes his head. "You're right," he murmurs.

I shrug.

"It's fine. I got over it. Mostly." I try not to sound too bitter.

I really got over it. I was angry for a long time, now I'm not. I accepted my mistakes and learned from them. It helped me to become the woman I am today. It wasn't only bad things that came from that experience.

"You know I would never do something like that to you, right?" he asks after a while, sounding genuinely concerned that

I would think something like that about him. If I've learned anything about Harrison these last few months, it's his honesty. He has too good of a heart to be a Hollywood star.

"I know." I smile at him.

"I want to use my money to give you something that you really want and deserve. You deserve to be on the top of those fucking hills. You should be celebrated like the fantastic director you are. That's what I want to do with my money, nothing else," he explains, and I believe him.

"I know. And that's why I can't accept. I would feel like I did it because of a man. Not because I did something great. Pulling off a good movie is easy if you have the right screenplay, but the journey that leads you to direct that movie is what counts. Being good is not enough. Working for it and achieving that result is what it makes you great," I explain and I see in his eyes that something clicks in his brain.

Realization. Harrison finally gets what I mean.

He nods. "Like when I first started this job and I had my father's last name attached to my ass. People thought I got there because of my last name and I worked harder than anyone else to prove I deserved this place. I'd feel like an impostor if I hadn't done that," he confesses and I feel almost relieved.

I didn't think Harrison could have struggled in a similar way. Our backgrounds are so different that I always assumed we couldn't have the same problems growing up. But once again, he proved me wrong.

"I didn't know that," I whisper.

"It's not something I flaunt." He smiles shyly. "But I want to say that I want to help you out. I want to find a solution that doesn't involve me dropping money on your doorstep."

He looks at me expectantly, like his life depends on my answer. My heart thunders in my chest. I've never had someone look at me like that. The happiness bubbling up in my chest makes it hard to speak.

"Listen, Harrison, I don't want you to feel obligated to do something like this because we sleep together," I start, but he puts a finger over my lips.

"I love you, Sienna. I'm doing this because I would do anything for you and *with* you."

His words hang in the air and he looks almost surprised by what he just confessed. And I am too. Not so much at his words but at how they are affecting my heartbeat. It seems like my heart wants to jump out of my chest and leap into his hands. It's exciting and scary at the same time.

I don't know what to say. Nothing comes out of my mouth because I'm too overwhelmed by my feelings tripping over each other to make sense of what is happening.

"Are you breathing?" he asks with a worried smile.

I nod.

"Listen, I don't expect you to say it too. It just came out and I think my brain was just catching up with my heart and you were here in front of me so…" he blurts out, almost apologizing for opening his heart.

"No, Harrison. It's not like you think. It's just, I wasn't expecting to have my heart squeezing in my chest hearing that. It's not what you said that made me speechless, it's the reaction I had hearing those words that knocked me out. I felt relieved that you said it because I was terrified I was going to lose you. I just realize that I would be gutted if you walked out of my life right now," I explain in a breath.

The smile on his face is so broad I don't think his cheeks can contain it. He grabs my hand and drags me to his chest, holding me tight.

His fingers sink into my hair and he fists it, tilting my head toward him. His eyes bore into mine as he slowly lowers his mouth to caress my lips. His kiss is full of a feeling that makes my legs weak.

We've exchanged a lot of kisses, but I've never been kissed like our souls are interconnected, like the sun won't rise tomorrow if we don't put our hearts in it. His tongue brushes my lower lip, asking me to open for him. It feels so right, I don't hesitate one second to give up my mouth, my heart, and my soul to him.

Perfection, I can only describe this moment as perfection. I never understood what people feel when they say that they have butterflies in their stomach. I always considered it a juvenile way to romanticize a feeling that's actually plain and simple. Now I get it. I can feel deep down in my belly those feathery feelings in a physical way, when I lace my legs around Harrison's waist and he carries me on the couch behind us.

He lays me down on my back and, without missing a beat, kisses me senseless. His lips are so perfect on mine I can't get enough. I stroke his tongue, matching his slow movements. It's like he is savoring me for the first time ever. He's taking his time to enjoy this moment.

We've always had an explosive sexual connection. We frantically chased our orgasm trying to get rid of the burning desire that consumed us. This time is different. It's like we're blowing on those glowing embers. It's not consuming like the high flames, but it's something more dangerous. Something that will last longer than a flame, longer than a raging fire destroying everything in its path. It's something that lasts longer, burning below the surface, branding us so deep we won't be able to get rid of the scars.

His lips travel down my neck, my shoulder, my breast. He bites my nipple lightly through the fabric of my bra and I shiver. It feels so good.

Harrison sits on his heels and runs his gaze over my body. I grab the hem of my tank top and pull it over my head. I drop it on the floor next to the couch, followed by my bra. I never move my eyes from his, and when he gets rid of his t-shirt, it's like he is baring my soul to me. There's a vulnerability in his gesture I haven't seen before.

When we finally drop every layer of fabric and stand naked in front of each other, a deep breath leaves my lungs. I've never felt so connected with a person like I am right now with Harrison. I can feel his feelings for me in every goosebump on his skin, every quiver of his muscles, every heartbeat that thunders against his chest. I can feel *him*.

He puts on a condom and lowers himself between my legs. He sinks slowly between my thighs and the feeling is so overwhelming I almost cry. I'm used to his girth, his length, his hot flesh, but I've never felt so desperately full like this. It's not physical. It's the meaning this act carries that make my legs tremble.

He thrusts in long, slow strokes, building our pleasure without a rush. He takes his time, lingering slowly when his length is fully buried in my core. I feel him deep inside me and enjoy the connection that ties us in a knot of feelings.

He pumps me slow, deep, with a purpose. He is branding me with his love, his care, his desperate need. I always thought that making love was something that only hopeless romantics experience, but now I get it. This is different. This is something that transcends physical attraction. When the orgasm hits both of us at the same time, it's not like a storm wrecking your body, but a river slowly and steadily pushing through it, changing it with the relentless power of water.

I will never be the same.

I will never experience the excitement of wild sex in the same way, knowing that I can get this powerful feeling that shakes my body to the bones. The pleasure is so intense that when I come down from my high, I'm dizzy.

Harrison collapses on top of me, trying to catch his breath. He turns his head just enough to look me in the eyes and find the confirmation that we are screwed. If this is making love, I don't think we're going back to explosive sex anytime soon.

I kiss his lips while he slips on the couch besides me. We stare into each other's eyes, trying to figure out what to say or do. There are no words to describe this moment, and while happiness and love and hope fill my chest, there's a small part of me that is terrified. A tiny voice in my head is whispering its fears: *If all of this ends, you won't survive this time.*

And the part of my heart that is listening to this voice knows it's right.

CHAPTER 24
Sienna

The solution to our problem comes five days after our fight. Or at least, we hope this is a solution. Harrison suggested a compromise on our views about our private life being public. We're not selling our story to some tabloid but we are going to take advantage about the buzz surrounding our relationship and book interviews to talk about our movie.

"Are you nervous?" he asks as we drive up the Hollywood hills.

"A bit. I'm not used to the cameras. Or at least, not staying in front of them." I let out a deep breath.

He briefly smiles at me before putting his eyes on the road in front of us.

"It's a podcast. Nothing major like a talk show. You'll be comfortable, trust me," he tries to reassure me.

Rationally, I know I have nothing to worry about, but my stomach seems to not get the memo. I don't have a good track record when it comes to selling my work. I don't know how other people can be so confident when talking about what they do. I know my work is good, but every time someone asks me to talk about it, I downplay everything because I feel like I'm rambling about it.

"I know it's a podcast, but he's an influencer with millions of followers. I don't think talk shows have as much reach as he has," I point out.

He chuckles. "Yes, he has a large following, but he also does his interviews in his home office. That should make you less intimidated by the cameras and microphones."

"A home office in an uber-mansion in Hollywood," I laugh, my nervousness going down a notch.

We stay silent for a long moment while he drives slowly up the hill. There's something soothing about how Harrison drives.

"Why don't you have a driver?" I ask out of the blue.

"What?" He looks at me with a confused smile.

"You're a billionaire, why don't you have someone driving you around?" I've always wondered this about him. He really is down to earth for a billionaire. Yes, he has a lot of things that scream money, but he never flaunts them.

"A lot of reasons." He stares ahead thinking about it. "I love cars, and I really like to drive them. I'm extremely protective with my cars, and I don't want anyone to drive them. And I have the weirdest schedule in the world. I don't want to keep a person on standby on those late nights when I finish shooting some scene."

"That make sense."

"Why do you ask?" He sounds curious.

"Because you don't act like some rich douche. You have literally more money than everyone I know put together, but you live like a normal person."

He shrugs. "My parents always lived up to the standards of rich people. Always impeccable when in public and at home. Never a hair out of place. I was honestly tired of being perfect all the time growing up and I just decided to value being comfortable more than appearances when I moved away from my parents."

He doesn't realize it, but some of this perfection is ingrained in his DNA. He is more casual, he doesn't have someone doing everything for him, but he's never messy. His house is tidy not because there's someone picking up after him, he cleans the countertop when he spills coffee and puts his dirty clothes in the hamper instead of on the bedroom floor.

He grew up being respectful of his things and the people around him and I think this makes him richer than anyone else in the world, even those with more money than him. There aren't many, but there are a few.

We arrive at the ultra-modern house and park in the back next to a shiny green sportscar. I take a look in front of me and my breath catches in my throat when I see the downtown skyline through the massive window next to the front door that gives me a view of the ultra-modern living room.

"Is that an infinity pool over there?" I mutter to Harrison and he chuckles.

"He has quite a few toys around this house."

"Why am I always the poor one when we talk about this industry?" I mumble.

"That is going to change soon, trust me." He winks at me while the door flies open and a smiley nerdy guy with thick-rimmed glasses greets us.

"Welcome to my home!" he chirps with a high-pitched voice I recognize from his YouTube videos.

"Thank you for having us," I say shaking his hand.

"It's an honor," he says, inviting us in and guiding us down concrete stairs just inside the front door. "I know Harrison's movies, of course, but when he talked about you with such enthusiasm, I had to watch your movies and, let me just say, you are quite the hidden gem!"

I feel my cheeks burn with embarrassment. I glance back at Harrison walking behind me and I find him grinning.

"Thank you. You're really kind," I blurt out, not sure how to answer his compliment.

We enter his office after walking down a hallway with concrete walls and old black-and-white photos of Los Angeles. It's a modern house, but it has a warm feeling. The office is no different from the rest of this place. The black walls are brightened by splashes of color from a lot of art.

Harrison and I sit down on the couch where two studio microphones wait for us, while Mark sits on an armchair in front of us. He already has a microphone attached to his electric blue polo. He grabs an iPad from the wooden coffee table and sets his green eyes on us.

"Shall we start?"

"Sure!" Harrison says while I nod. I'm not sure how my voice will come out.

He points a remote control toward a camera on a tripod and the things comes to life as my stomach clenches in a tight grip.

Mark starts introducing us but I'm so nervous I only hear half of it. I smile and I'm sure I look like I'm having a stroke. My face is so tight I can't even blink. I'll go blind, my eyes will dry out by the end of this interview, I'm sure of it.

"So, talk to us about this movie." He smiles at me and I'm paralyzed.

I turn slightly toward Harrison and he is expectantly waiting for me to answer, at least until he realizes I can't even open my mouth. His eyes widen slightly, then he clears his throat and launches into an explanation about this wonderful movie we're making, his words, not mine. Apparently, I become mute as soon as I have a camera in front of me.

I'm so embarrassed I can feel my cheeks burn. *Get a grip, Sienna!* I try to convince myself that I can do this but only when Harrison's hand slips on the couch cushion and grabs mine do I truly relax enough to say something.

My voice comes out a bit insecure in the beginning, but as I explain what my vision is for this movie, the tension slips away enough to let me talk freely and, a half hour later, I can even joke. It's strange how physical contact with Harrison can calm my nerves so much that I can face one of my biggest insecurities without too much trouble.

"But let's talk about the less fun part of making a movie. Money. You struggled a bit to find funding for this movie, right?" Mark frowns like this is almost a tragedy.

I let Harrison handle the answer. He's better equipped to do that. His poker face is perfect to get you to open your wallet.

He nods and puts on his serious face. "Making an indie movie is never easy. You don't have a lot of people willing to take a risk with a production that could lead to nothing. But we have a really great script, a fantastic director." He smiles slightly at me before giving his attention to Mark. "We know it will do great and we found someone who gave us what we needed to start. Still, we're actively looking for other investors. We're talking about a movie that has Oscar buzz surrounding it. If you know what I mean."

Mark is completely enraptured by his explanation, and his eyes widen like saucers at the Oscar mention. He's almost dreamy as he scrolls his iPad for the next question.

"Well, you believe so much in this movie that you personally financed it, is that right?" he asks Harrison.

I feel his hand tense under mine on the couch. What is he talking about?

Harrison rubs a hand on his jaw like he always does when he's nervous. He looks completely at ease on this couch, but I know him well enough to recognize when he's on pin and needles.

"Well, I found a company that could invest in it, yes." He sounds like he wants to dismiss this argument fast.

"Yes, but you're one of the shareholders, so basically you put your own money in it," Mark says and my blood runs cold.

I look at Harrison and the guilt painted all over his face is answer enough for me.

"Yeah, sort of." He tries to dismiss it, but I can't dismiss it. Not a chance in the world I can forget about this detail.

I move my hand from Harrison's grip, and put it on my lap, trying not to fidget too much. I don't miss him flinching when I rip my hand out of his tight grip.

The rest of the interview is a blur. It goes on for another twenty minutes but I don't remember one single thing about what we talked about. Only one thing goes on repeat on my mind: he betrayed me. He did the only thing I asked him not to do. He paid his way into this movie and he forced me to work with him.

And I thought I was the asshole for how I treated him. How stupid am I to fall for a man like this twice in my life? Am I so dumb that I don't recognize people who try to scam me?

"Sienna, wait, please!" Harrison calls when I'm already out of the gates of Mark's house.

"Why? Do you want to feed me some other lie?" I grit through my teeth.

He flinches and I feel the pain deepening in my heart. He doesn't even try to deny my accusation.

"Can we talk about it?" he pleads.

"There is nothing to say," I spit.

"There is a lot to say," he counters.

"Oh, now you have a lot to say. Not when you betrayed me by putting money in a project I openly asked you not to." I see red. If he comes closer, I'm going to punch him. I swear.

I feel so betrayed I can't even breath.

"It was before I even knew you. I didn't know you didn't want me to," he tries to explain.

Technically, he's right. He couldn't know I didn't want him to save my movie, but it doesn't justify him going behind my back. He forced me to fire the lead actor to make space for his massive ego.

"And you didn't think it was something you should have told me after? *Four days ago*, I told you what happened with my ex and you didn't think that was a good moment to come clean?" Damn. Four days ago he told me he loved me. What a fool I am.

He says nothing. He stands there with guilt all over his face. He knew exactly what he was doing and he chose the easy way.

"You know what hurts most, Harrison? That you are the most honest person I know. You are always straightforward, candid in everything you do. But I'm not worthy of your honesty. I'm so low on your priority list you don't even bother to tell me the truth. I had to find out from a complete stranger that you betrayed me in the worst possible way." I'm so spent that my words come out in a whisper.

"I didn't want to lose you. I knew if I told you you'd walk away and I couldn't do it. I love you, Sienna. And the thought of you disappearing from my life was scary enough to make me do something stupid." His voice cracks and my heart bleeds with every sound.

"You want to know the irony in all of this? You didn't lose me because of the money, you lost me because of the lie. If you had talked to me, I would have probably freaked out and yelled at you, but I would have gotten over it. But now, Harrison, I can't trust you. And that is something I can't get over." I turn around and walk down the empty street.

I don't look back once. I don't know what he's doing but I can't hear his car or any other sound. And maybe that's what breaks my heart even more. No matter how angry I am with him, what guts me most is his absence.

"I fucked up!" I blurt out when Leonard opens his front door.

He frowns, stares at me for a long moment, then shakes his head. Why do my friends look like disappointed fathers whenever I talk to them lately?

"Sienna found out I paid for the movie when we first started and she's furious."

He steps aside to let me in. He leads me to his office and I sit down on the leather couch while he pours a couple of whiskeys from the wet bar in the corner. He hands me one and it's my turn to frown.

"It's ten in the morning," I point out, grabbing the glass.

"Considering you're interrupting my work day, I say I have a good reason to start drinking so early." He raises an eyebrow, challenging me.

"It's Sunday," I remind him.

"So what?" He appears genuinely confused about my statement. Does he ever stop working?

I shake my head and drop the topic. We stay silent for a while, Leonard staring at me like there's a movie playing on my face, showing all of my thoughts.

"So, we're not going through the 'I told you so' argument, right?" He hides his smug smile behind his glass.

I give him the stink eye and the traitor chuckles. I need support, not someone kicking me while I'm already down.

"How did it happen?" he asks when I don't elaborate.

"We got an interview for a podcast on Friday and the guy dropped the bomb, asking me if I believed in the project, considering I invested money with my company," I summarize.

He chuckles and I flip him off. "I don't know what's worse, you finding the only journalist doing his job well or her discovering you lied to her on the camera."

"Tell me about it," I groan.

Hearing it out loud from my friend's mouth sounds even more horrible than I thought. I acted like a hideous pick. I snuck into her movie exactly like her ex did, and then betrayed her in the same way. It doesn't matter that I did it with good intentions. At first, I was thinking only of myself and what I needed and I completely disregarded her project. She chose another person for that job and I don't even know his name.

Another layer of shame dawns on me. Since when have I become so self-centered that I stab my colleagues in the back to get what I want?

"So, are you going to do something about that?" he asks, dragging me out of my self-pity.

I shake my head. "I don't know what to do, honestly," I admit.

"Well, groveling is a good start," he points out.

"It's not even close to what I need to make amends."

"So, be creative."

"I don't know what to do. Any suggestions?" I study his face while I sip my whiskey.

"You're asking me? I've never had a relationship in my entire life. I don't even know where to start."

"Good point. But you are the one running an empire. You have a keen eye for problem solving." Now I'm just messing with him.

He grunts. "Let me Google it for you, Harrison." He flips me off.

I chuckle. At least my mood improved a bit coming here.

"Listen, Harrison, I don't know how to help you, but if I was in your shoes, I would probably start from the beginning. I would probably fix my original mistake," he suggests.

I look at him, not really sure about his advice, but it's worth a try to at least think about it.

"Okay, now that I'm done asking for your help, can we order pizza? I can't drive after drinking whiskey on an empty stomach."

"You have got to be kidding me," he whispers, grabbing his phone.

"Well, next time give me a Diet Coke if you want me out of here sooner."

He mumbles something I can't discern but there's a hint of a smile on his face. I don't feel guilty for forcing him to take a break from his job. Sometimes I feel like he focuses so much on his companies because he doesn't have anything else worth living for. All alone in this empty mansion, I know for a fact that sometimes working yourself to death is a better option than facing your loneliness.

***

I'm in my car driving home when my phone rings. My heart jumps in my throat hoping that maybe Sienna decided to give me a chance. My heart sinks when I see David's name flashing on the screen. The sense of disappointment is overwhelming and when I answer I sound almost angry.

"Hey, David, what's up?"

There's a moment of silence. "Did I catch you in a bad moment?" He sounds puzzled.

"No, sorry. I'm driving and a dickhead just cut in front of me," I lie. Apparently, it's becoming easier and easier.

"Well, I don't want you to hit someone because I'm distracting you."

Please, David, get to the point. I don't have all day. "No worries, I can handle two tasks at time. What's up?" I try to sound more cheerful.

"Listen, I listened to the podcast interview you and Sienna did for that movie. I want to invest." He gets straight to the point and I almost choke.

I always forget that David is a producer. Not a big shark like someone in Hollywood but he has good movies on his resumé. I always meet him at parties, most of the time he's wasted, which is why it didn't click immediately that he could be interested in investing in it. I thought he was going to invite me to a night out.

"I'm listening."

"I have a budget sitting around I want to invest and you sound pretty sure you have a big hit on your hands. I want to hear more about this movie and why it's so special. If you're putting your own money in an indie movie, it *has* to be good."

The irony. What got him to decide to jump in the boat is me investing in my own movie. I want to laugh at how the universe is fucking with me right now.

"I would be happy to have a chat with you. Let me call Sienna and I'll call you back, okay?" I don't even know if she'll answer my call.

"Perfect! I'll wait for your call. Don't hit anyone in the mean-while." He chuckles and I can't stop a smile forming on my face.

"This is Los Angeles, dude. Nobody pays attention when they're driving."

He laughs. "I'll wait for your call."

He hangs up and I find myself staring at the phone for way too long for someone that should pay attention to the road in front of him. But I feel the uneasiness sneaking up my chest when I think of calling Sienna. I take a deep breath and try to call her, but it goes straight to voicemail. I try a second time with the same result.

"Fuck this." I pull up to the traffic light in the left lane and make a U-turn.

I drive to Sienna's apartment and I'm so focused on what I have to say I don't even know how I got here. I just hope David wasn't right and I haven't hit someone in the process.

I knock on the door and nobody comes to open. I knock a sec-ond time, not sure if they heard me or if they're not home at all. The curtains on the windows next to the door move just slightly but it's enough to know that she's home and avoiding me.

I knock again. "Sienna, please, can you open up? I know you're in there and I need to talk to you."

Nothing.

I knock again. "Please, I really need to talk about something important." My plea comes out softly.

The lock on the door clicks and hope rises in my chest, only to be crushed when Harper appears.

"Harrison, she doesn't want to talk to you, she doesn't even want to see you." Her stern voice is chilling.

Considering we have to work together on this movie, how does she plan avoiding me forever?

"I don't want to apologize again," I blurt out and Harper raises a scolding eyebrow and crosses her arms in front of her.

"Excuse me?"

I take a deep breath to calm my nerves.

"I got a phone call from David, a producer who wants to invest in our movie. We need to meet with him to discuss it and I want Sienna to be there," I explain.

"Is this just another way to put money in your movie? Does this David even exist?"

I gave her the stink eye. Okay, I messed up once, but I'm not *that* big of a jerk.

She raises her hands in mock surrender. "Just asking. You don't have the best track record when it comes to lying."

"I lied because I didn't want to lose her, not because I want to scam her," I spit out, a bit annoyed. "I made a mistake, I know it, and I apologized. I'm not a bad person. I'm human."

She seems ashamed about her remark and shakes her head. "Listen, she doesn't want to talk to you right now, but I will tell her that."

"Thank you. It's kind of important, so if she could give me an answer soon, I would appreciate it," I plead.

She nods. "I'll talk to her right now. I'm sure she'll call you as soon as she can."

I nod. I can't ask for anything better than this. She's pissed and I get it. I turn around to walk to my car.

"Harrison!" Harper calls after me.

I look at her and all her fighting attitude is gone. She smiles softly.

"Give her time. She got burned badly last time and you're the first man she trusted after him. I know you're not like him, and she knows it too, but she needs time to process what happened. Be patient with her."

I nod. "I'm not going anywhere. When she's ready to talk, I'm here to listen. I know that I messed up. I realize how bad it was, and I don't expect her to forgive me just because I apologized. Words means nothing if I don't act on it."

She smiles at me and waves before watching me walk to my car and jump in it. I meant what I said. My apologies are empty words if I don't do anything to make her trust me again. And I'm determined to fix what I broke in the first place.

CHAPTER 26

Sienna

I watch Harrison going through his lines like he always does when he leaves his personality behind and steps into his character's head. It's a pleasure to watch him deliver a scene that is almost perfection.

We're at the end of this week and reshooting the final scene that wasn't working. I was right to insist to go back on set. These are the most amazing shots we got so far. They're dripping with raw emotion and go straight to your heart.

Harrison is the most amazing actor I have ever worked with. Hands down, the most committed. And it shows. And he's also dedicated to the cause. He has connections I never dreamed of and he is not shy to use them to make this movie amazing.

We would never have David on board if it wasn't for Harrison. I have to admit, he's the one who makes a difference not only because he's great at his job, but because he has the resources to bring an indie movie to a whole other level.

"Cut!" I call and everyone holds their breath to see what my verdict is.

"What do you think?" Ellen's expectant voice makes me turn to her.

She has a smile on her face I can only compare to mine. She knows this scene is gold.

"It's the best scene I've ever shot," I admit and she lets out a breath.

"I agree. He was spectacular on this one. I don't know what happened since the wrap, but I think that weekend in Aruba was regenerating for him." She winks, grinning at me.

My heart squeezes in my chest. If she only knew. So much has happened since we started filming this project that it seems like we took years to do it. I hated Harrison, then I liked him, then I loved him, broke up with him, and now we're in a limbo where we're civil with each other but our relationship status is far from being clear.

I still love him, I miss him, but I can't get over the fact that I don't trust him, not completely. He lied for *months* and when he had the chance to come clean, he decided to lie a bit more. I can't get over this so easily.

"We are done here, folks. That's a wrap. Again!" I shout and everybody cheers.

I watch Harrison smile at Viola. He briefly glances in my direction, but I pretend to be busy fixing things in my backpack so as not to give him an opening to come and talk to me. I'm not sure I can keep cool while we're with other people and I need to keep a professional conduct on set. It's not that I think Harrison will make a scene, it's that I don't trust myself when I'm with him.

"So, are we going out to celebrate?" Ellen asks and I want to dig a hole and disappear.

I knew this moment was coming, but I hoped they would just go home and forget about me. Not going to happen, but a girl can dream, right? I need to be more social, I can't keep hiding my awkwardness to avoid human contact. Especially in this industry where connections are everything.

"Listen, folks! We're going out to celebrate, if you know a place that takes parties of thirty plus people, you're welcome to suggest it!" I holler.

People look at me a bit surprised but happy about my idea. They are silent for a few long moments, but then someone starts to drop names of places and, an hour later, we're on Sunset Boulevard in a place with a mechanical bull in the middle of the space. It's loud, packed with people, but perfect for the crew that joined us for a beer and buffalo wings.

Harrison is at the table, a few seats down from me. This place is so noisy we can't talk and that's good for me. I don't want to make small talk with him just to appear civil in public. We never did small talk. We fought, we fucked, we had deep meaningful conversation but small talk never happened.

"So, what's the deal with you two?" Ellen asks.

I was expecting this question at some point. I didn't confide in her about what I had with Harrison, but she's smart and it doesn't take a genius to understand that we had at least a fling.

"No deal." I shake my head. And it's true. There's nothing between us right now if not awkwardness.

"You went from ripping out your throats, to ripping off your clothes, to nothing?" She seems genuinely puzzled.

I shrug. How can I explain it all?

"I don't know. It just didn't work out."

She shakes her head and raises her eyebrow. "You're not fooling me. It's impossible that what you had just cooled down. It's like Hell freezing overnight. There were people betting on you getting married by the end of the year."

I roll my eyes. "Not going to happen."

"Well, maybe not, but the tension between you two is palpable. And I'm not just talking about physical stuff. I never saw two minds challenging each other so much like yours do. It's like when you're together you're in a creativity bubble that pulls off Oscar-worthy movies. What you two have is rare and I don't believe it just died down."

Ellen's words strike a nerve. I always thought this connection was in my head but she saw it too. It's real. It's like we were born to complete each other in an intellectual way. We make great things together, but that doesn't mean we're perfect for each other on a sentimental level.

"He lied to me," I blurt out.

She glances at Harrison laughing with a camera operator and then frowns in my direction.

"It was good-intentioned…sort of, but still, he lied to me," I explain when she seems unconvinced.

I can't blame her. When you get to know Harrison, it's difficult to think of him as a liar. He's so blatantly honest sometimes it's too much to handle. Nobody believes he's capable of tricking you.

"Is it something so massive that you can't forgive him? Did he apologize?"

I nod. "He did and I understood where the lie came from, but he did the only thing that burned me once and I can't get over it."

"Did he cheat on you?" she asks, surprised.

I roll my eyes. "Have you me Harrison? Does he look like someone who would cheat?"

"No, definitely not." She chuckles. "Well, I don't know what he did, but I hope you two sort it out, because you have a good thing going and it's rare to see something like that in Hollywood. You remind me of Roberto Benigni and Nicoletta Braschi."

"The Oscar winners?" I have been compared to many persons in my life but never to an icon like the Italian actor and director and his wife, actress and producer. They're like a mythological figure in a world of shallowness like ours.

She nods. "There is something special about those two. They met forty years ago and never left each other. It's not just about love. Every movie they make, they make together and put a bit of magic in it that only they can make. It's like a chemical reaction when they're working together that creates something special and unique you can feel onscreen. You can't have that kind of alchemy with someone else. And I can see that in you two."

Her words hit me square in the face. I look at Harrison and, as though he feels me staring at him, he turns around and smiles. It's a sad one, like he's lost hope in something he wants. Is he the agent for our chemical reaction? Am I throwing away something unique and special I can only have once in a lifetime?

I know that when we're together, we unlock a level of creativity we can't achieve alone, but I always thought it was all in my head, it's the first time I've been with someone so kindred to my creativity. But Ellen saw it too, and now I'm questioning my every decision.

***

"Can I give you a ride home?" Harrison's hopeful voice startles me.

I'm waiting for Ellen to come out of the bathroom to finally go home. We called it a night a few minutes ago after spending the evening chatting, laughing, and simply enjoying the fact that this movie is basically done.

"I'm waiting for Ellen." I smile at him but it dies on my lips when I see the hurt in his eyes.

"Can we talk, Sienna, please?" he whispers.

There are a few people on the curb next to us and I don't want them to eavesdrop on our conversation.

"I don't feel like talking right now, Harrison."

The hurt in his eyes morphs into disappointment. I know he deserves an explanation, or at least a clarification, about where we're going from here, but I know myself too. I know that I will be overwhelmed by this entire situation and say something I don't want to and ruin everything. Words can do more damage than any physical blow.

"Will you ever give me a second chance? Or is it just one mistake and I'm out with you?" I can almost feel the pain in my own chest.

I've never had a man bare his feelings so openly to me. I was always the one trying to protect myself. I never found myself in the position of protecting someone's else feelings. I'm certain that if I'm not careful with Harrison right now, I will break something in him, in *us*, I will never be able to fix.

"I can give you a second chance, Harrison, but not right now. I really understand why you lied to me, and I know you are not like my ex, but I'm not ready yet. While my brain trusts you right now, my heart does not. It retreated behind that wall I built years ago and it's scared. If I give you that second chance right now, I will ruin everything. I will second-guess your every word, every gesture, poisoning a relationship that could be great. I need to convince my heart that it's safe to come out again from behind that wall, but it's not something you can do. It's something that *I* have to do and I need time," I explain, and I can see his shoulders visibly relax.

He nods, understanding. "I'm here when you're ready. But I will fight to convince your heart that I'm worthy of trust. That

I'm a person who won't hurt it. I won't hurt you."

His words carry a fierce conviction that almost make me re-consider my decision. Almost. Because Harrison teaches me that there are good people in this industry, but now I have to become one of them, because my anger and my resentment made me one of the bad guys.

Harrison deserves to be with the hero, not the villain.

CHAPTER 27

Harrison

I sip my iced tea while I wait for Sean, my potential new agent, to show up. He's ten minutes late. By Los Angeles standards it's not a big deal, but I'm a bit annoyed anyway. I have more time to overthink my conversation with Sienna last night and when I overthink, there's a potential for disaster. I'm famous for complicating easy situations.

She asked me for time to trust me again. I have every intention of giving her that, but I also have every intention of giving her a reason to do it. I don't assume that she'll do all the work and I'll sit here, waiting for a solution to fall into my lap.

"Sorry, I'm late. There was an accident on my way here," a tall bald man says, sitting in front of me.

I smile and shake his hand. "This is Los Angeles; traffic is crazy here." *That's why we leave extra time to be on time.* I encountered the same accident on my way here, but I was at this table ten minutes earlier than our appointment.

"Fortunately, you're unemployed right now so I didn't mess up your schedule." He chuckles as he orders his drink to the waitress.

What the hell does that mean? I'm between jobs but that doesn't mean I don't have anything to do. Does he have no respect for other people's time?

"I'm actually still involved in my current job," I point out. Not that I have anything to do until we start promoting the movie in a few weeks, but still, my time is as valuable his.

He smirks. "Yeah, that indie movie. It's not like the crazy schedule of a Hollywood big hit. You know? You're more relaxed...more like hippies," he says in a condescending tone.

I don't know how he is to work with, but he's rubbing me the wrong way already. Who does he think he is?

"So, tell me about you. Kevin said you're one of the best around." The truth is, I don't even know him. I talked to Kevin when we discussed David coming on the project with new funds and he asked me what happened with my old agent. Long story short, he suggested someone he knew and I decided to give him a chance.

I should have known. There's a reason I don't like Kevin and there's a big chance I won't like his friends either. This one is no exception. His order didn't even arrive yet and I already want to stand up and leave.

"You could say that! I only work with the best because I'm the best. My clients soar because of me. I have almost twenty years of experience in this industry and I've never failed once," he brags.

He's humble too. What a surprise! I can't believe I willingly stepped into this nightmare. I've had my agent since I started my career and I forgot how hard it is to find someone you feel comfortable with.

"I'm sure they're happy that you're helping them." I'm not sure if they're too happy with his implication that they're nothing without him.

I already know that this encounter is going nowhere, but I'm curious to see just how badly he messes up this appointment.

"They sure are. They're also happy because I'm very honest with them. Sometimes I come off as rude, but there's no doubt I always tell them the truth to make them better," he announces. I don't know if he really believes what he's saying or if he's so arrogant that he considers other people stupid and incapable of understanding he's just mean.

"Oh, really?" I sip my tea.

His face turns serious. "I have to be honest with you, it will not be easy to turn your career around. After you stooped to making this indie movie, it won't be easy to get back up to where you were before. It wasn't a wise choice," he starts.

"But don't worry, with a couple of movies similar to the old ones, I can bring you back to the old glory." He says it like I'm a kid who's failing in every class he enrolled.

This guy is something else. How can he be so cocky with a potential client like this? How does he even find clients acting like this? I can't believe someone would actually put their career in the hands of a pompous prick like him.

"What make you think my career is actually going down-hill?" I smile calmly and sip my tea again.

He scoffs. He actually dares to scoff in front of a potential client. "Everybody knows when you agree to downgrade to indie movies it's because you're not receiving any more decent scripts."

"I actually wanted to be in this movie, and I was the one who invested in it in the first place because I believe it's a damn good movie," I point out in my angelic attitude.

He looks at me like I just confessed to enjoying licking shoes for fun. I would laugh at his shocked face if I wasn't so disgusted by his personality.

"You had to pay to do that movie? That's worse than I thought. I'll have to work harder to bring you back. I'm not even sure it's possible," he says, outraged.

This time I laugh out loud and he seems even more confused.

"Don't worry, you're not my agent and you never will be. I invested in that movie because I believe in it. You couldn't tell the difference between a good script and a grocery list, so I didn't think you'd understand my choice," I point out.

His mask drops and the sneer behind it reveals his true personality.

"He told me he dumped you because you're a diva, but I thought he was just an incompetent asshole. Turns out, it's true." His snarky remark puts me on high alert.

"Who told you that?" My smirk never leaves my face but I'm boiling inside. I have an idea of who's spreading this gossip.

"Who do you think? The agent that dumped you because you're a lost cause. He told everyone that you're willingly sinking your career, against his advice. He had to dump you before you dragged him with you. I thought he was exaggerating, but it looks like he was right."

I take a deep breath and smile, taking him by surprise.

"You know what? I fired him because he's exactly like you. He doesn't want the best for me, he just wants the money. The problem is, just like you, he wouldn't recognize an Oscar script if it hit him square in the face. Thankfully, I have a good eye for those scripts and I go after them when I find something I think is worth it."

He scoffs. "Oscar script? It's an indie movie. You don't even have the budget to go after an Oscar."

"What you underestimate is that I'm a billionaire. Money is not a problem. I can work for free and I would be happy with that. The problem is having an agent that recognizes talent. You clearly aren't a good fit, but don't worry, I'll thank you when I get my Oscar for opening my eyes and not making the same mistake twice." I pause for effect. "Wait, you won't be at the Oscars because none of you clients are ever invited, let alone you. Never mind, forget I said anything," I say and then stand up, leaving him gaping after me.

As soon as I get in my car, I call my lawyer.

"What's up?" He answers on the second ring.

I chuckle. "Do you answer like that with all your clients?"

"No, just the dumbasses who call me when I'm on vacation." He laughs.

I laugh too. "Listen, your dumbass client has a question."

"I hope it's a dumb one." I can hear the smug smile in his tone.

I roll my eyes. "Do you think there's grounds for suing that prick of my ex-agent? He's shit-talking about me, saying he dumped me because my career was imploding."

"Are you kidding me?" He's serious now. "I don't know if we can sue him for defamation, your career is actually soaring so he's not doing you any damage. Not yet, at least. But I'll look into it, see if there's something we can come up with. I can't wait to nail that prick for real. He shouldn't be allowed to work in this industry. He's a pain for everyone trying to survive in Hollywood." He's in full lawyer mode now.

"Jeez, thank you. He was my agent until two seconds ago." I chuckle.

"I told you to dump him a long time ago, didn't I?" he points out.

"Yes, you can say 'I told you so.'"

He laughs. "Listen I need to get back to my wife before she kicks me out of our cottage. I'll call you if I have something."

"Thank you. And apologize to your wife on my behalf."

***

I walk into Aaron's new streaming company offices and look around at the colorful walls. I love this place. Since he opened it a while back, I can't stop thinking that this was the best career move I've ever witnessed. The way this man can bring magic to life is incredible.

"What are you doing here?" he asks, looking up from his computer.

I'm on the guest list of people that can come and go into this place without being announced by the security gate guard, and he's always puzzled when I show up at his door. He'll probably cancel my name from the list if I keep showing up unannounced.

"I just met Sean Lind and I needed a colorful place to re-charge and release my anger."

His brows knit. "Why would you see that prick?"

I sigh. "Because I casually told Kevin I don't have an agent and he suggested one of his friends."

He rolls his eyes. "Of course he did."

"I've never heard a more pompous prick talking."

"And considering who your agent was, that's saying a lot."

Seriously? Why did it take so much for me to fire him? It seems like everybody hated him but me.

"Anyway, I'm still without an agent." I plop on the chair in front of his desk.

"Why do you need an agent?" He's genuinely curious.

"What do you mean?"

"You're not at the beginning of your career; you don't need to book as many auditions as you used to. Directors and produc-ers come straight to you when they have something good, and you've been in this industry long enough to know where to find a good project. This movie you're in is proof that you don't need anybody to get where you want."

"I don't know. I feel like I'm missing something. That the perfect screenplay is somewhere out there and I'm missing out," I admit.

He raises an eyebrow. "Or you think you're missing something because nothing out there is worth your time."

"So, what, I give up acting?"

"Or you create what's missing. If you see a gap in the market where you can fit in, don't wait for someone else to fill that void. Do it," he suggests, and my heart picks up peace.

Sienna also thinks I can do something as huge as filling that void, and a strange feeling starts to fill my chest. When one person has faith in your talent you feel empowered, but that's it. You assume they really like you and want the best for you. But when another person has the same faith in your skills, you start to think maybe there's something about you that you can't see, something worth trying.

"You mean like writing a screenplay?"

The grin on his face is worth a thousand words, and I don't need an answer. Maybe this is where I have to start, where I need to pick up to fix my life. This is where I made my first mistake with Sienna, maybe this is the sign I need to fix that mistake.

CHAPTER 28
Sienna

"You can go home, you know, right? I'll call you when I finish," Nolan tells me for the tenth time this morning.

We finished the reshooting a week ago. I was here with Ellen and Christopher last week to rewatch it to make sure that it's actually as great as I think. Now we have to put it all together and Nolan can't wait to get rid of me. And it annoys me to a level I didn't know I could reach.

"I'm sure you can, but I'd prefer to stay here. There's just one last scene you have to edit and I don't want to go back and forth in Los Angeles traffic." I try to keep a calm tone, but it's difficult considering I'm getting angrier by the minute trapped in this tight space with him.

I understand he'd rather work alone, but I need the movie to be done. He takes his sweet time when he's working in here alone, and I'm honestly tired of giving him extra space just because he's a weird genius who hates people. I'm asking to stay here for one last scene, not the entire movie.

He huffs but says nothing. He stares at his computer for a long time then starts to work on the scene. It took him four hours for a six-and-a-half minute sequence and I want to rip my eyes out. I know he did it to spite me because I stayed here with him. I've done his job countless times when I had projects on a tight budget, so I know exactly what needs doing and most of what he did wasn't necessary.

Nolan is a very good film editor, but he's also very difficult to work with. I'm sure he's better than me at his job, I'll give him that, but he's also a petty person who makes your life a living hell if you don't do what he wants. What he doesn't know is that I've met countless men that didn't want to have a woman as their boss and I'm thick-skinned. I can stay here all day long and make him regret messing with me.

"Okay. It's ready," he grits through his teeth.

"Go back four scenes and let it play six scenes after this one," I order.

He turns to look at me like I just asked him to delete the entire movie and redo everything, but I stare him down until he looks away. If he thinks he can intimidate me, he's dead wrong.

He does what I asked, and when the movie comes alive on the screen all my frustration disappears. This is the part where the whole movie makes an abrupt U-turn and we question everything we thought was going to happen. Harrison is perfect. He's so flawless I get sucked into the movie and forget to watch for something that doesn't work.

When Nolan stops the scene where I asked him, I'm not even breathing. "Can you please start it again?" I ask when I realize I haven't paid attention to the editing.

He plays the scenes again, and for the second time my attention is drawn to Harrison and not the entire movie. Since when did I became one of those teenagers that go crazy for the movie star? I know sleeping with him clouded my judgement a bit toward the movie, but this is ridiculous.

"Can you start it again, please?"

He throws a questioning glance at me but does what I say. I watch the scenes again and I'm barely aware that I have to tell Nolan if it's good or not. I struggle to focus on my task, but apparently the third time is a charm because I can finally assess the editing and find it good.

"It's good. We have the final edit." I smile but he doesn't reciprocate.

This man makes me uncomfortable.

"Good. I'll send the file to Kevin." He goes back to his computer without looking at me.

Is he for real right now? "I'm waiting here for my copy too. I have a hard drive you can put it on."

As soon as the words leave my lips, he looks back at me, horrified. "I'm not putting the movie on your hard drive. What if you lose it or someone steals it? It will be out there and it will be my fault."

I take a deep breath to keep from punching him in the face. "First, I'm an adult, I don't go around dropping hard drives like a toddler. Second, you're putting this movie on a server somewhere you don't even know the whereabouts of and that's safer than giving it to me? Offline? Third, I'm the director of this movie. You give it to *me*, then *I* eventually give it to Kevin. You don't go straight to him without my approval. I'm the one who found this script, found Kevin to produce it, and I'm responsible for it. The first person who should watch it and decide if there's anything else to fix is me, not Kevin," I hiss.

I'm honestly tired of his sexist behavior. He can be a genius, but if he thinks he can walk over me, he's delusional.

"I've always dealt with him when there was a problem," he spits back.

I've long suspected Kevin knew more than I wanted him to because he has his ass-kisser in this production, but hearing him say it out loud hurts.

"That was you first mistake. *I* am the director. You come to me, not him. Like it or not, I don't care." I stand up and give him the hard drive.

He stares at my hand for a long time and I'm worried he'll throw it against the wall, but he grabs it and reluctantly connects it to his computer. Then he downloads the movie on my hardware and hands it to me.

"You don't need to put it on the shared server. I'll do it when I'm sure it's good enough."

He turns around and looks at me furiously. I point toward the door. He reluctantly stands up and I lower down to shut the computer off. When I turn toward him, I see his anger brewing.

"Your keys," I say, reaching out my hand.

He is outraged. "Are you serious?"

"More than serious. I'll let you know when we need to put it on the server," I say firmly.

"Do you think that I'm going to wait around for you to go on vacation with your superstar boyfriend before doing my job?" he scoffs.

I'm so close to punching him in the face I have to make a fist at my side. "That's exactly what I expect my employee to do. I decide when and where to do the job and if I ask you to wait, you'll wait." I'm tired of fighting with him.

People forget that I'm the one who got this movie. They're working here because of me, because I wanted them. I took responsibility for every decision and I demand respect for that. I always give people freedom to work as they please because I believe everyone should do their job as they see fit, but I'm tired of being treated without respect because they mistake my kindness for weakness.

He grabs the keys from his front pocket and throws them on the desk, then storms out of the room. I feel relieved. I've never felt so good telling someone they have to do what I say. When I lock the door behind me, I feel like a weight has lifted from me.

***

"What happened, why are you crying?" Harper asks worried, sitting on my bed where I've been lying down since this afternoon when I watched the entire movie for the first time.

"I watched the movie." I hiccup.

"What movie? The one you made?"

I nod.

She frowns. "Is it that bad?"

I shake my head. "It's too good."

"You're crying because the movie is too good?" She's puzzled.

I nod again.

"What does that even mean?" She's completely lost.

"Watch." I start the movie from the beginning and she settles down next to me to watch it on my computer.

I can't explain how I feel, how watching it from start to finish gutted me. And I directed it! Usually, I know exactly how a movie I'm shooting will turn out. I have a vision about what I want and it's never far from the outcome.

This time I completely underestimated the emotional impact of this project. And underestimated the impact Harrison's talent had on the main character. I don't know if it's because I fought with him in the beginning and lost track of the actual film, or if I actually love Harrison and the pain on the screen seems way too real, but it got me like a punch to the gut.

I never cry watching a movie, let alone one of my own.

Half an hour into the film Harper grabs the tissue box, and by the end she's sobbing so hard I doubt she can see anything on the screen. I know, because I'm ugly-crying too.

"Jesus Christ. Even without the soundtrack and the sound engineers putting their hands on it, it's almost overwhelming. How is it even possible it's this good and not finished?"

"Isn't it?" I thought maybe Harrison had just fucked my brains to oblivion and I couldn't see the movie for what it really is, but she's crying too. "I mean, it's a good movie, right? My judgement isn't clouded by my relationship with him, right?"

She looks at me and shakes her head smiling. "Since when are you so insecure about one of your projects?" Her voice is soft.

"I don't know, since I fucked the lead actor, I suppose. It's strange. I have no idea what got into me, but I can't separate my personal and professional life in this movie. Harrison is so into this character I can't separate the two of them. I can see part of him in that movie, shades of his personality I've come to know during these months. I can't tell if I'm seeing him or my protagonist," I try to explain but I realize my thought are so confused I can't even explain them to myself, let alone someone else.

Harper wipes her eyes with a tissue and puts her arm around my shoulders, dragging me to her side. "I think that you're just in love and you don't know how it feels anymore. After Dickhead you never let anyone in, and now that Harrison has made his way into your heart, you're confused. It's normal. It's good, Sienna."

She's right. The turmoil inside of me was there before watching the movie. The film just magnified what was stirring inside my heart since Harrison took down the walls.

"I fucked up. God, I fucked up so bad with him that I don't even know if he wants me anymore," I murmur, hearing the desperation in my voice. Or maybe it's just the realization of what I have done.

"I'm sure he didn't give up on you. I don't know him like you do, but he seems like a guy that doesn't mess around. He told you that he loves you and I'm sure he didn't say it just to make small talk. And he seems stubborn, something tells me he won't give up on you," she says standing up and grabbing my computer. "Call him and I'll keep this in my room, so you don't watch this movie again and bawl for another two-and-a-half hours."

I smile and don't complain about my computer. She's right, I would have watched the movie again. I stare at my phone, trying to gather the courage to call Harrison. What can I say, besides apologizing for acting like a crazy person? I know he understood why I reacted that way, but *I* am the one who feels like I betrayed him. No, betrayed isn't even the right word to describe how I feel. I didn't give him the chance to prove I can trust him.

I grab the phone and, without another thought, dial Harrison's number. It goes straight to voicemail. I'm so surprised that I don't even say anything before hanging up. I try a second and a third time with the same result.

An ugly feeling settles in my stomach. Why can't I get a hold of him? I take a few moments to consider my options and come to the conclusion that I don't have many. I call the only other person who has his number.

"Hi Kevin, I'm trying to call Harrison but it goes straight to voicemail, do you know if he's having some problem with his phone?" I ask as soon as he picks up, and I realize how childish my words are when I hear them out loud. Why should I call Kevin to ask for him? I'm having sex with him, I could just go to his house. I sound like a teenager who got dumped by his crush, asking his friends if they know where he is. God, I feel stupid.

"No, I got a call from him this morning, I assume his phone works." I hear rustling in the background and I hope Kevin is doing something important and not giving much thought to what I'm asking.

"Listen, I watched the edited movie and it's great. I'm in touch with the sound engineer and the guy coordinating the soundtrack," I add, hoping to move the attention to something less stupid than my love life.

He chuckles. "I know. Nolan was furious when he called me."

That asshole had the guts to go to him as soon as I called him out. "Speaking of Nolan. I don't want him near the movie for any reason. I'll put it on the server and if he asks you why he can't have the key, tell him he pissed me off and he's fired. His name will be on the credits, but he's done with this movie," I say firmly, trying not to give too much space to the anger rising in my gut.

Kevin chuckles again. "Finally, you grew some balls," he says before hanging up.

What does that even mean? I stare at the phone in disbelief with more questions than before. The man who always belittles me is now proud of me and the one who always supported me sent me straight to his voicemail. Did I step into an alternate reality where my life turned upside down and I didn't notice it?

CHAPTER 29
Harrison

This doesn't work. The dialogue it's too stiff, nobody talks like that. I rub a couple of fingers over my eyes and feel the burn making my view blurry. I should go to sleep, or at least use some eye drops. I look out the window and the sun is shining high in the sky. What time is it?

I put my eyes back on my computer and stare at the page. I'm almost finished, but the more I read what I wrote, the more I think it's a bunch of bullshit. How does Sienna think I can do this? The dialogue sounds childish and the scenes are...I don't even know how to describe them. Insignificant? I knew it wouldn't be easy, but now I'm doubting every single scene of this screenplay.

I had a great idea for the movie. Something that came straight from my heart but now I'm doubting I even have a heart to follow. Maybe it was just a dream and I'm fool to follow it. Not everybody has the skill to actually achieve their dreams.

"Are you fucking serious?" Aaron's voice startles me to the point that I almost drop the computer.

My heart hammers in my chest as I turn around and find Aaron and Leonard looking at me in disbelief. "Are you trying to kill me? You can't sneak into my house like that. You scared the shit out of me!" I shout back, more startled than angry.

Aaron scoffs.

Leonard looks at me like he wants to kill me. "Sneaking up on you? We fucking rang the bell like maniacs before using our keys to get in!" he spits.

"Oh. Really?" Now I'm confused. "I didn't hear it."

They shake their heads, walking to the couch and sitting down. It's weird to see them so worried. And I have no clue why. Did a bomb explode in the neighborhood and I didn't notice it? My eyebrows knit together, trying to understand what's happening.

"We thought you were dead. We've tried to contact you for the last three days, but your phone goes to voicemail. We thought you were filming or something, but you usually call back when you listen to your messages. So, we came here to check. You scared the shit out of us, too," Aaron explains and I'm even more confused. Three days? How did I miss three days?

"I don't know what to say. Was it really that long?"

They look at me like I'm crazy and, to be honest, I feel a bit nuts right now. It's like I walked into my own mind and forgot to come out. I feel out of touch with reality and it's unsettling. I feel completely lost and all I want to do is crawl into bed and sleep until it's gone. Maybe the sleep deprivation is what's making me feel thrown under a bus.

"Where's your phone?" Leonard asks.

I have to think about it. I normally check my phone often when I'm not on set, but right now I can't remember the last time I saw it. After a ten-minute search with Leonard whispering "unbelievable" at least ten times under his breath, and Aaron turning my living room upside down, I find it under the couch cushions.

"It's dead," I announce trying to turn it on without success.

"Since when?" Leonard asks.

"I don't know." I shrug.

"When was the last time you plugged it in?" Aaron pushes.

"I don't know." I sit down on the couch again.

"When was the last time you slept, or ate…or took a shower?" Leonard makes a disgusted face.

"I. Don't. Know." I repeat, exasperated.

They stare at me for a long time, no doubt thinking I'm out of my mind, but I really have no idea when it died or when I last walked away from the couch. I remember I went to my bedroom to grab the power cord for my laptop, but I didn't stop to sleep or anything.

"Are you on drugs?" Aaron is worried.

"What? No! I started writing this screenplay and just…lost track of time."

Aaron smirks. "You're writing a screenplay?"

I feel a bit shy talking about it. It's something I've never done and I'm not sure I'm any good at it. He's the best producer around and could destroy my script reading just the first page. I'm not sure I'm ready for him to put his hands on it.

"And you lost track of three entire days of your life?" Leonard sounds outraged by the idea.

"I…" I try to explain but he raises a hand to stop me.

"If you say 'I don't know,' I'm going to slap you."

I close my mouth and say nothing.

"Unbelievable," he whispers again.

We look at each other for a long time. I'm not even sure what to say. This whole screenplay thing just took me by surprise. I thought I was going to lose focus as soon as I put my hands on the keyboard, but I actually started to write and never stopped. Is it supposed to be like that? I've never done it, so I have nothing to compare it to.

"You need to eat. Please, go to take a shower while we order pizza," Aaron says with a grin.

There is a strange, proud look in his eyes I've never seen before. He always considered me an excellent actor. He was never shy about telling me what he thinks of my movies, but he seems especially excited about this step in my career. I don't say anything, not sure what I'm supposed to tell him, so I take his suggestion and shower before eating something. My stomach grumbles, and I realize I'm starving.

"I almost fell asleep under the shower," I admit when I come back to the kitchen where they put the pizza boxes.

"I can't believe you forget to sleep and eat and do things a normal person does to survive." Leonard seems to want to scold me.

"It's not like I've stayed on that couch for three days. But I just grabbed something from the fridge and ate it in front of the computer. I have bodily functions I need to pay attention to, you know, like going to the bathroom," I tease him.

"So, tell me about this screenplay." Aaron finally gives in to his curiosity.

I shrug. "I didn't finish it yet. It's a story I've had in my head for a while and I finally had the guts to write it down." I don't want to go into detail before it's finished, but I can see he's dying of curiosity.

"Can I read it when it's done?" He's like a kid asking for a new toy.

I roll my eyes and bite into the pizza. God, I was really starving. "After Sienna reads it. She's got first dibs on the screenplay," I say without any doubt in my voice.

He grins. I don't know if he's happy because he's going to read it or because I'm considering Sienna for my next project. To be honest, I don't want anyone else to direct that movie.

"So, you're doing this to win her back? Isn't this plan a bit complicated?" Leonard points out chewing at his pizza. He puts his on a plate and uses a fork and knife, like the psycho he is.

"I'm doing this because I need to, not because of some elaborate plan. I feel like my actor career run has run its course and I want to try something new." It's the truth. I want Sienna to be the first to read it, but if she doesn't want me back, I'm not going to throw away what I built.

"You're not acting anymore?" Leonard frowns.

"I'll still be an actor, but I want to branch out a bit. More or less like you did with the different companies you have. I want to try my skills at something I actually enjoy."

I went head-first into this project, but now that I think about it, it doesn't feel like a job. It's more something I needed to get off my chest and I had fun doing it. Sleep deprivation included.

Maybe I won't have anything more to say after I write this screenplay, and my writing career dies there, but at least I'll try it and see how it goes.

"You should sleep and go back to it tomorrow…or in ten days when you wake up. You really look horrible," Aaron points out, chuckling.

"Maybe I should, but I feel like I can't go to sleep until I figure it out. My brain feels like it's in overdrive. Does that make sense?"

This is foreign for me. I've always been someone who never stays up at night worrying about things. I take my time getting ready, doing what I need to prepare for my job, and then go to bed so I'm in perfect shape the next day.

I've never been an over-thinker like this about something I'm working on. Now that I think about it, it seems more like an obsession than a healthy change of career.

"Tell me about it. Sometimes I need to run for miles on a treadmill to get tired enough to fall asleep without thinking about some problem with one of my companies. And considering how many I have, it's basically a nightly occurrence," Leonard mutters in a rare confession.

I've never heard him talk about his job like something he's worried about. He usually tells us how to be profitable, how to invest our money. It always seems so easy for him that sometimes I forget that having an empire to run must be stressful.

I glimpse at Aaron and spot the surprise on his face too. I'm not the only one getting a glimpse at the human behind the mogul mask.

"So, what convinced you to write the screenplay?" Aaron diverts the topic from Leonard. We both know he hates appearing vulnerable and when the question leaves Aaron's lips, Leonard's shoulders drop just a bit, relaxing at the turn in conversation.

I shrug. "Sienna thought that I could do it. She believes I'm smart enough to pull off this and I thought I'd give it a try."

He nods and smiles. He looks almost proud of my decision and I can't wrap my mind around it. I was always considered the good-looking one, not the smart one.

"She's right. I don't know why you didn't start sooner. You're unbelievably talented but you're the only one who doesn't believe it," he points out and I almost blush.

"Stop it. I feel like an impostor. I reread what I wrote and it sucks!"

He laughs and Leonard grins.

"Trust me, when you start to edit your first draft you'll doubt your entire career!" Aaron chuckles.

"Thanks. I needed the support," I mumble.

The smile fades a bit to give way to a serious face. "Don't give up. When everything seems like it sucks, take a walk and come back later. Don't throw away something this huge because of doubt. It's normal, it happens to all of us. Just keep going and trust your gut. You have enough experience as an actor, you'll have no problem figuring out what will work and what won't."

I appreciate his tips. He's one of the most knowledgeable people in this industry and everything that comes out of his mouth is pure gold. Even if it's just encouragement. He doesn't push you into doing something if he thinks you don't have the skills and knowing that is enough to make me believe in myself a bit more than before.

***

It's almost ten when Aaron and Leonard leave my house. I suspect they stayed for so long to give me a break and take my mind off the screenplay. I understand their worry. I completely missed three days of my life, and that's not even near to being normal behavior for a sane person. Especially someone like me who has never been so obsessed with something I forget how to live.

But I need to finish this. I know if I go to bed I'll lose my momentum and won't be able to write down everything in my head. I just need a little push and then I can go to bed. A bed without Sienna. Maybe that's why I can't face going into my bedroom without feeling lost.

I have no interest in walking into that room without the only person I miss more than air, food, or sleep. She is the reason I can pour my feeling onto the page, or a computer screen, and without her the only thing I can do is write those feeling into this movie.

Maybe I'm just a lovesick fool, or maybe I needed this wake-up call to put things in perspective. Whether the reason, this feels a lot like that fate I never believed existed.

"Okay, now you're just ridiculous." Harper's voice from behind startles me.

"Are you insane? I almost peed my pants!" I scold, more to divert the subject from what she caught me doing.

"Sienna, you are stalking his Instagram! You are ridiculous, get your shit together and ask him what's going on." She doesn't back down.

I hate when Harper takes it upon herself to be the voice of the reason. Because I know she's right. I can't contact Harrison and I'm stuck in a loop checking his social for any news. I even checked the gossip websites to get a glimpse at where he might be.

"It's been a week and I have no idea where he is. He could be dead right now and I don't even know it." I whine like a kid that doesn't want to do her homework.

She huffs and grabs my phone from my hand. "I repeat: you are ridiculous. You are an adult, just go to his house and check what's going on."

The problem is, if I go to his house and he doesn't open his door for me, I'll be crushed. It's why I didn't go there in the first place. I messed up and I'm scared to know just how badly.

Her scowl softens in a warm smile. She knows me well enough to understand my fears without me voicing them.

"Go, Sienna. I'm sure there's an explanation for his radio silence."

"What if he decided I'm not worth all this trouble?" I blurt out.

Harper is a bit surprised by my confession. I'm not known for talking about my feelings.

"I doubt that Harrison is giving up on you. But if he decided to not go further in this relationship, you'll survive it and even learn from it. You messed up. It's okay, you're smart not to repeat the same mistake twice."

This is what I fear the most. I already learned my lesson and I'm not sure I'll find someone like Harrison ever again. He's a rare gem and I threw him away.

I stand up from the kitchen counter, hug Harper, grab my phone and keys and walk out of the apartment.

"Go get your man!" she shouts after me and I smile.

I don't go get my man, but I do drive to the only person I know who will give him a message for me. When I open the door to his office, Aaron is surprised to see me but the smile never leaves his face. He's come a long way since being called 'the Butcher' here in Hollywood.

"Sienna, what a surprise!" He seems genuinely happy to see me, standing up and reaching out to shake my hand. His grip is firm but not imposing. I like the person he's become in the last few years.

"Sorry. I didn't want to show up without an appointment, but I don't know where else to go."

He frowns and sits down in his chair, beckoning me to do the same in the one in front of his desk. I accept his invitation because I'm so nervous I'll start to fidget if I stay standing up.

"Is everything okay?" He seems worried.

I look down for a moment before having the courage to look him in the eyes.

"Yes and no. I think Harrison blocked me from his phone because I can't contact him. I'm here to ask you to give him a message on my behalf, if it's not much trouble for you. I get it if you don't want to be mixed up in these things," I ramble nervously.

He smiles and shakes his head. My words die in my mouth and I start to think I've made a terrible mistake coming here.

"He didn't block you on his phone. He has it turned off," he says, with an amusement in his words I can't understand.

"I'm an adult, I can handle the truth, Aaron." Mostly. "You don't need to sugarcoat things."

He shakes his head, chuckling. "I'm not joking. His phone died and he forgot to turn it on."

I raise my eyebrows, calling out his bullshit. "For one week straight?"

"I swear! Leonard and I went to his place to check if he was still alive. We were worried too." He seems honest and I don't know if I'm more surprised or worried.

"Is he okay?" I can hear the urgency in my voice.

"He's perfectly fine. A bit obsessed with something but nothing bad."

"Oh. So, he's not avoiding me?" I'm confused now.

He smiles. "No, he is not. Come with me."

"Where are we going?"

"I'm driving you to his house. I don't know if he'll open the door."

"So, we're breaking in?" Now I'm a bit concerned.

He chuckles. "I have the keys."

"Oh. I have my car here."

"So, you'll drive. I'll ask my driver to come to pick me up." Of course, he has a driver!

One hour and countless questions from me about Harrison's obsession later, we are driving through Harrison's gates and parking in front of his door. Obviously, Aaron didn't tell me anything about what Harrison is doing, saying that it's a surprise.

I hate surprises.

When I walk through the door my heart thunders in my chest. I don't know what I expect to find and this makes me nervous enough to want to run inside and run back home in equal measure.

When we walk through the living room doors, I'm taken aback at the disheveled state Harrison is in. He's hunched over his computer, hair sticking up and his face a sick shade of gray.

"You told me he was fine!" I say turning toward Aaron and startling Harrison.

"He is fine." Aaron chuckles as Harrison stands up from the couch.

He's wearing a dirty, crumpled t-shirt and stained gray sweatpants. He looks far from fine.

"What are you doing here?" he asks confused, approaching me.

I notice the dark circle under his eyes and turn toward Aaron, giving him my most scolding glare.

"He looks bad, but I promise he's fine," he says, waving at us and walking out of the house from the same set of doors we came in and murmuring, "I'll leave you alone, I don't want to watch you making out," or something like that.

Harrison grabs me by the shoulders and I finally turn toward him. All my nervousness transforms into worry.

"What happened to you? Why is your phone turned off? And why do you look like you went through hell and back?" I ask in a rush.

"Geez, thanks!" He chuckles.

"I'm serious, Harrison. What happened? I'm worried about you," I say seriously and his laugh sobers up.

He guides me to the couch and I sit next to him. There are glasses on the coffee table and plates with half-eaten meals. It looks like he's been living on this couch, forgetting about the rest of the house.

"I did a thing," he blurts out without explaining further.

I wait for a long moment, then I grab his chin and force him to look at me. He seems almost shy and it scares me more than knowing he won't forgive me.

"Harrison, you are freaking me out," I plead.

He takes a deep breath. "I wrote a screenplay."

I stare at him not knowing what to say. I expected a lot of things, bad ones, but this was not on the list. I'm happy because I always knew he had it in him, but I'm also puzzled because he hid it from me.

"Why didn't you tell me?"

"Because I made a mistake and I tried to fix it, but I'm not sure this screenplay is good enough to fix it," he rambles and I don't understand.

"What? Stop there. You wrote a screenplay because you thought you could fix things between us?" I ask, dumbfounded.

He blushes. He actually blushes, looking down at his hands in his lap.

"I realize I fucked up when I stole your movie." He raises a hand to stop me when I try to argue. "Let me finish, please."

I nod.

"I stole that movie from you. Because you didn't want me in it and I imposed myself. I get it. I made a mistake and there is no other way to fix it other than giving you another movie good enough for you to direct," he explains and my heart cracks a bit.

What he did is so huge and so amazing there are no words to describe it. He found a way to literally start over and fix his mistake. Nobody has ever done something like this for me.

"Harrison, I came here to apologize to you," I say and he frowns. I know he can't understand so I continue. "I don't trust myself when I'm around you. I always second guess my judgement because I'm so in love with you that I don't know if I'm blinded by my feelings or if what I'm doing with you is actually good."

"I don't know if this is good or bad." He smiles.

"Sometimes it's good and sometimes it's bad. Sometimes I'm so insecure that I don't know if I'm doing a good job or not. When we work together, I'm sometimes lost because those feelings are so strong I don't know anything else. But I have to learn how to separate my work life from my personal one and I can't do it without you. When you didn't tell me how much you were involved in this movie, I thought I made a mistake in trusting you. I thought my judgement was clouded by my feelings and I…freaked out."

He nods and takes his time to think about it. He's not pushing me away, but he's not letting me off the hook either.

"Are you going to say something?" My voice is small, and even if I try to put a smile on my face I'm sure he can tell how nervous I am.

He smiles. "I wrote this screenplay because I wanted to start fresh with you. I messed up, you have trust issues—for a good reason, but still, you don't trust me—so I think we should try to start over. Go home, read this script, and then come back and tell me if you want it or not. Maybe it's not good enough for you and you'll decide to not direct it, or that you don't want me in this movie. It doesn't matter, we can discuss it openly, no expectations. And maybe we can start from there with our relationship too," he suggests.

When I came here, I thought I would have an answer: yes or no. Nothing in between, but I actually like this solution even better. A new starting point. A new solid cornerstone for our relationship. Not the sand castle of lies it was built on before.

"Okay. I like this plan," I agree and he finally seems to relax.

***

I stay up all night with my printed copy of the script on my legs and a pencil in hand, leaning against the headboard of my bed. As soon as I read the first page, I knew I wanted to direct this movie. It's clever, sarcastic, and witty. It's a movie that will make you laugh and punch you in the gut at the same time.

Harrison has a brilliant mind and I want to make it shine for everyone to see. This is the movie I've always dreamed of directing, all that laughter soaked in melancholy, staying with you for days after you leave the theater.

I knew he could write a good script, but damn, this is an excellent one. I want to be the one to direct it and I want him to star in it.

I make notes in the margins, how I imagine doing the scenes, and the more I reread them, the more I'm convinced this is even greater than the one we just shot. It's different, less of a tear-jerker, but it makes you think on a completely different level.

If the last one showed us Harrison's acting skills, this one shows us his soul, and I feel the burden of that on my shoulders. I can't screw up this one.

CHAPTER 31
Harrison

"She didn't call me," I murmur as I stare out the window of Leonard's office downtown.

"This habit of yours of showing up without an appointment is annoying," Leonard points out.

When I turn around, he's staring at his computer without paying attention to me. I know I'm bothering him, and it's so much fun. I like to piss him off, especially now that my best friend, Raphael, has been elected Senator and doesn't have much time for me anymore. I'm not complaining, he's still my best friend and I know he has more important things to do than hang out with me, but I'm a social person and I need to interact with people.

"And you're not helping me with my crisis," I counter.

He finally raises his eyes to me. He is borderline pissed. If I keep this up, he'll call security.

"It's barely been twenty-four hours, Harrison. Give her time to read it," he scolds.

"She had plenty of time to read it, but maybe she doesn't like it and she doesn't know how to tell me." I sit down in the chair in front of his desk and sigh.

He looks at me like I'm a bug he has to kill with his thousand-dollars shoes.

"Does she seem like someone who doesn't tell you what she thinks?" he points out and he's not wrong. She went for my throat the first time we met, but that was a different time, we didn't have a relationship.

"No, but now she's in love with me and she doesn't want to hurt me."

The truth is I'm terrified I wrote the worst script ever and she died laughing. How can writers survive with so much pressure? At least when you're an actor, you can gauge the casting director's thoughts looking at their face. I've had a million doubts since yesterday when I gave her the screenplay.

Leonard snorts and goes back to work.

"Do you think she'll call me?" I ask again, more to push his buttons than to get a real answer.

"Do you want me to call security? You are a pain in my ass. Yes. She will call you when she has something to tell you. You asked her to start over, she's taking her time doing it."

I don't know if he's trying to be helpful or just wants me out of this place, but he's not entirely wrong. Starting over is not that easy and requires time.

"Well, I'm going home to see if she's there," I say moving to the door.

"Finally. I thought you were going to follow me home," he murmurs.

I grin. "Do you want me to?"

He throws me a deadly glance. I take it as my cue to leave the office before he kills me.

"Harrison!" he calls before I walk out. "She will call you. Give her time, but I'm sure she will call you."

I smile at him. He always plays the grump, but he cares. Maybe not for many people, but he cares for his friends.

I nod before turning around and walking out of his office.

When I park the car and walk into my house, I'm disappointed to find it empty. It's not even possible that she'd be here. She doesn't have the keys and unless Aaron helped her in, she can't sneak in here and wait for me. But somehow, I hoped to find her here. My heart wanted her so badly, my reason threw away the logic.

I walk into my empty living room and turn around, taking in the silence of this place. It's fantastic to have privacy here in Hollywood, but sometimes life can be lonely.

I lay my eyes on the computer and I'm tempted to open it and reread the screenplay. I don't, only because I know I'll find something to fix, something to change, another word that fits better in every dialogue exchange.

Every time I read it, I see how imperfect it is, but Sienna already has it, with all the imperfections and the flaws I put down. I could give her a new version but for what? Yet another chance to tell me it doesn't work?

I'm so focused on staring at my computer that my phone ringing startles me. Aaron's name flashes on the screen and I'm tempted to send it straight to voicemail. But maybe Sienna called him like she did yesterday. She has no reason to, but clearly my heart didn't get the memo and it's hammering in my chest.

"Hey! Why are you calling? Couldn't use your keys to barge into my house like the last two times?" I joke but there is a subtle question in my words: Is he going to bring Sienna here again?

He chuckles and I can hear traffic noise in the background. "Move your ass out of that house and come to The Jail. We need to talk."

"Who says I'm at home?" I hate how well he knows me.

"Do you really think Leonard wouldn't tell me you were there today? He whined the whole time and was ecstatic when you went home." I can hear the grin through the phone.

"That asshole," I mumble but I can't keep a smile off my face.

"Move your ass and get here," he orders.

"Can't we do it tomorrow? I'm tired." And I want to be home if Sienna comes here.

"No. I'm already here and I don't want to dine alone."

"Don't you have someone waiting at home?" Now I'm just messing with him.

"Not tonight. She's filming a late scene."

"So, I'm your booty call?"

"Shut up. Come on," he chuckles.

"Give me a few minutes to get there. I just got home."

"My driver is already at your gate," he says and I'm a bit surprised. He never sends his driver.

"Is this a kidnapping? Did you think I was going to bail?" I joke but now I'm just curious about this dinner.

When I walk into the restaurant, the first person I spot at the table is Alan Leery and his lanky figure. Weird. Then I lay my eyes on the seat next to him and see Aaron, which is even more weird. But what throws me off completely is who I see seated across from them. I'd recognize that raven mane anywhere.

Sienna turns around like she can feel my eyes burning into her back. She smiles at me and I don't know if this is a strange party I'm walking into or an ambush.

Aaron follows her gaze and finds me staring at the most peculiar dinner I've ever been invited to.

"Finally, you're here," he says as I take the place next to Sienna who reaches out her hand and squeezes mine under the table.

"I don't know if I should be happy or worried you're here," I confess.

Alan gives me a smug smile and I don't know how to feel. He and Aaron are the most powerful producers in Hollywood.

They've worked together many times and have brought home Emmys and Oscars like it's the easiest thing in the world. Which is why I feel so nervous about this meeting.

"Do you want to do the honors?" Aaron asks Sienna and she straightens her spine, like she's tasked with a very important responsibility.

She nods and turns toward me. "I read your screenplay and I think it's the most brilliant script I have ever had in my hands. It's clever, sarcastic, deep, and has what it takes to become an instant classic. I'd do anything to direct it and I've already begun asking help from the best producers I know," she says firmly.

Her words have a strange effect on me. My heart hammers in my chest, the blood rushes to my ears, my hands become clammy, but the most unsettling feeling is disbelief at her words.

I hoped my script was good, but this is way beyond my expectation. The potential to become a classic? She's crazy, right? I mean, she's obviously in love with me and blowing her compliments out of proportion.

I turn toward Aaron and Alan and they're both grinning.

"I don't understand," I blurt out and Sienna squeezes my hand harder.

"Sienna asked us to read your screenplay and it's one of the best I have come across in my entire career," Aaron confirms and I feel my breath leave my lungs, emptying them for a long moment.

"Are you serious?" I ask, turning to Sienna.

She nods. "I think your script is magic and I wanted to be sure you move forward with it. I know you doubt your writing skills and I wanted to have Aaron and Alan on board to show you I'm not joking around with this movie."

I laugh and rub a hand over my face. "I thought you were going to say it was a shitty screenplay," I confess and they all chuckle. "I'm serious. I thought you hadn't the courage to tell me that it sucked and I was moping all day trying figure out how to look you in the eyes again after I made you read that shit."

They all laugh.

"I can't believe you don't see how good it is." Alan speaks for the first time.

I shake my head. "This is the first time I've written a screenplay and I'm not sure about anything."

"Bullshit. It can't be you first script. It's too polished to be the first thing you've written," he scoffs in disbelief.

"I swear, I've never written a single word before a little more than a week ago."

He gapes at me and I look at Aaron. The proud smile on his face makes my chest tighten. Is it possible to have your heart explode from happiness?

"Why on earth didn't you write sooner?" Alan seems genuinely curious about my reasons for staying away from manuscript writing.

I turn my gaze to Sienna. "Because I never had someone pushing me to use my skills. Not many people believed I could do it. I'm just a pretty face in Hollywood."

Alan shakes his head and scowls at me. "He did a number on you, that shitty agent you had, didn't he?" He stares at me as though trying to figure out something.

"Fortunately, someone got a hold of you before you wasted your career on meaningless movies." Aaron winks at me and smiles behind the glass of water he's sipping.

It hasn't fully settled in my heart and brain, what's happening at this table tonight, but one thing I'm sure of: this is a turning point in my life. I don't know how big it is, and I don't know if it's for the best. The only thing I know is that I want to discover it with the woman sitting next to me holding my hand.

I wrote that screenplay to get those feelings off my chest, the ones crowding a space too small to fit them all. It turns out, my heart is full of new emotions that make me happier than I ever thought I could feel again in my life.

"We need to talk," the four words a woman never wants to hear from her partner, leave Harrison's lips as soon as I answered the phone this morning when I woke up.

It's been three days since our dinner with Aaron and Alan and it's been a whirlwind of phone calls, meetings, and planning. This new movie is coming along faster than I thought and I'm already overwhelmed with everything I have to do to complete the one we just finished shooting.

The perk is that I'm working with Harrison. I came to the conclusion that I love working with him. It's not just an emotional connection with the person I love, but a natural chemistry we have when it comes to being creative together.

We discussed my notes about how I want to do the filming, we discussed my vision, and we put together a few names for the technical side of the project—who we want as director of photography and who we imagine bringing the soundtrack to life. It was more "dream casting" than a real talk, but we had fun with it.

It was refreshing and intimate and I'm glad Harrison suggested starting fresh with our personal life. No lies, no doubt, nothing to stain this blissful collaboration.

So, I'm not worried about those four words as I drive to his house. He's not going to dump me. He just needs to talk about something serious and we're not going to do it on the phone. No hidden meaning or overthinking our situation.

When I park in front of his house, he's already at the front door waiting for me. I can't help but smile, walking to him.

"Hello, gorgeous," he whispers before grabbing my waist and pulling me to his chest to kiss me properly.

I slip my arms around his neck and kiss him back. When his tongue slides over mine, a moan escapes my throat. "If you keep kissing me like this we won't get far from this doorway." I peck at his smiling lips.

"Well, isn't it good that I live alone and we can get naked anywhere we want?" He smacks my butt as I walk in front of him toward the living room.

"Do I have to remind you that you asked me to come here to *talk*?" I raise an eyebrow at him while I sit on the couch.

He grins and sits next to me, pecking the skin on my neck, making me shiver. "Damn! You are sexy when you talk business."

"Harrison! Focus!" I order swatting away his hands trying to grope my boobs.

He chuckles but finally sits back and puts on his serious business face. "I've thought a lot about it and I think we're making a mistake with this movie," he begins, and I frown.

"With the screenplay you gave me?" I don't understand.

He shakes his head. "No, the one we just finished."

"Oh. Okay. Really? What do you mean?" I ask, puzzled. I think it's a great movie, I can't see where we could do better.

"We shouldn't go after minor or indie festivals. Some of them require exclusive rights for the premiere. We can't release it in movie theatres before the festivals and this stops us from aiming for more."

"Aiming for more? Are you serious? We're talking about big indie festivals that will give us international visibility, do you want to throw all our hard work away? I don't understand where you're going with this." I try to follow his reasoning but can't make sense of it.

His gaze is intense, like he's trying to download his vision for the future of this movie into my brain. I swear, I'm feeling so dumb right now.

"I think we should aim for the Oscar, along with Cannes, Berlin, and Venice film festivals." He drops the bomb and watches me intently.

I stare at him, confused. Is he serious right now? This is impossible even for him. It's not realistic.

"We don't have the kind of money to pull off something like that. We don't even have a distribution company to reach the bigger theaters in Los Angeles, let alone the entire country. We are counting on those minor festivals to raise visibility and find someone willing to invest in distributing it. You're talking about a whole other level of promotion," I try to explain.

Harrison, more than anyone else, should know how this works. We need to create a new level of buzz around the movie for it to be considered for a nomination. Even if we find a few theaters in Los Angeles willing to show our movie for a week— the basic requirement for the Oscar—we don't have a budget to push it.

"I know, but I also know someone who has the money and the connections to pull this off." He grins.

"Who?" I mean, he is a big Hollywood star and can probably drop a million names right now, but I'm the small fish he has to guide into the shark tank.

"Aaron."

I feel stupid for not having thought about him. Of course, Aaron has the money and the connections to do whatever he wants in this industry. He's already won Oscars and Emmys with his production company. I often forget that his is not only a streaming company. He's a producer and his job is to make successful movies.

"He's already into the next one…" I toy with the idea.

"And I would trust him with my life," Harrison adds another pro to the virtual list.

"He'd ask for something in return." I try to play devil's advocate, but I'm not so convincing.

"Yes, but I'm sure it's something good for us too. He's not one to fuck someone over for profit."

Until a few weeks ago, I would have had doubts about Aaron, but after talking to him for the new movie, I feel I can trust the guy.

Two hours later we're all sitting around the dining room table eating Chinese and explaining to Aaron what we're thinking. Or, rather, Harrison is explaining, I'm scarfing down noodles and Aaron is looking at us like he just won the lottery.

"So, what do you think?" Harrison asks in the end.

I sip the water to swallow the prawn I'm munching and wait for Aaron's response. Harrison assured me it wouldn't be a problem, that he'll certainly say yes, but I can't stop myself from feeling a bit nervous.

Aaron is his friend, but in this case, he's a producer and a businessman first. He won't throw his money into this without being certain it's a good investment.

"I think I'm interested, but I have some conditions," he says without beating around the bush.

We both nod. We knew this was coming.

"Name it," Harrison says with the same determination. He's definitely better than me at negotiating.

"The first one is more to satisfy my curiosity than a real request. I want to see the movie," he says with a grin.

Harrison seems almost nervous about it but nods. I never understand why he's so shy with his friend; he's a great actor, he should be proud to show him what he's doing.

"I hope you have time tonight, because I have it here. It's still missing the credits and the final round of edits, but it'd in a pretty decent shape right now," I say. At least the sound is great and we have a fantastic soundtrack. Thank God I pushed to work hard and fast with this one.

"Good. I can stay." He smiles.

"What else?" Harrison asks, and I'm a bit more nervous about this one.

"After it hits theaters for a while, I want the exclusive rights for my streaming platform. We will negotiate price and length of the exclusivity, but I want it first," he says without hesitation.

I feel my chest expand with a deep breath. I can deal with that. I had a bunch of absurd requests in my mind, thinking the worst.

"That's it?" I ask.

He smiles. "That's it."

I look at Harrison and he grins. "Deal!" he tells his friend.

A shiver of excitement runs down my spine when realization sinks in. I can aim for the Oscar. It never crossed my mind that this movie could be so big as to gain the attention of the right people. I knew it was unbelievably great, but that's not enough when you have to compete with the greatest in Hollywood. You need luck and you need money. And I haven't had a lot of either in the last ten years.

Now it's my turn to shine and I can't wait to show the world what I can do, what *Harrison and I* can do. Because this movie wouldn't be the same without him.

It's exciting and terrifying at the same time.

CHAPTER 33

Harrison

The phone rings on my nightstand and I groan. Sienna is sound asleep in my arms but if this keeps going, she'll wake up. I relax a bit when it stops, but the reprieve is short because it starts to ring again.

"Please, answer that phone before I throw it out the window." Sienna's gruff voice wakes me up completely.

"Yeah, sorry. I'm trying to find the strength to turn around. Your perfect body is quite inviting in the morning," I whisper, kissing her neck.

She wriggles her ass against my morning wood.

"Not helping." I groan.

She smiles and turns around to kiss my lips.

"Answer that fucking phone so we can have sex," she orders.

I grab my phone from my nightstand when the third call starts and Aaron's name flashes on the screen.

"What?" Maybe I'm a bit rude, but right now Sienna is slipping under the sheet with a mischievous smile. I want this conversation to be very, very short.

"Are you still asleep?" He sounds puzzled.

I can't see Sienna under the white sheet, but I feel her lips wrapping around my raging erection. I try to stifle a groan but I'm not very successful.

"Sort of," I grit out when she starts to suck me like a lollipop. Jesus Christ.

"Are you fucking right now?" From the urgency in his tone, he seems outraged.

Another grunt on my part. "No."

"Jesus Christ. Tell Sienna to come fast because you both need to be at my office in an hour. I found a distributor and we need to pitch your movie."

"You what?" I sit up so fast I'm terrified Sienna will bite my dick off.

She slips out from under the sheet and scowls at me. *"Aaron,"* I mouth and she asks to put him on speaker phone.

"Aaron, this better be very good news because you just ruined the best wake-up blowjob Harrison will ever have." She winks at me and I laugh.

"Jesus Christ, you're worse than him and that's not a compliment, Sienna."

She laughs too. "I know. So what's up?"

"You have to be in my office in an hour because the CEO of Iris Distribution is coming to hear about your movie." I can hear the smile in his voice.

There is a moment of stunned silence on our part. There are a lot of film distributors in Los Angeles, and not all of them offer services for indie movies. But if you want to go big, there is only one you have to go to: Iris Distribution. Having the CEO come to you? It never happens.

"How?" I blurt out. "How could you have the fucking CEO at your disposal one day after we told you we want you on board for this?"

He chuckles. "I called in some favors. But the point is, you don't have much time, you need all the help you can get to pull this off."

He's right. When you try to go after the Oscar, you plan for months, if not years, in advance to come up with a marketing strategy that will push the movie. We switched goals when the movie was already done. It will be hard work to find a way to climb to the Olympus of Hollywood.

"We'll be there in forty-five minutes," I say hanging up and looking at Sienna in disbelief.

"It's impossible to be there in forty-five minutes," she points out.

"I know, but I'm counting on Aaron to make an excuse for us."

An hour and fifteen minutes later, we rush into Aaron's office. Sonny Lambert, the imposing fifty-five-year-old shark and CEO of Iris distribution, is waiting for us with a glass of amber liquor in his hand. We are both out of breath. Aaron grins behind his glass of what I hope is just water at eleven in the morning.

"Finally, you're here. I was starting to think you didn't want to show me your movie after all." The man's thundering voice fills the office.

I open my mouth to try to find an excuse but Sienna beats me to it. "Next time send the chopper you used to get here to pick us up and we'll be on time." She smirks at him. "Until then, we have to deal with Los Angeles traffic."

She's not a fan of the guy, from the tone she used, but at least she can handle him. I didn't even notice the helicopter on the roof of the building if she hadn't pointed it out.

The man bursts out laughing and beckons us to sit. "Damn, you are a feisty one, aren't you?"

I'm ready to grab Sienna by the waist if she decides to rip out his eyes. She's playing a dangerous game in this room but Aaron is grinning so I hope everything is fine.

"I don't suck producers' dicks, so I have to make them listen to me in other ways." She pulls off a sweet fake smile that makes my cock throb in my pants. Damn. I like when she stands up for herself. And I like it more when I'm not on the receiving end of her sharp tongue.

"And smart too." He seems almost pleased. "Keep this one. You won't find another one like her," he says to me.

I don't know what's happened in the two minutes since we stepped foot in this room, but I try my best to not mess up the power play going on here.

"I'm not planning to let her go any time soon." I throw an almost arrogant wink at Sienna, just to let the jerk know that I wear pants too. He seems the type that doesn't like weak men.

"So, are we talking about this movie?" Aaron chips in and I'm glad he interrupts this conversation that's becoming quite dangerous.

"How good is this movie? Aaron says it's a blast," the jerk asks.

I doubt Aaron used those words, but I don't point it out. We agreed in a call with Aaron on our way here to let the movie talk for us. It's the best way with someone like him.

"We're not here to convince you the movie is good, because we know it's more than good, it's phenomenal and it will have Oscar buzz surrounding it as soon as it comes out, " Sienna says. "But those are just words. Harrison's and mine. We're involved in this movie, it's obvious we think it's good. Everyone who makes a movie thinks theirs is the best. But saying it to you it doesn't mean it will sell. We can't judge our own movie. But you can. You built an empire putting success after success out there. You're a smart man, so, when you see it, you'll understand what you have in your hands."

There's a moment of silence after she finishes and I'm not sure how it's going. This man is unreadable, at least for me. I haven't had the chance to meet him before this encounter, and I can't tell if he's an arrogant, pompous jerk or if he just acts like one and is actually a cunning fox. I suspect it's the second, but I wouldn't bet on it.

He moves his eyes from Sienna to me and fortunately, to Aaron. We're all staring at him. Sienna with a smug smile on her face, like Aaron. I seem to be the only one on pins and needles, a strained smile on my face. I hate to come unprepared to meetings, but my friend here didn't give me much of a choice.

"I hope this is really a good movie, or I'll sue all of you for wasting two hours of my time," he grunts, but I'm almost one hundred percent sure it's just an act to flaunt the advantage he has on us. He knows perfectly well he can change the fate of this movie.

Aaron turns on the TV in his office and I hold my breath. We still have to polish it, and for two entire hours I sit still, staring at the man, trying to gauge his thoughts. Needless to say, he doesn't give away anything at all. There's a reason he became CEO of an empire: he has the perfect poker face.

When the screen goes black, you can hear a pin drop in the room. I'm not sure Aaron and Sienna are breathing. I'm certainly not. We're looking at him trying to figure out what to do next. He doesn't show any emotion, but I think it's because he doesn't have a heart.

He turns toward us and scowls. Not exactly the reaction I was hoping for. My stomach clenches in a painful grip. We screwed up. We fucking screwed up.

"You want to distribute it for one week in Los Angeles so you can be nominated for the Oscar?" he asks.

Aaron already laid out our goals before we got here, and now I'm sure we overestimated our movie. Maybe Aaron was too happy to finally work with me that he completely misread our potential? We should have asked for a smaller fish, aim for less pretentious targets.

I look at Sienna, her expression unreadable, same as Aaron. Am I the only one freaking out right now?

"I'm not doing it," he adds.

There it is. Our dreams going up in flames. I look down at my hands and I can't think of anything to say. The disappointment is so massive it's burning a hole straight through my chest.

"I'm not going to waste my time and resources for something that small. You have a gold mine right under your ass and you want to just do the bare minimum?" he asks.

Wait. *What?*

"I want to go big with this one. I want national distribution. Or, even better, we should try for worldwide. You have the potential to make history at the box office and I'm not passing this up just because you want to be eligible for an Oscar nomination. I won't even discuss an offer for anything less," he says firmly and we're all completely speechless.

It's Aaron who breaks the silence. "There's no time for a campaign so massive. How could we pull off something like that? We'd need to find the contacts for worldwide distribution, it would take months."

He's not wrong. We're risking biting off more than we can chew and ruining everything.

My stomach dips like I'm on rollercoaster. What he's considering is gargantuan, with a lot of work for a team we don't even have. I glance at Sienna and she's studying the man like she's figuring out a puzzle. The small smile tells me she's close to solving it. Or she's losing it. At this point, I'm not sure of anything.

"Okay, let's do this," she says firmly.

Aaron and I turn toward her, trying to see if she's joking or not. She looks at both of us and smiles, shrugging.

"I know, it's risky and we could fail. But, what's the worst thing that could happen? We won't be nominated for the Oscar? It would suck, but we'd have worldwide exposure for the movie. When I started this project, I assumed it would be an indie movie. This is already a victory for me. If we're nominated for the Oscar, that's just the cherry on the top," she points out, and I can't disagree with her.

Working on this project was strange in that I saw the potential and wanted more. It's amazing that we've come such a long way since that party in January, but I lost focus of the fact that this started as an indie movie. Now we're talking about distributing it worldwide. That's not just big, it's impossible. We've already done the magic, we're already winners.

"Let's do this!" I blurt out and feel my chest expand with happiness and fear and a hundred different feelings I can't name.

Aaron crosses his hands behind his neck and leans back in his chair grinning. "Let's do this."

"Get ready to flaunt your dick all over the world," Sonny smirks at me.

My eyes fly to his, wide like saucers. I completely forgot about my full-frontal nude scene.

"Shit."

CHAPTER 34
Sienna

The crowd outside the iconic movie theater on Hollywood Boulevard is loud. Barriers along the street keep the fans on the other side of the oriental-designed building. They're screaming Harrison's name, mostly, but they're calling my name too.

It's the first time in my life that I have a movie premiere for one of my projects, let alone one this massive. Nervousness grips my stomach and I'm struggling to stand up without crumbling on the red carpet.

We did it. We worked overtime to bring this to life. Sonny used his connections to sell the movie overseas and we actually pulled off the kind of launch usually seen with blockbusters.

"Are you nervous?" Harrison grabs my chin between two fingers and gently forces me to move my wide eyes from the crowd to his face.

"Terrified," I admit.

"Are you going to throw up?" He smiles at me.

"Probably."

"Can you try not to do it in front of the cameras?" He chuckles.

"I can try, but I can't guarantee anything."

This time he laughs and it's enough to relax my nerves a bit. I'm not completely chill, but at least my stomach doesn't hurt.

"Are you ready to walk over there?" he asks, pointing to the red carpet.

I nod but I don't trust my voice coming out firm. My mouth is so dry I can barely swallow. Harrison grabs my hand and gently guides me to the other side of the tall divider and flashes start to go off, blinding me.

It takes me a few moments to adjust to the blinding lights but when I do, I take in the importance of this moment. People are going crazy, shouting, asking Harrison for autographs and selfies. They all have the small version of the movie poster in their hands and I'm mesmerized by how Harrison seems comfortable with all of this.

I stay a step behind, a couple of security people we hired guiding us through all the chaos. We only need to follow their instructions and I'm glad because my legs tremble and my brain is completely gone.

A hand on my lower back gently pushes me toward the barriers where fans are. It's the assistant tasked with following me around and guiding me to what I have to do.

I walk in front of the crowd. They're mostly looking at Harrison, but one teenager, a scrawny thing with thick glasses, is trying to get my attention. I smile at her and she blushes.

"Can you sign this, please?" she asks in a trembling voice and giving me the poster with Harrison's name already scrawled on it.

She's asking for my autograph? Is she serious? "Mine?" I frown and she smiles shyly.

"If you want to. But if you don't want, it's okay," she scrambles to explain.

I finally smile at her and grab the poster and sharpie. "I'm totally fine, it's just…I'm not used to people asking for my autograph," I confess.

She smiles and grabs the pen and poster I'm handing back. "I think you'll be doing it a lot tonight." She points her finger to another person asking for a selfie with me.

She's right. It takes me a while to reach the backdrop with the sponsor's logo where we pose for the cameras.

"Is it always so chaotic?" I ask Harrison without dropping the smile on my face. God forbid that a photographer thinks I'm sad and does an entire story on the reasons why I was grumpy at the premiere of my own movie.

"Yes." He smiles and peck my lips, causing a blinding flash feast.

"Do you get used to it?"

"Mostly," he admits.

I turn toward the cameras and hope that at some point in the future I won't feel like a freak show during these events.

When we finally step into the movie theater, I can't see anything for a long moment. The blinding lights outside contrast with the dimly lit entrance, not to mention the movie theater, forcing me to blink a couple of times to adjust my eyes and see who's surrounding me.

I recognize a lot of famous Hollywood faces, people I could only dream of having at a premiere of one of my movies, and everyone is ready to reach out a hand and compliment us. It doesn't matter that they haven't watched the movie yet. The important thing is to be seen by us.

How much things change in a span of a few months. Some of these people didn't even acknowledge me at Kevin's party, but now they're tripping over each other to shake my hand.

We don't stay long in the lobby, we walk into the room where rows and rows of red chairs wait for us. The back of the theater is already full of people who won tickets for tonight, average people who want to see the movie, while the front rows are reserved for Hollywood bigwigs and journalists who will stay for the question-and-answer session after the movie.

Some cheer, everyone murmurs when they notice us entering the room, but the most palpable feeling is expectation. My stomach is knotted tight, and I think my lungs are too. How else can I explain why I'm barely breathing? I realize people around me are talking, asking questions, and that I'm giving answers, but I'm doing it on autopilot. There is no way I'll remember even half of the conversations I'm having tonight.

Kevin gives a small introduction to the crowd, explaining that we will answer their questions after the movie, but I can barely follow his speech.

This is it.

This is the acid test we were waiting for and I'm not sure I'm ready for the reaction. Every person so far who's watched the movie has said it's incredible. But they're all people working in the industry, they have a technical eye to judge it.

Behind me are rows and rows of real people, fans, who are here to enjoy this experience. *They* have to like it, not the producers or the CEO's of some company that has to work with us. Those people behind me are the ones who will go home and tell their friends to come out and watch this movie.

What if they don't like it?

I'm relieved when the lights go out and the screen lights up with the movie, because everything goes silent and everyone is focused on Harrison's outstanding performance and not my face.

I can't focus on the movie and I know Harrison can't either. From time to time, I catch him glancing back and looking at people's faces. Are they enjoying the movie? Are they glued to the scene?

Nobody talks, nobody even breathes. A lot of them are clutching their popcorn buckets but not eating. By the halfway point in the movie, there is not one eye dry in the place. By the end, they're sobbing. Is it too sad? Did I make one of those movies where you finish it and then say, "Never again?"

I can't tell if they like it or not, and when I catch Harrison's questioning eyes, I shrug. Apparently neither of us knows what's going on in their heads.

When the final credits scroll to an end and the lights turn on, I grab Harrison's hand and squeeze. I'm not a super expert of Hollywood premieres, but I know when the movie ends, you get some sort of reaction. A cold one, maybe some booing, but complete silence? What does that mean?

I turn to Harrison and we both turn around. Fear is gripping my stomach.

The first clap comes from the back of the theater, followed by some others a few rows down. In a matter of a few seconds, the entire theater is standing up, clapping like maniacs, cheering and whistling their approval.

A standing ovation.

We are getting a freaking standing ovation and I can't even stand up myself. Harrison wraps his arms around me and I bury my head in the crook of his neck.

"You did it!" he whispers in my ear.

I did it. *We* did it.

The world is spinning so fast I don't know how to stand, but Harrison's firm grip grounds me.

Now I know for sure, deep in my heart, that we are the perfect team, and nobody will stop us. This is just the beginning.

Now is our time to shine.

EPILOGUE

Sienna

Three years later

I watch Harrison sipping his iced tea, lounging on the deck chair with his computer on his lap. He's been there since this morning when he woke up at six to write his new masterpiece. Fortunately, I moved into his house a couple of years ago and he has enough rooms to work anywhere. He doesn't keep me up late when he's in his "writer mood."

He's wearing his glasses that make him look oh-so sexy. I take my time enjoying the view of his perfect abs and those little two wrinkles forming between his eyebrows when he focuses on his computer.

I've come to love those two wrinkles because it means he's doing exactly what he loves most: writing.

It turned out, his first screenplay wasn't just a fluke. After he won the Oscar for best actor for his performance in our first movie together, where I won as best director and the movie as best picture, he didn't end his winning strike.

His first screenplay got a "Palme d'Or" at Cannes and a "Leone d'Oro" at the Venice film festival. He also got nominated for best original screenplay at the Oscars. He mostly stars in his own movies, but he's not so interested in acting anymore. It will always be his first love, but he won't grow old with it.

I walk down the paved path and he raises his eyes to mine when he hears me coming. His smile is so warm and genuine I want to melt here on the pool patio. I will never get used to how much love he puts in those glances that melt my heart.

"Here are my two favorite girls," he says, grabbing my hand and dragging me next to his deck chair. He kisses my seven-months pregnant belly then scoots over to make room for me to sit. He wraps his arms around my shoulders and kisses my temple.

"Your favorite girl here almost destroyed my ribcage this morning, kicking like she wants to come out right now," I complain.

Sometimes this pregnancy is easy because I have Harrison by my side helping me out, sometimes it's hard because, apparently, I'm carrying Satan's spawn and I don't have a second of rest.

"Clara says lunch is ready." I peck him on the lips.

"I'm coming. Almost finished with this scene."

"How's it coming?"

"It sucks, as usual, but you'll make a great movie no matter what I give you." He grins and I push his leg out of the chair.

"You always say it sucks and then the Oscars put down the red carpet just for your movies." And I'm not kidding.

His writing style is so clever and tasteful he's becoming one of the best screenwriters I know. He's making a name for himself as a screenwriter and people are taking him seriously.

I fell once for his brain and his skills and I'm falling every day for the great man he is.

"Aaron asked if you want to slow down a bit, you know, considering you're almost at the end of the pregnancy." He glances at me, trying to figure out if I'm going to freak out about it or not.

"I'm pregnant, not sick. I'm one of the lucky women that doesn't have a complicated pregnancy. I'm not even particularly tired. I'm enjoying what I'm doing and I promise that at the first sign of discomfort, I will stop. Okay?"

I know what people think about a working mom, especially one that has a billionaire as partner: I should stay at home with the kids and leave the work to him. I'm not that kind of woman. I will never teach my daughter that it's okay to be emotionally or financially dependent on a man.

I'm lucky enough to have a flexible job that allows me to have my daughter with me all the time. I'm not giving up my career to be a mom and conform to what society asks of me. I have the chance to be both and a partner that understands the importance of sharing responsibility. I'm not giving up on that.

"Okay. I trust you."

"Good. Now are you coming to lunch or not? I need my umpteenth meal of the day to have the strength to carry this watermelon and to plan a new movie," I point out.

He chuckles and helps me to stand up.

"Let's go get you fed," he whispers in my ear as we walk up the stairs.

Happiness fills my heart and I can't stop a smile from taking over my face. A few years ago, I would have never thought my life and my career would be shared with a man.

After what I went through, I thought my path was one I would walk alone. I was wrong, God was I wrong. I just hadn't met the right man yet.

They call us the *power couple* here in the Hollywood Hills. When we're together, we're able to create something special that translate into record-breaking box office weekends and almost guaranteed success.

But we're not a power couple. We're just two people who found a deep connection on a creative level. We bring out the best in each other and create something that looks a lot like magic.

I will not teach my daughter that she *has* to have a man to be happy, but I will teach her to find someone that empowers her, that makes her a better version of herself. Nobody is perfect, everyone makes mistakes, but it's what you learn from them that makes you a bit closer to perfection.

Harrison helped me to trust people, I helped him to trust himself. This is why we love working together, not to prove we're a power couple, but because we have the power to make each other better versions of ourselves.

BOOKS BY ERIKA VANZIN

ROADIES SERIES (Complete)

LOS ANGELES BILLIONAIRES

About the author

Erika Vanzin is the Italian Amazon bestselling author of the rock star romance Roadies Series.

After traveling around the world with her husband, she settled down in Seattle, enjoying the marvelous Pacific Northwest. She brought from Italy a couple of suitcases, fifteen boxes full of books, and her most successful novels translated into English.

While she is not writing, she enjoys reading books, watching the Kraken hockey games, and working on DIY projects.

Keep in touch with Erika via the web:

Website: https://www.erikavanzin.com/

BookBub: https://www.bookbub.com/authors/erika-vanzin

Goodreads: https://www.goodreads.com/author/
show/14437720.Erika_Vanzin

Facebook: https://www.facebook.com/erikavanzinauthor

Instagram: https://www.instagram.com/clumsyeki/

TikTok: https://www.tiktok.com/@authorerikavanzin

Twitter: https://twitter.com/ErikaVanzin

Newsletter: https://hello.erikavanzin.com/welcome/

Acknowledgements

First and foremost, a big shoutout to my husband and chief cheerleader, Dario. Thanks for putting up with my bad moods when my writing doesn't come out the way I want. You're my rock, and let's be real, you make an unbelievably great coffee to fuel my writing escapades.

To the amazing Staci, my editor extraordinaire, thanks for transforming words into a well-crafted book. Your patience and sharp editing skills are a powerful combo!

Thank you to Katiuscia, my Italian wizard. You saved me from countless embarrassing language blunders. Bravo!

Annalisa, the proofreading maestro, you deserve a medal for catching all those sneaky typos and grammar gremlins. Thank you for keeping my book polished!

Annalisa and Chiara, my fabulous friends and unpaid therapists—thanks for putting up with my meltdowns and providing endless spicy pics and encouragement. You're the real deal.

Jess and Martina, my dynamic duo of publicity prowess, you're the wind beneath my authorial wings. Thanks for turning my book into the literary talk of the town!

Last but not least, a massive thank you to all you awesome readers out there. You're the reason I'm not just talking to myself in a room full of paper and ink.

Much love and kindness,
Erika